FAMILY BUSINESS

FAMILY BUSINESS

Helen Cannam

This first world edition published in Great Britain 1999 by
SEVERN HOUSE PUBLISHERS LTD of
9–15 High Street, Sutton, Surrey SM1 1DF.
This first world edition published in the U.S.A. 1999 by
SEVERN HOUSE PUBLISHERS INC of
595 Madison Avenue, New York, N.Y. 10022.

British Library Cataloguing in Publication Data

Cannam, Helen
      Family business
      I.   Title
      823.9'14 [F]

      ISBN 0-7278-5448-8

All situations in this publication are fictitious and
any resemblance to living persons is purely coincidental.

Typeset by Hewer Text Composition Ltd.,
Edinburgh, Scotland.
Printed and bound in Great Britain by
MPG Books Ltd, Bodmin, Cornwall.

For Lorna Brough

One

Doctor Charles Poultney was a great advocate of the therapeutic value of fresh air. Even today all the long windows of Dale House stood open, completely invalidating old Sam Peart's early morning struggle with the central heating boiler. The curtains shivered, the flowers in the many vases trembled in the icy wind, the family retriever curled himself in a huddle in the most sheltered corner of the drawing room behind the doctor's favourite armchair. The soft domestic sounds – the rustling of tissue paper (just removed from wedding gifts) and the gentle hum of busy people – were all submerged by the noise of the wind, louder even than the familiar distant springtime roar of the river.

In her bedroom Pamela was shivering as, attended by her mother, her six bridesmaids and Emily the maid, she dressed for her wedding in the gown that was the triumphant result of an Easter trip to London.

"Stop shaking – I can't catch hold of the buttonholes," said Diana, the middle Poultney sister, who was trying to fasten the tiny pearl buttons at the back of the bride's white chiffon overdress. Like the other bridesmaids – Pamela's younger sisters and four of her friends – she herself was already dressed in a full-skirted, puffed-sleeved peach satin gown, which she thought very unbecoming.

"Nerves," said their mother in her most brisk and sensible tone. Whatever her emotions on this day when her firstborn was to be married, she did not think it appropriate to allow them to appear on the surface. "Take a deep breath, Pamela. That's right. And another."

1

"She's cold," objected her sister. "So am I. Frozen. At this rate we'll all be blue by the time we get to church."

"Don't exaggerate, Diana."

"Then please may I close the window?" Ignoring her mother's objections (which didn't in any case have the emphatic note that meant opposition was not only unwise but useless), Diana went to the window and pulled it shut. She stayed there for a time, leaning against the comforting warmth of the radiator and taking the opportunity to look down on the changed scene outside. The lawn, which was the only level part of the garden, had been almost entirely obliterated by a marquee, erected two days before. Around its nearer edge (flapping noisily in the wind), she could see men and women hurrying to and fro with trays, on which were glasses, or food shrouded in white linen cloths, or piles of table napkins, or yet more vases of flowers. A dozen additional staff had been taken on for the day to augment the usual household quota of cook, housemaid and gardener-handyman. Bradley's sister Lily was one of them, Diana knew – one of Bradley's many sisters, to be exact. She wondered which she was: from up here the women, all white-capped and white-aproned, had little individuality to mark them out. Besides, she'd never met Lily, or any other member of Bradley's family.

She raised her eyes beyond the shuddering summit of the marquee, to the tops of the trees that edged the lawn, and then through their bare branches to the slate and stone roofs of Wearbridge, and the fells rising from the further bank of the river. Somewhere among those roofs or those hills Bradley was busy with whatever he did on Saturday mornings.

"Diana! Look! What do you think?"

Pamela was ready at last. She stood in the centre of the room, suddenly transformed from a fresh-faced, brown-haired girl of no great beauty to a radiant creature in a figure-clinging gown of white chiffon over peach satin, with a long lace veil falling to the floor from the close-fitting, pearl-scattered juliet cap on her newly permed hair. "Golly, Pamela – you look stunning!"

Her sister smiled shyly.

Enraptured, Diana gazed and gazed, while her imagination

2

rearranged the scene. *I am there*, she thought, *not Pamela; I am the bride, with that pretty cap on my obstinate black bob that won't take a perm, and the warm tints of the gown putting some colour into my pallid, peaky face, so that for once it's not all green eyes and black brows. I am that lovely bride. I am an offering fit for my chosen spouse, my soulmate; for Bradley Armstrong.*

She saw him then, too, as clearly as if he were here in the room; not dressed as a conventional groom (that was hard to imagine), but as she had first seen him, on that hot day last summer. At home for the holidays and with nothing much to do, she had accepted a lift from her father, in the hope of being allowed to drive (she'd not then passed her test). He was on his way to the sanitorium, and would pass the house where her friend Lydia Garthorne lived. But first they had to stop for petrol at the pump in Front Street.

No one had come to serve them, so she'd got out of the car and walked through the archway that led into the yard behind the garage. It had been baking hot in that enclosed space and, she'd thought at first, empty, except for a red lorry parked to one side, with the words *Jackson Armstrong* painted on it in dark green edged with yellow. Just in case the garage man was busy in one of the shabby outbuildings, she had called, "Cooee!" and then realised that there was somebody in the yard after all, bent under the raised bonnet of the lorry, just out of sight, but quite embarrassingly close. At her call, he had straightened – and she'd realised that he was stripped to the waist.

She had occasionally seen boys in that state before – or one boy at least, her brother Robert, all white, scrawny, thirteen-year-old flesh. This boy was nothing like Robert. He was older, of course – perhaps twenty to her sixteen – and his body was tanned and smooth, the muscles moving under the warm skin, the sun gleaming on the red-gold hairs of his broad chest. He was, quite simply, beautiful. She had experienced his beauty in her mind, as something to feast her eyes upon, rather as she would on a fine thoroughbred horse, admiring the perfect combination of muscle and form and hidden power. But she had felt it too in her body. At first it was as if something had struck her in the stomach and then exploded, fanning sensation out to the uttermost part of her limbs and organs, finding in the process new senses to wake to life. The universe seemed to have shrunk and yet grown, so that it had become only and entirely this one piece of human perfection. She had felt what she saw with an intensity that was almost like touching.

All this had happened in a moment, which had yet seemed to go on for ever. The next moment she saw that he had blushed, and then was grinning, a little sheepishly, but with a boyish charm that had only increased her inner turbulence. She had been quite unable to speak, or even to remember why she was there. Oddly, he had seemed almost as incapacitated as she was, and had mumbled something incoherent that, even at the time, had made no sense, and which she could not now recall. She only knew that in some way that sudden encounter had been a beginning.

Remembering the scene, she could feel it all again, as disturbingly as ever.

"Dido, come on! You haven't put your head-dress on!"

"*Diana*," Evelyn Poultney corrected her youngest daughter, more from habit than conviction. She deplored nicknames, but this was not the day for a strict application of rules. Besides, Angela was in a mood of exuberant high spirits that probably meant she had not even heard her mother. She had taken the circlet of carnations that Emily was holding out, and now placed it carefully on Diana's head. "Very pretty," said Evelyn approvingly. "Now, the bouquets please, Emily."

By the time they were ready to leave for the church it had begun to snow. The bridesmaids, a giggling huddle, ran up the churchyard path, heads bent against the sharp icy flakes, halting in the porch to rearrange head-dresses and shake off the powdering of white. Inside the church, it was warm and crowded, heavy with the scent of flowers. The organ was playing sweetly. Diana felt a prickle of tears behind her lids and a great choking love for her family, and especially for Pamela. For once Bradley was driven out of her thoughts.

He was returned to them, sharply, as the bridal party emerged

4

after the ceremony into a furtively restored sunshine, to process down the path to the gate. As tradition required, it had been closed against them by a group of townsfolk – not all of them children – who would not let them pass until the customary coins had been scattered for them by the bridegroom, who looked acutely uncomfortable at being forced into such a rustic and light-hearted role. He was, Diana thought, a very stuffy young man.

It was then that Diana, suddenly glancing beyond the watchers across to the far side of the road, saw Bradley Armstrong leaning against the window of the Rose Tree Tea Rooms. Startled, she felt the colour pour into her face. She was so confused that though she thought he grinned at her she couldn't be quite sure.

Then she saw his lips move, exaggeratedly, as if he were mouthing some important message. He gestured with his thumb too, towards the lane that led down to the river bank. She watched, and he repeated the words. "Tonight, down there, third tree." She knew that was the message, because it was the arrangement he had made before, on the two occasions they had met since the dance last Christmas when he'd first kissed her. She was about to shake her head, indicating that a meeting today was out of the question; then she decided against it, and simply smiled instead. After all, it might just be possible, you never knew.

She almost forgot Bradley during the long and leisurely wedding breakfast in the marquee, and afterwards when Pamela, smart but ordinary in her going-away frock and jacket, came to say goodbye to the members of her family, lined up on the front steps to wave her off. "Bye, little sis," she said as she passed Diana. "Be good."

Diana remembered the things that, in spite of the five years between them, they had shared – the secrets, the squabbles, incidents at boarding school and during the long holidays. There had been others – especially her schoolfriends – who had been closer to Diana, but none, apart from her parents, who had for so long been a part of her life, even if in recent years they had seen little of one another.

5

Pamela suddenly kissed her. It was, Diana believed, the only time in their lives they had ever kissed: the Poultneys were not a demonstrative family. She felt a mixture of embarrassment and emotion, and was afraid she was about to cry. She forced a grin. "At least you won't be able to order me about any more."

"No, and I bet you can't wait to move into my room," said Pamela, also repudiating sentimentality.

That was quite true, and made Diana instantly feel thoroughly cheerful again. She waved with enthusiasm as the bridal couple were driven away in the car that took them to Wearbridge station for the first part of their honeymoon journey to the Scilly Isles. Now, at long last, she, Diana, was the eldest unmarried daughter of the family – Miss Poultney, instead of mere Miss Diana, if one were to be very correct. Tomorrow she would move all her belongings out of the room she shared with Angela and into the slightly smaller but very pretty bedroom that had been Pamela's; reserved for her even after she went to work in London. She would be an adult at last, a person of consequence.

Much later, tingling with boredom after hours of polite conversation with rarely-seen relatives, her head aching slightly from too much champagne, Diana sat slumped on a stool near the drawing room door, much too hot (though by now she'd changed out of her bridesmaid's dress) and wondering if she would ever be able to make her escape, as she had hoped. Her mother, passing on her way back from waving off some departing guest, glanced at her with concern.

"You look tired, my dear," she said. "Bed time, I think."

Diana stood up, and stretched. "I couldn't sleep a wink," she declared. "I think I need some fresh air."

To her mother that seemed a wholly reasonable wish, if one had been confined for hours in a drawing room thick with the smoke of pipes and cigars and cigarettes. "Put a coat on then. It's cold outside. And don't be long. We have to be up for ten o'clock church tomorrow."

It was as easy as that. Diana knew her mother thought she intended to go no further than the garden, but she was sure no

6

one saw her slip out through the orchard gate into the steep cobbled lane that ran down the other side of the garden wall.

It was windy still, but not snowing. It was later than she had thought and almost fully dark, a clear starlit night with no moon – fortunately she'd thought to bring a torch with her from the drawer in the hallstand. She walked down the lane, across the market place and on towards the river bank, beyond the reach of the gas lamps that lined the main street. The water gleamed faintly in the night, emphasising the contrasting black of the riverside walk. What if he wasn't there after all? She did not like the thought that she might be all alone in this dark place.

He was there. She saw him almost at once, standing under the third of the large sycamores that had been planted just before the war. She smelt the tobacco smoke before she saw him, though she could just make out his dark figure, like a distorted growth on the black trunk of the tree, and the glow of his cigarette end.

"Bradley?" She saw the tiny point of light fall to the ground in a shower of sparks, heard him crush the stub with his foot. Then he took a step towards her. She halted in front of him, looking hungrily up at the pale glimmer of his face. "It's cold," she said. She felt his hand, rough and manly, close about hers.

"Let's walk then."

After a moment his arm slipped around her shoulder. It felt heavy and warm and set her shivering with excitement. She could hear his breathing even above the sound of the river. A little further on he suddenly stopped and turned her to face him and bent his head and kissed her. The kiss was wholly pleasurable, yet her body was so full of turmoil that it hurt. She'd felt them before, these sensations between the legs that were both painful and a little frightening. She knew that this was the area that had something to do with having babies, though she was not sure what. Some girls at school said a kiss could make you pregnant.

"It looked a grand wedding," Bradley said at last, with what seemed supreme irrelevance. "Must have cost your Dad a bob or two."

Diana suppressed the thought that to remark on such things was really rather vulgar, and gave Bradley a confused account of the day's events. She found it oddly difficult to remember much about them.

"Aye well." His arm tightened about her again. "So now you'll be going away."

"On Thursday, yes. First thing. Mother's coming with me, for a week or two."

Bradley was silent for a time, as if awed by the immensity of the forthcoming journey. "France – it's a long way."

"It's only for a year." She tried to sound cheerful about it, but in truth she felt as if she were facing a life sentence. Besides, she knew that France was intended to be only the beginning. After that, her French perfected, she was expected to come back to England, but not to Wearbridge. There would be an appropriate course at a secretarial college in London, and then employment with some respectable firm, of solicitors perhaps, one of whom at least would be known to her parents. A year or two more, and then would come the moment for her marriage to some eminently suitable man, from a background similar to her own – very possibly the junior partner in that same firm of solicitors, with whom she would conveniently have fallen in love. That was precisely what Pamela had done, in the appropriate order; today's wedding having been the highly satisfactory culmination of the process. But for Pamela there had never been anyone else. For Diana there was Bradley, and she knew she would never love anyone but him as long as she lived. "I shall come back," she said with a sudden surge of renewed confidence. "That's a promise."

"What if there's a war?"

That again! thought Diana impatiently. Even the wedding guests had seemed to talk of nothing else but the possibility – the probability even – of war with Germany. "I hope there is," she said. "Then I'll have to come home." She didn't really believe there would be a war. What was real and immediate was Bradley, his nearness, the sound of his breathing, the weight of his arm about her shoulder. War was just a word, though one heard off and on all her life. The dreadful 'war to end all wars' had brought her parents together, the doctor and the volunteer nurse in the grim field hospital in Flanders. But that was simply something people talked about, something that had happened long ago, before she was born.

"But then I'd have to go away," Bradley pointed out. "A single man, twenty years old – I'd have no excuse."

That was something she'd not considered, and she felt a sudden sense of alarm – perhaps she did believe war was possible, after all. She was on the point of asking if a married man would be less vulnerable, but even with all the champagne inside her was not quite bold enough to put it into words. Yet what she said instead was just as bold. "I love you."

Bradley nudged her back against the high wall of Wearbridge castle grounds and kissed her again, and while he did so slid his hand to her throat, where he tugged gently at the buttons on the front of her linen frock, loosening first one then another, in descending order. She heard herself make an odd noise, a sort of moan, as the hand slipped inside the gap it had made and felt its way under her brassière to her breast. The touch of his fingers, closing about its roundness, almost overwhelmed her.

Then he stopped kissing her, and with one hand still on her breast (she was not sure how he managed it) was steering her on again, quite fast now, purposefully, towards the place where stepping stones crossed the river by the ford.

She was past thinking about what was happening. She was all feelings. Her aching, throbbing body simply allowed itself to be led, to the water's edge, over the stones, one by one. On the further bank he urged her quickly up the hill a little way, then through a stone stile into a wood at the foot of a sloping field. There, under the trees, he halted again at last, and began once more to kiss her, while, inexorably, he pressed her down towards the soft sheep-cropped grass. She did not resist at all, could not have done, for her legs had lost all power and simply crumpled under her.

He had her frock open all down the front and was kissing her between her breasts and then over them. Some little part of her mind told her she should have been ashamed, but the response of her body was too strong for shame. She thrust her own fingers deep into the thickness of his hair, pulling his head closer. She did not feel in the least cold, but rather too hot, far too hot.

She felt his hand move down her leg, grope its way to the hem of her skirt, ruffle it upwards. This, she knew quite well, was forbidden, utterly forbidden. No nice girl ever allowed a hand below the waist.

She did not care. Whatever it was that would normally have made her resist had quite deserted her. The hand reached her knee, moved on, came to the space above her stocking, then slid inwards. She heard herself moan again.

He was struggling with her knickers, trying to pull them down. "Don't!" she heard herself say then, but feebly, with no conviction at all.

"S'all right," he murmured breathily. "We'll get married."

It *was* all right then, quite all right, even though he pulled her knickers right off and pushed them out of the way. She felt the air cool on that most private part of her, which was so hot, which hurt so much. Then, a pause, and he was on top of her, between her legs. She felt his flesh on her flesh, something hard pushing into her. It hurt, intensely so for a moment, so that she cried out, yet she could not have stopped it, would not have wanted to. She lay still while he thrust and thrust and lost himself in her. Once, in triumph, he cried her name.

It went on for what seemed a long time. In the end, she found herself wishing he would stop, which at last he did, falling limply against her in exhausted satisfaction, a great heavy-breathing weight. Then he pulled free and rolled away.

"Best get dressed," he said. "You'll catch your death." He got to his feet.

She wanted tenderness, sweet words and caresses – some kind of reassurance, now it was over, that it really was all right. His matter-of-factness was a little chilling, and the way – as she could dimly see – he was pulling up his trousers, fastening belt and buttons, not even looking at her. She found her knickers and put them on (there was something sticky between her legs), stood up and made sure her stockings were straight, and her skirt. Then his arm was about her again and he kissed her, lightly this time.

"Come on, lass. Time to go home." Now there was some tenderness in his voice, though not as much as she would have liked.

They walked most of the way in silence, though Diana's head was crowded with confused thoughts and unanswered questions. By now she felt thoroughly sober again, and a sick anxiety began to gnaw at the pit of her stomach. Whatever the truth about the mechanics of conceiving children, she was quite sure that what she and Bradley had just done was more than enough to make it happen. That did not mean it had, of course, or she did not think so, but she couldn't be sure. Once or twice she glanced at Bradley, but she could see only that he was not looking at her. Though his arm was still round her, she felt that he was remote from her, out of reach.

It was not until they reached the shadow of the lane running up towards the orchard gate that she found the courage to speak. "Bradley, what you said – you know, just before . . ." She floundered into silence, then stumbled on again. "I just wondered – did you mean it?"

"I always mean what I say." She could not make out his expression, but his voice sounded easy enough, casual, assured. Then he kissed her, and she knew it was all right.

Even so, she didn't sleep very well that night.

Two

At first, Diana told herself it was the distinctive odour of French drains that was making her feel sick, on top of a longing for Bradley that was physical as well as emotional.

She had been feeling unusually tired even before she left home, but had put that down to all the things it had been necessary for her to do in readiness for her sister's wedding and her own impending journey. Then of course it was only natural to feel tired after a long train journey, involving several changes, and a nauseating Channel crossing, and yet more trains, French ones this time. Then there'd been the arrival, at the end of a long night, at Périgueux, near which they were to stay, and the meeting with strangers, and the exhausting effort of talking French all the time – even, at her mother's insistence, when there were no French people present – and the strain of adjusting to yet more unfamiliar surroundings. The house was a charming small château, the Pommarède family (Monsieur, Madame and five little ones) were ceremoniously welcoming, the rocky wooded countryside was beautiful, the weather perfect, the food a revelation, and Diana's room was a delightful round tower room with a bed like a wooden boat and a narrow window looking out on the topmost branches of an unfamiliar tree in which a nightingale sang every evening without fail. But none of these things made her miss Bradley the less, nor did they staunch the physical symptoms.

By the time Diana had been in France for a month, she felt no better. On the contrary, the weariness and nausea were worse than ever. Sometimes she was actually sick, especially first thing in the morning. If it wasn't the drains (and she began to doubt it) then perhaps it was due to the smell of French cigarettes, or the

13

unfamiliar food, much though she liked it, on the whole. Before long, inevitably, her mother began to grow anxious about her. Evelyn Poultney had been due to go home by now, but refused to leave while Diana was so unlike herself. "If you don't improve soon," she said, "I shall insist that Madame Pommarède calls a doctor."

A week later, at the beginning of June, the doctor came. He gave Diana a thorough examination, asking her many questions in French and broken English, which she answered as best she could; after all of which he said gravely, "*Mademoiselle, vous êtes enceinte.*" Diana's schoolgirl French was not quite up to understanding what he said, but the expression of horrified disbelief on her mother's face translated the words for her more than adequately. Besides, she'd known all along, in her bones.

There was a hurried, anxious discussion between her mother and the doctor, before he took his leave. Then Evelyn Poultney sat down on the edge of the bed beside her daughter. "How is this possible, Diana?" She sounded coldly accusatory.

Diana could feel her face going redder and redder. She felt more sick than ever, but it was a different sickness. "I didn't mean to. It just happened."

"It does not 'just happen'! Come now, I want the truth. Is it since we came to France?" She was clearly going over the past weeks in her mind. "No, I don't see . . ."

Diana bent her head, so as not to see her mother's troubled face. "It was the night of Pamela's wedding – I went out."

"Then who went out with you?" Diana knew her mother was running over the male wedding guests in her mind, the cousins and uncles and family friends, alarmed at the possibility that any of these might so have betrayed her trust.

"No one. It was Bradley Armstrong. I met him."

Evelyn stared at her daughter. "Who—?" It was clear that the name meant nothing to her.

"Bradley Armstrong. From Springbank Farm. You know, they have the garage in Front Street, and lorries."

After a painful silence, her mother said, "How long has this been going on?"

Diana tried to explain, though it all sounded so slight a thing, and she knew her mother couldn't take it seriously, except in its consequence, of course – clearly that was very serious indeed. Trying to make it better, Diana said at last, "We love each other. We're going to be married anyway. I know he won't mind if it's very soon."

She was astonished at her mother's reaction to that assurance. "No! Diana, he must not know of this, not under any circumstances. Do you understand?"

Diana didn't know what made her do what she did next. She had no time to think about it or to plan, but for some reason she found herself saying, "I've already written to him." It was a complete lie. When she was a little girl, her grandmother used to warn her that if ever she were to tell a lie she would develop a pimple on her tongue. She had believed it then, implicitly. Now she had an uneasy conviction that tomorrow, as a mark of her untruthfulness, she would wake to find that the tell-tale pimple had erupted. She ran the tip of her tongue round the inside of her mouth, checking, and then worried in case her mother should guess what she was doing.

"How can you have done? There's been no time. You've only just seen the doctor."

"But I knew. I guessed." That at least was true.

"And yet you said nothing to me of your suspicions? You told them to this boy before your own mother knew a thing? Oh, Diana!" Hurt, bewildered, dismayed, Evelyn went on, "You told him by letter then? When was this?"

"Yesterday." There ought, she felt, to be two pimples, after lying on such a scale.

"And you've posted the letter? You're sure about that? That it's gone?" She frowned at her vigorously nodding daughter. "Oh, Diana, I wish you had not! All we can hope is that the letter goes astray somehow." Clearly, she thought this unlikely. "Do you suppose he will keep it to himself? You did ask that much of him, I take it?"

Diana shook her head. "I expect he'll tell his family. They'll need to know he's going to be married." Somehow she was beginning to believe her own lies.

"Diana, the Armstrong boy may marry whom he pleases, but he is not going to marry you! Is that clear? It is out of the question."

"But, Mother, I'm going to have a baby. He must marry me!" She was shaking, feeling suddenly isolated and afraid. Since this nightmare began, she had never imagined that her parents might oppose her marriage to Bradley.

"There are other arrangements that can be made. But if he knows . . . Oh, I wish you had kept quiet!"

"Mother, I want to marry Bradley, really I do. I love him."

"You only think you do. It's just an infatuation. You're very young. This isn't the kind of feeling that will last. I do know what I'm talking about, Diana. After all, you have nothing in common with him."

That seemed to Diana the oddest of objections. What after all did Cinderella have in common with Prince Charming, or Romeo with Juliet (except warring parents), or Elizabeth Bennet with Mr Darcy? "I love him and he loves me. That's all that matters."

"But it isn't, believe me. Besides, how well do you really know him? You've met – what, about three times, at the most?" She ignored her daughter's murmured *four*. "You can't know someone in that time. Nor love them, not with a true and lasting love. And you can't ignore the fact that his background is quite different from ours. Such things matter, believe me. Oh, they're a decent enough family and I'm sure he's an agreeable young man in his way. But it's a question of standards and upbringing. Such things are important, whatever some people might like to claim. If you were to marry him, you would soon realise I'm right, but by then it would be too late. No, we must try and get round this somehow . . . There's another thing." Evelyn was sounding increasingly desperate in the face of her daughter's obstinacy. "What if you were to lose the baby? Miscarriages are not unusual, and then you'd find yourself trapped, for no good reason."

"It's not a trap to be married to the man you love," Diana asserted.

"Indeed not. I would be the first to agree with that." Her face brightened slightly, as a new angle occurred to her. "You may well find he'll try and wriggle out of marriage. I'm afraid boys from his background are often like that. At the very least, he'll be only too pleased if we find a way for him to evade his responsibilities." She began to walk about the room, thinking aloud. Diana heard her speak of a clinic in Switzerland – 'your father has a contact there' – of adoption, of how it would be better for the child, for them all. No one need, in the end, be any the wiser. She sat down again and laid a hand over Diana's, but her daughter shook her off and stood up, confronting her.

"No! I'm not going to give up my baby. I'm not going to pretend it hasn't happened. I'm going home and I'm going to marry Bradley. And I shall be happy, we'll both be happy, and so will our baby. You can't stop me! I'm nearly eighteen – I'm not a child any more."

Rather to her surprise her mother did not argue. She simply looked terribly weary, though Diana felt neither sympathy nor remorse. "Let's leave it for now," Evelyn Poultney said at last. "Think about what I've said. We'll talk again later. In any case, it's time for lunch."

Diana had no need to think anything over. She knew that she must go home and marry Bradley, and that was that. As far as she was concerned there was no argument her mother could bring that would move her.

As soon as she was alone, she sat down at the table and took her box of notepaper and picked up her pen, intent on making true the lie she had told, by writing at once to Bradley. Then she hesitated. What if her mother should accidentally see what she was doing and realise there had been no earlier letter? Worse still, what if Bradley should react as Evelyn had implied he might, and even perhaps take flight at her coming? Of course he wouldn't, she knew he wouldn't, but some part of her urged her to wait, to save the revelation until she was face to face with him, where she could not be gainsaid.

She had no idea what her mother told Madame Pommarède

about the doctor's visit, but their hostess was very kind towards the girl for the few days left before their departure. Diana wondered what her reaction would have been had she known the truth.

But at least Evelyn had agreed to take Diana home with her. "Perhaps your father will make you see sense," she said, just to show that after all nothing had been settled.

The journey home was unpleasant in the extreme, with all the discomforts of the outward voyage accentuated by Evelyn Poultney's coldness towards her daughter. She was obviously concerned for Diana's health, anxious that she should rest when she could, and eat sensibly, and take regular but moderate exercise. But her disapproval of her daughter's behaviour was expressed in every rigid line of her body. She spoke only when necessary. There was none of the casual talk that had enlivened their journey to France, no pointing out of landmarks, or recollections of the history of this place, or anecdotes about that. She never smiled, and her tone was, at the very best, cool in the extreme. Diana wondered once or twice if she herself would actually survive the journey without breaking down. More than once she felt close to tears, but knew that any public display of emotion would only lower her still further in her mother's estimation. After all, it was lack of self-control that had brought all this on her in the first place.

She tried not to think of what would be waiting for her at the end of the journey. Her mother had not said what her father's reaction had been to the long and clearly painful telephone call made before they left the château, but Diana knew he must be at least as distressed as her mother was. Sometimes, perhaps when drifting off to sleep, she would find herself thinking it was all a bad dream, from which she would wake to discover none of it had happened. Sometimes she would tell herself that the doctor might have been mistaken, and she was not pregnant after all. But the perpetual sickness, worse first thing in the morning, belied that tenuous hope. It was not that she did not want to marry Bradley, but she hadn't wanted it to be like this, with so much misery surrounding her. Everything was horrible, and she wished she could turn back the clock and blot it all out.

As they came nearer to home, a new fear, growing from seeds sown by her mother, began to obsess her. What if her mother was right, and Bradley refused to marry her? What then could she do? By coming home she would have destroyed all her best hope of easily concealing what had happened, putting it behind her and starting afresh. She would be facing the worst of both worlds.

But it won't be like that, she told herself. *He will want to marry me. He loves me, and I love him.* Then she caught her mother's eyes on her, and they seemed to have an ironic questioning look in their hardness, as if warning her that the love on which she depended was an illusion. She shut her own eyes again hastily, hoping she might escape into sleep.

She did sleep, and had a confused, episodic dream in which she was sometimes at home in Dale House, and sometimes at her grandmother's lovely country house in Surrey – the place where her mother had grown up, and where they had often stayed as children. Wherever it was, her grandmother was always there, following her about and demanding to look at her tongue, her face dark and accusing, like that of a witch in a fairy tale. Granny was in fact slight and fair and small-featured, like her daughter, but all the same Diana, in her dream, knew it was she, and that she must not be allowed to see her tongue, on which an enormous pimple was growing and growing, until it filled her mouth. By this point it was obvious to everyone, and she found herself running in terror down the lane beside the house, and rounding the corner. And there was Bradley striding towards her, and she knew that at any moment he was going to see the grotesque thing in her mouth and turn from her in anger and rejection.

Only then, mercifully, the train drew into a station with a squealing of brakes and a noisy rush of steam, and Diana was jolted awake. "Darlington," said her mother. She was already on her feet, reaching for her coat from the rack, while a porter – who had materialised in the way such people did for Evelyn Poultney – lifted down the heaviest suitcase. A hoarse voice called out beyond the grimy windows, reminding passengers to change here for Wearbridge.

Sleepy, shivering in the sudden cold air, Diana followed her mother and the porter to the platform where their connecting train waited. *Nearly back to Bradley*, she thought, trying to grope her way out of the troubling dream. But she could only see the expression he had turned on her in its final moments. Had it been a warning?

Dr Poultney was waiting on the platform when they reached Wearbridge, late in the afternoon. "Good journey?" he asked his wife, without smiling. He scarcely glanced at Diana, though he took those of the suitcases that the porter could not be expected to carry.

"Not too bad," replied Evelyn. They went with him in silence to the car. No one said anything, either, on the way back to Dale House. Staring out of the car window, Diana was almost surprised to see that the town still looked as it had always done: solid stone houses ranged on the hillside, the flowers in their neat gardens the only brightness in the grey afternoon light. Something, she felt, should have changed, as she had.

The doctor carried Diana's cases up to her room, that new room she had moved into with such pleasure, and had so far slept in for only four nights. "Tea in the drawing room in ten minutes," he said before he left her. It was a command, not an invitation.

She changed out of her travelling clothes into a pale green cotton frock and a warm jacket (it felt more like February than late June), and ran down the stairs, as softly as she could, hoping no one would hear her.

Her mother was standing in the drawing room doorway, clearly waiting for her. She glimpsed her father already seated in his favourite wing chair, one hand irritably fondling the dog's head. She could already imagine the unpleasant scene that was about to take place – or that her parents intended should take place.

At the foot of the stairs, she ran straight ahead, past her mother, on towards the front door. "I'm going to see Bradley."

Her mother took a step after her. "No, wait!" Then, despairingly, "Oh, Diana!"

Her bicycle had got well to the back of the outhouse, behind all the other bikes and various garden tools, so that it was a struggle to extricate it, but she was already mounted by the time her mother came round the corner of the house. She pedalled away as quickly as she could.

She had never seen the place where Bradley lived, though she knew roughly where it was, on the northern bank of the river just this side of the village of Ravenshield, which was about eight miles west of Wearbridge. It turned out to be large by the standards of the Dale, and very old, a long low stone building, with the dwelling quarters at one end and stabling and cow byres at the other. Sheep and a few horses grazed in the surrounding fields. She propped her bicycle against the garden wall and knocked nervously on the door, which was opened by a handsome woman in a large apron. The smell of baking – something sweet and fruity – wafted out with her. Did she know what Diana and her son had done together?

"Mrs Armstrong?" Diana felt appallingly nervous, though the woman looked friendly enough. "Is Bradley at home? I'd like to speak to him, if I may."

She thought the other woman looked faintly surprised. "He's not back yet. He had a load of stone to lead down to Bishop for Mr Wilkinson. He shouldn't be long. It's Miss Diana, isn't it? I can give him a message if you like."

"I really must see him."

"Then you'd best come in and wait."

Better that, however terrifying, than to go home and risk being prevented from seeing Bradley; Diana stepped into the kitchen. It was, she thought, a room of which her parents would not have approved at all. Its great black range threw out an overpowering heat and (apart from various oil lamps) it was lit only by two tiny windows, which were firmly closed and looked as if they had never been opened; the sills were cluttered with potted plants and other oddments. But the room was spotless, brightened with copper pans and polished brassware, the flagged floor scattered with colourful rag rugs, various good things strung from the great beams – bunches of herbs, hams, freshly ironed washing. The table on which a girl of about her own age had just placed a newly-baked pie had a surface worn with daily scouring. The smell of baking submerged but did not quite overcome the sharper smells of carbolic soap and well-aired linen.

Mrs Armstrong was taking off her apron. "Come through to the parlour. Our Lily, put on the kettle, there's a good lass." She led the way across a flagged passageway to a small panelled room, as dark as the kitchen but cheerless, with its look of shiny disuse, its firmly closed piano and its unlit fire, to which Mrs Armstrong at once put a match. "Please sit down, Miss Diana."

Diana did so, on a prickly horse-hair sofa by the fire now crackling and snapping its way towards warmth, and Mrs Armstrong left her, to get the tea, Diana supposed. She felt acutely uncomfortable. She would much rather have stayed in that warm and friendly kitchen. At Dale House, Bradley would almost certainly have been admitted no further than the kitchen – that was his proper place, as hers was the parlour. She wondered how much, if anything, Bradley had told them about her. She supposed they knew that he'd danced with her two or three times last Christmas, but they were still treating her, respectfully, as Doctor Poultney's daughter. They could not, of course, know the very worst. She felt sicker than ever when she wondered how they would react to her news, when they knew it.

A tray arrived, bearing a silver teapot, and cups of flowered bone china, and a fruit cake on a pretty plate. Diana sipped the tea poured for her, nibbled at her piece of cake (which was delicious, though she was too nervous to be in the least bit hungry), and tried to think of something to say. She wished Bradley would come home and rescue her from this uncomfortable situation. Except that she was afraid that she might then simply be plunged into something even more uncomfortable.

"Poor weather we're having," Mrs Armstrong said. She too was clearly struggling to find some suitable topic. "We have to hope it fairs up by haytime."

"It was too hot in France," said Diana.

Mrs Armstrong looked surprised. "Have you been to France then?"

Diana stumbled over a short and entirely misleading account of a recent holiday, which bore little relation to anything that had happened to her. She began to think Bradley must never have mentioned her at all to his family. What did that mean? That she was not important to him?

It seemed hours before she heard feet clattering briskly in the passage, coming nearer. Then Bradley was at the door. While his mother scolded him for not leaving his boots on the doormat, he stared at Diana, who somehow managed to indicate that she must speak to him alone.

They went outside, into the chilly evening wind. A lorry had been parked in the yard, and Bradley led the way to its far side, where, out of range of the farmhouse windows, he turned to face her. "What are you doing here? I thought you wouldn't be back before next year."

Is he glad to see me? Diana asked herself. She had – in her more optimistic moments – imagined him running to clasp her in his arms, but he showed no sign even of wanting to touch her. She glanced round to check that no one was within earshot, and then, her heart thudding, said baldly, "I'm pregnant." It sounded horrible, crude, even sordid.

Bradley stared at her, his lips forming a silent whistle. "Mine?"

What a strange question! "Yes, of course."

He laughed, an odd rather embarrassed laugh; his face was flushed. After a pause, during which she felt increasingly that she couldn't breathe, he flung an arm about her shoulder. "Then I'd best make an honest woman of you."

Diana rested her head on his chest, and felt as if she had come in out of the storm.

Three

Diana and Bradley were married, very quietly, on the last Saturday in that chilly June, in the parish church at Wearbridge. Her parents, accepting the inevitable, had insisted that the wedding should take place as soon as possible, before their two younger children came home for the school holidays. They paid for a special licence, so as to avoid the three week delay for the reading of the banns. Henceforth, they indicated, though not exactly cast out, Diana was only in the most tenuous way to be considered a part of the Poultney family. They had no wish at all to admit Bradley to it. She felt that if her parents had been able to think of a good excuse, they would not even have been present at the wedding.

The Armstrong family, all staunch Methodists, took a much more cheerful view of things. Once they had expressed a nominal disapproval of Diana's condition, they simply accepted her as their son's bride, as joyfully as if everything had taken the most respectable course. They made it clear that if her parents were not willing to celebrate to the full, then they would make up for the deficiency, as far as lay in their power.

As she walked into the church on her father's arm – feeling his shame in her somehow seeping through the sleeve of his coat into her hand – Diana recalled painfully how she'd imagined herself as a bride, not quite three months before. This time, the church was more than half empty, and her own relatives were limited solely to her parents. She wore a pale blue frock and a little blue hat – pretty, and almost new, but scarcely bridal – and carried a posy of some kind of blue flowers, chosen by her soon-to-be-mother-in-law. Bradley, waiting in the front pew beside his elder brother Jackson, who was best man, wore his old-fashioned grey Sunday suit, which Diana thought must be the most unattractive outfit he possessed. His hair had been slicked flat against his head, and he looked pale and very nervous, quite different from the confident, assertively masculine figure who had first overwhelmed Diana. It all added to the sense of unreality that had been with her to some degree since her going to France, and had intensified during the past uncomfortable days.

Afterwards, they went back to Springbank Farm, where they sat down to a hearty lunch in the kitchen. There were neither speeches nor champagne (the Armstrong parents were total abstainers), but plenty of good food and strong tea, and a cheerful atmosphere that was balm to Diana's spirit, infected as it was by the miasma of disappointment that had hung over Dale House since her return from France.

There were few presents for the young couple, though Diana's mother had given her a cookery book, and (discreetly, when no one was looking) a book on infant care. "I'm afraid the Armstrongs are the sort of people who rely on old wives' tales," she'd said. "This will redress the balance." Diana had been a little comforted by what she took as a sign of concern, even perhaps of love, which her mother would not allow herself to demonstrate in any other way. Later, when lunch was over and – duty done – they came to take their leave, Evelyn Poultney kissed her daughter, and stroked her hair, a furtive, uncharacteristically tender gesture. Her father, more restrained, shook her hand. "Good luck, Diana." She closed the door at once, not wanting to watch them drive away. If they no longer wished to look on her as their daughter, then so be it. This was now her home, and this her family.

The celebrations went on all afternoon and for most of the evening, with a bewildering number of Armstrong friends and relations coming and going (Diana wondered if she would ever remember who everyone was), and food constantly replenished, and the kettle always on the boil. Late in the afternoon, Uncle Billy (who was really some sort of distant cousin) sat down at the parlour piano and called for a song, and everyone within earshot

joined in. By the end of the day a succession of songs had given
way to solemn hymns, which Diana found rather depressing. By
now she was exhausted and wanted only to be alone.

But she wouldn't be alone, she reminded herself, even when
this day was over: Bradley would be there, today and for ever,
her husband, her mate. It was what she had once dreamed of, but
now that it had happened, she felt full of apprehension. Today, in
church, Bradley had seemed little like the Bradley she had
thought she knew. In his own home, he was more himself,
but so cheerfully preoccupied with the throng of guests that
he'd scarcely exchanged a word or a look with her, even when
introducing her to yet another cousin or aunt. Everyone seemed
to be trying to make her feel welcome, but there were just too
many people. Seeing all the strange faces, hearing the gossip
about people she didn't know, she felt she was an outsider. Like
Bradley, she had been born in the Dale, yet it struck her today
that they had grown up in what were, in effect, totally separate
worlds, which scarcely overlapped at all. None of the people she
knew (apart from her parents) had been here today, and none
were talked about. In a way, that was a relief, because she knew
what they must think of her, and, if nothing else, the Armstrongs
were kind and seemed glad that she'd become one of them.
Except that she did not feel like one of them.

The young couple could not afford a honeymoon, so when it
grew dark Bradley simply came in search of Diana and said
softly, "We can go up now." His breath smelt of beer. Diana
wondered where, in this teetotal house, he'd found the opportunity to drink. But it seemed to have relaxed him and released
the last hidden traces of the man she knew. His hair was ruffled,
his tie had been cast aside some time before, he looked flushed
and his brown eyes were bright with suggestion. When she stood
up he put an arm about her and shouted to the company,
"Goodnight, all!" With laughter and jokes following them, they
made their way by candlelight upstairs to his bedroom.

He opened the door for her to go in ahead of him. She had
expected to see a room which, in its long-acquired clutter, was
thoroughly stamped with his personality, just as Robert's room

at Dale House was full of the books he loved – *Biggles* and Kipling and Captain Marryat – and the objects he'd collected and the toys he'd once played with. But even in the dim flickering light of the candle she could see that this room contained no books at all, no ornaments and no treasured possessions – or none that were visible. Perhaps he'd tidied everything away in preparation for her coming. Certainly the room was tidy, every surface shiny with polish. There was a small wardrobe (poor quality, Diana noted), two cane-bottomed chairs, a washstand with basin and ewer – put in especially for her, Bradley told her later, since he was used to washing in the scullery or even outside at the spring – and a hard narrow bed, which reminded her suddenly of the beds at boarding school . . .

That was it! All day there had been something just under the surface, a memory she couldn't quite bring to consciousness, which had its echo in what she'd been feeling today. Now she knew what it was – that first day at boarding school, when she was eight years old, and how strange it had been, a new and unfamiliar world in which everyone seemed to know everyone else and she knew no one. Except that then she had been one among seventeen or so new girls, all equally strange, and able to turn to one another for sympathy. Here she was the only new girl.

But at least she had Bradley . . . *How can you possibly know him*? her mother had asked, on that horrible day in France. Recalling the words, she tried to push them from her mind. Yet her hands were shaking as she undressed for bed, and she could think of nothing to say. She didn't look round at Bradley, who was (presumably) undressing too. When, wearing her pale green pyjamas, she did look round at last, she saw that he was already in bed, watching her from the pillow with an expression she could not read.

Shivering a little, she slid in beside him. The sheets felt smooth and cold. The bed was very narrow and she exclaimed as its hard edge dug into her flesh.

Bradley grinned and pulled her close. "We'll have to sleep in the middle. It's that, or be black and blue come morning." Then he blew out the candle.

Darkness enfolded them, as it had in the wood on the night of
Pamela's wedding, a friendly, comfortable, familiar darkness,
blotting out all that was strange. Diana felt Bradley's hands
begin to explore the fastenings of her pyjamas and she giggled,
snuggling up to him. Everything was going to be all right. This
was the Bradley she knew and loved.

Much later, he sat up and reached for the cigarettes lying on
the floor on his side of the bed. He didn't offer her one. She had
smoked occasionally until last Christmas, when he had told her
he hated to see women smoke. Craving his approval, she had
given up at once. Now she lay in the crook of his arm and
watched the glow of his cigarette in the darkness, and felt truly
happy, for the first time that day.

"How soon do you think Fell Cottage will be ready?" she
asked at last.

"Oh, it'll not take long, you'll see."

Fell Cottage was a tiny stone house on the northern edge of
Springbank's land, just over the brow of the hill. Built originally as
a lead miner's cottage in the days when there were more than a
mere half dozen working mines in the dale, it had in recent years
been used to store tools or stock, but Bradley's parents had offered
it to their son and his wife. As soon as it was cleared out, repaired
and redecorated, the young couple would be able to move into it.
Bradley assured her it would suit them fine, though Diana hadn't
yet seen it – her parents had discouraged meetings between the pair
of them before the wedding; almost, she thought, as if keeping
them apart might somehow restore her lost virginity.

"I'll take you up there tomorrow," Bradley promised. "After
dinner."

Sunday dinner was the pivot of the week at Springbank Farm.
Bradley assured Diana that only grave illness or sudden death
could excuse any family member from attending (and that
included the spouses of all the sons and daughters: Jackson's
wife Amy and their infant daughter Irene, Tom and Willy who
were the husbands of Vera and May, and Bert, engaged to Lily;
only Annie, the eldest daughter, in service in a country house in
Northumberland, was absent). Made hungry by equally com-

pulsory chapel and a very long sermon from a local preacher whose accent was, to Diana, completely impenetrable, the family assembled about the kitchen table in an atmosphere which was at once relaxed and formal to tackle a massive roast joint that made yesterday's wedding meal seem almost frugal. The men carved, carried dishes, enlivened the company with jokes – many, kindly enough, at the expense of other members of the family. The women, as a matter of course, helped with the preparation of the meal and the table laying, and with the washing up afterwards, but there were so many of them that there was very little for Diana to do. She was well able to share the conviviality without actually exerting herself very much. The strangeness of yesterday seemed like an aberration.

Afterwards, she and Bradley walked over the fields under a grey sky to inspect their future home.

Diana, full of high expectations, tried very hard to hide her disappointment. Fell Cottage was not at all as she'd imagined. She had known it was no cosy thatched retreat with roses round the door, nor ever would be, on that hill top where only the scrawniest hawthorn could survive, bent by the wind. Bradley had told her, too, that a great deal of work was needed, but his manner had not led her to expect quite this scene of near-dereliction. Outside was a yard with pigsty, coal house and earth closet (*netty*, Bradley called it), all half-ruined, and a walled, weed-grown enclosure that might once have been a vegetable plot. Inside, the house consisted of barely more than two rooms, linked by the remains of a staircase – the scullery was too cramped to count as a proper room. The interior walls had once been plastered, but damp and the buffeting of animals and weather had worn much of it away, and what was left was blackened and cracked. The floors were caked with a thick uneven layer of mud and dung. The only improvement that had been made so far was a new front door, which at least partly secured the house from the elements, or the attentions of mischievous children. But the roof was in a bad state of disrepair, and it was clear that the rain still came in that way. It all smelt horrible.

"Needs some work, as you can see," admitted Bradley, though he sounded very cheerful about it. "Jackson'll give a hand, and my dad, when he can. We'll soon have it put to rights." It was hard to imagine, but Diana tried to believe him.

For the time being, she was thankful for Springbank Farm. She had, she thought, found a second family there, one whose love was proof against disapproval; and whose life had a richness undreamed of in Dale House, for all its modern comforts.

On Monday morning, Bradley nudged her awake before it was fully light. She thought he was about to make love to her, while everyone else was still asleep (the bedroom walls were uncomfortably thin, and she was afraid his parents in the next room must hear everything). But by the time she had fully opened her eyes he was half out of bed, sitting up and pulling on his shirt.

"What's the matter?"

"Time to get up."

She glanced at her watch, laid on the chair by the bed. "It's only five o'clock."

"And I've to go to work."

"Am I coming with you?"

"Course not. But you can't lie in bed."

Diana was about to ask why not, then thought better of it. That was, she reflected, one way in which life at Springbank Farm was not like boarding school: there, from the very first, it had been made clear what was expected of her and what (most definitely) was not. Here, so far, she had been left to work out the rules and boundaries for herself.

Yawning, she began to dress. "What am I going to do all day?"

"It's Monday," he said, as if that were explanation enough. Then, perhaps realising it wasn't, added, "Washday."

She discovered very quickly what that meant. Breakfast seemed to be over almost before it had begun. The men soon disappeared, leaving the house to the women. Mrs Armstrong must have been up for some time, for she was already busy in one of the small rooms built on the side of the kitchen. Diana sat alone at the kitchen table, drinking a last cup of tea, while Bradley's youngest sister Lily, unmarried but courting, began to clear the dishes away. "Let me help," said Diana, draining her cup and getting to her feet. Lily gave her what she thought was an odd look, but said nothing and moved towards the back kitchen.

Elsie Armstrong, coming back into the room, had heard Diana, and said briskly, "Why, of course – you're family now. Just get on with it, lass." She swept up a towel that hung on a hook near the fire and disappeared again before Diana could ask what she should get on with.

After a moment's consideration, Diana piled up her own breakfast dishes and followed Lily into the scullery, where she was already swilling crockery in the stone sink. "Is there a teatowel somewhere?" she enquired. Yesterday there had been too many people in the kitchen for her to notice where such things were kept.

"I can manage these. You go and help Mam in the wash-house."

She found the wash-house, by following the odd rhythmic slurping noise that came from it. It was not a big room, and it was filled with steam from the great boiler set over a fire in the corner. Elsie Armstrong was standing beside a waist-high tub, plunging a large implement up and down in grey soapy water in whose depths lay a bundle of something that had once been white, and might, presumably, be white again, eventually. "There's those things to sort," she said, without looking round. She merely tilted her head towards a heap of clothes piled on the floor.

Diana looked at them helplessly. Was she supposed to sort them according to who they belonged to, or what kind of garments they were (there seemed to be everything she could think of, almost the entire wardrobe of everyone in the house, she suspected), or what they were made of, or what colour they were, or how badly soiled they were? She had no idea. Some of the clothes were very dirty, and smelled of stale sweat and cow dung and oil. She lifted up something that seemed cleaner than most – it was a nightdress, she realised – and looked at it, wondering what to do next. She gazed round the room, but no clue offered itself.

Elsie glanced at her, sighed (though she also smiled, as if at a half-witted child), held the handle of the tool she was using towards Diana and said, "Here, you do the possing. I'll see to those."

'Possing' was not as easy as Elsie had made it seem and Diana kept splashing herself, but at least she had some vague idea what she was supposed to do. It seemed an age before her mother-in-law looked into the tub and declared that the washing was ready for rinsing. That, she found, was just the beginning. When the rinsing was done (and it took a very long time and made her hands cold and sore), there was bleaching and mangling and starching to do, and then the washing had to be carried out into the cold wind and hung from the long washing line in the orchard behind the house; and then there would be another bundle of dirty clothes waiting to be put through the same process. With every task she struggled to complete, Diana hoped that she would soon be released to go upstairs, or even into the cheerless parlour, to read or write a letter, or occupy herself with one of the other simple personal activities that she had taken for granted at Dale House. But if ever she was seen to be standing idle, even for a few seconds, Elsie would direct her to another task. "We're not done yet," she would say. That, Diana quickly decided, was the understatement of the year.

It was not, of course, that she minded helping about the house. After all, she was part of the family now, and glad to be so. Even at Dale House they were generally expected to make their own beds (except when there was linen to be changed) and set the table for meals. But she found herself feeling just a little resentful that Elsie Armstrong should take her readiness to help so much for granted. She would have liked to be asked. She would also like to have felt they had some consideration for her condition; instead of which no one ever thought to ask her how she was. In fact, in the past days the sickness seemed to have gone, and she felt very much better, for which she was heartily thankful. But even Bradley appeared unconcerned about her health.

Most of all she would have liked to have the various tasks explained to her. But no one ever explained anything, and there

33

never seemed to be time to stop and ask. As the week passed, she found herself swallowed up in a relentless daily (and day-long) routine that left her no time for any kind of leisure. From first getting up in the morning (and no one ever lay in much beyond dawn) the women of the household were busy clearing ashes and laying fires, shaking mats, scrubbing floors, swilling the yard, cleaning windows and paintwork, turning leftover meat into some new dish, and endlessly baking. As well as the routine daily tasks, each day also had its appointed extras: Monday, of course, was washday; Tuesday was for ironing (unless the weather was so fine it had been done the day before) and a major baking session; Wednesday was the day for cleaning upstairs; Thursday for a thorough downstairs clean of every room but the kitchen; Friday for blackleading the kitchen range (a hateful task) and cleaning up afterwards; Saturday for the biggest baking of the week, and changing the bedlinen. Diana hovered behind Lily and her mother, trying to understand what was being done, struggling to carry out utterly unfamiliar tasks whenever a casual command was thrown at her: 'Rub that down, lass!', 'Those sheets want putting sides to middles!', 'The eggs want gathering, come on now!' Everyone always assumed that she would know by instinct where everything was to be found and what to do with it. Their bemusement when she had no idea how to carry out what to them seemed the simplest of tasks, or how to use the most common of domestic implements, turned very quickly to impatience.

Even at the end of the day, when the supper dishes had been washed up and put away, and she'd hoped for some time alone with Bradley, she found she was not allowed to be idle (and idleness was a term that embraced such activities as reading, or writing any but business letters, or playing the piano). If there was no mending to be done, then the women were expected to occupy themselves with the endless making of the latest clippy mat, hooking small pieces of old clothes into the canvas stretched on a frame by the kitchen fire. In due course, when finished, it would replace one of the rugs that scattered all the floors in the house – those colourful homely rugs Diana had once so much admired. If neighbours called, as they sometimes did in the evenings, the mat still had to be done, as well as cups of tea made and food set out on the table. Of course, morning and evening, everyone talked as they worked, but gossip (however entertaining) about people she didn't know was not much compensation for lost leisure time.

The cottage on the fell began to seem a much more attractive proposition to Diana with each day that passed. Not only would it provide an escape from housework, but she and Bradley would be alone together, in their own home. Here at Springbank Farm the narrow bed in Bradley's room was the only place where they had any privacy at all.

On her second Thursday at Springbank there was, to Diana's relief, a promised respite from housework. It was market day at Bishop Auckland, the nearest sizeable market town, and she gathered that the Armstrong women often made the journey there in search of essential major items of shopping – of which, it seemed, there were several outstanding at present. They assumed she would want to come too – as indeed she did, if the alternative was to polish the already over-polished furniture in the parlour, or scrub the spotless floor of the dairy. But Diana longed for once to escape from the Armstrong womenfolk, to have a little time to herself, to spend as she chose; or, better still, with Bradley.

"Let me come with you tomorrow, please!" she pleaded softly, as she and Bradley left the supper table at which the next day's plans had been discussed.

"I'll be at work. I've to lead stone to Spen Green, over Consett way. They're building a village hall."

"Then I could come with you in the lorry. Couldn't I? Please!"

He grinned suddenly. "I don't see why not. All right then." He had been talking quietly, but lowered his voice still more. "Mind, don't tell Mam." She was about to object, when he added, "Leave this to me." Out loud, he said, "Mam, Di's not feeling so good. You don't mind if she stays quiet here tomorrow, has a bit rest?"

Elsie seemed surprised, but agreed, and even suggested that Diana should go early to bed.

The next day, everything worked perfectly. The senior Armstrong women set off in good time to catch the bus, allowing Diana (for once permitted to lie in) to savour the rare treat of being all alone in the house as she washed and dressed. She set off down the hill, crossed the narrow wooden footbridge over the river, meandered through the flowery meadows beyond and reached the appointed meeting place beside the road in good time. For once in this cheerless summer it was sunny and almost warm, a perfect beginning to the day.

Bradley arrived almost as she did, and looked as happy as she felt. It was, Diana thought, as he helped her up into the cab, as if they were an unmarried couple again, meeting in secret. "This is fun," she said happily, as he moved off.

"Aye. Driver's mate, that's what you are today. So just watch that you behave, mind."

She knew what his sly look implied, and giggled. "I might or I might not," she returned. Desire, lately so often dampened by the discomforts of pregnancy or simple exhaustion, revived in her. Emboldened by it, she pressed a hand (briefly) on his thigh.

"You'll have me off the road," he warned, but she knew he didn't mean it. Then he added, "Dad wanted to send Jim with me – you know, Jim Stobbs the quarry manager; he was at our wedding." Diana dimly recalled a short, square-set man, with a face as rough-hewn as the rocks he worked. "Had a right job putting him off. Told him there'd be any number of men to unload at the other end. There'd better be, or you'll be in for some heavy work."

"Does the quarry belong to your father?" She knew it was a family concern, but had not yet worked out all the ramifications of the Armstrongs, and their various responsibilities. Nor had she seen much of Bradley's father, a slight silent man who scarcely seemed to know she was there. It was hard to imagine him running a business.

"Aye, for as long as I can remember. Came down in the family

36

somehow. Building stone mostly, for houses in the dale. Our cottage came from there, I reckon.''

"So is that his main work? Is that how he started?"

"Why, no. Carriers, carters, that's what the Armstrongs have always been, for hundreds of years. Horse-breeders too – goes with it, I suppose. That's what Jackson likes best. A horse man, he is. It's what he'd do all the time if he had the chance. He'd have liked Fell Cottage, you know."

"But he's got somewhere to live," Diana pointed out. She knew that Jackson lived with his wife and daughter in the flat above the family garage in Wearbridge.

"Aye, and a good snug flat it is too – more space than we'll have, by a long way. Amy likes it. But there's no land handy. For all he's a fair mechanic, Jackson couldn't care less about cars and lorries. If it's not got four legs, he's not interested. Still, there's no future in horses. Even he can see that. It's the lorries put bread in his mouth. And the car repairs."

"So your father hasn't had them long – the lorries, I mean?"

"He bought up some ex-army stock after the war. Just the one to start with, a Thorneycroft J-type – we've still got it, up at the quarry. Good vehicle it is too. Anyway, he could see horses and carts were finished, even though no one else could, that soon. Maybe marrying Mam put it in mind – her Dad had the garage. Elsie Bradley, she was then; you see where my name comes from. Her brothers were killed in the war so she inherited the lot. Blacksmith's it was to start off, then when cars came in there was more money to be made on that side. Anyway, it's all grown from there. Mind, hard work's what's made it, above all else."

Diana felt that she already knew more than enough about hard work. "Then you don't just use the lorries for the stone, from the quarry? Or do you?"

"That's most of it these days. Of course, things are bad. They've been worse since they finished the reservoir last summer. There was any amount of work while that was on the go, especially with the railway not going that far. But that's all done now. Dad's had to lay off drivers. I'm the only one left, apart from him, though Jim does the odd run now and then, and

Jackson when he can't get out of it. But it's the mechanicking I really like, the repairs. That's what I'd do all the time, if I could."

She recalled their first meeting and smiled softly. "Suits you too," she said, and saw that he knew what she was thinking.

He reached out and pushed her skirt off her knee, running his hand up under it. The lorry lurched to the other side of the road. Diana cried out, and he laughed, though the hand hurriedly returned to the steering wheel.

Fortunately there were more than enough men to help unload the stone at Spen Green. The coal mine which had been the sole employer for the isolated community had closed some time before, so the men, most of them unemployed for many years, were occupying themselves by constructing a much-needed meeting place for the village. They invited Bradley and Diana (who had to endure much teasing, little of which she understood, since the men's dialect was so strong) to share their midday meal, but Bradley refused. "Got to get back," he said. Diana knew that was not the reason at all.

He drove a few miles back the way they had come, and then turned into a narrow lane that ran down into a wooded hollow. There, he drew half off the road, switched off the engine, and turned to her. "Now, your wages, driver's mate."

Afterwards, hot and a little bruised (there was not a great deal of room in the cab), they shared his jam sandwiches and flask of tea (his *bait*, he told her). "Now, back to the quarry," he said, when they'd finished. "I'll drop you off on the way."

Diana tugged at his arm. "Let me drive – please! Just a little drive!"

He looked round at her, laughing, outraged. "You're a woman! You can't drive!"

"Yes I can. I've passed the test."

"That's different. This is a wagon. Women don't drive wagons."

"They did in the war. My mother told me." She felt, momentarily, a pang of recollection; just last year, a corner of the drawing room, a portion of heavy gold curtain behind, the evening sun on her mother's face. She could see the tiny flecks of powder on her fair skin . . . It hurt, badly. She was glad that Bradley quickly answered her, so she had no time to dwell on it.

"There isn't a war now."

"There might be." Even with all the distractions of the past weeks, she knew war was still feared and expected, even if she couldn't really believe it. "Go on, let me try – please!"

A pause, then: "All right, just this once. Not here, though. A nice safe straight bit of road."

He turned the lorry and drove back to the road, and eventually found a place which he declared would do. Then he jumped down and they changed places, and he began to explain the controls. She thought he was a good deal more nervous than she was.

"It's not so very different from a car, you know," Diana said. "And I'm not stupid." Slowly, carefully, she followed his instructions. They worked. The lorry edged forward, a little unsteadily. She gained courage and pressed more firmly on the accelerator.

"Steady! Not so fast!"

"Bradley, if I go on at this rate we'll not get home before next week."

"You needn't think you're driving all the way home!" He sounded genuinely alarmed, and she glanced at him, laughing. "Keep your eyes on the road!"

It felt wonderful, high up in the cab, with a clear view all around, and the power there at the end of her feet, and the touch of her hands on the steering wheel. At a steady, sensible pace she drove for perhaps two miles on that long straight road (a Roman road, so her parents had told her, when they'd come this way once), until Bradley's nerve snapped and he insisted she halt the lorry so he could take over again. It was only when he was safely back in control that he admitted she had really done quite well, better than he'd expected. "Not bad, for a girl," he said.

Diana felt exultant. His approval made her triumph complete. She could ask for nothing more.

"I'll drop you where I picked you up," he said as they passed through Wearbridge. "Then if anyone sees you, you can just say you've been for a walk."

Unfortunately, the first person to see them was Bradley's father, who had returned to Springbank to repair a wall near the road. They neither of them saw him until Diana jumped down, ran round the front of the lorry and suddenly found herself looking into his startled face.

"What's going on?" he demanded, glancing from her to Bradley.

"Driver's mate," said Bradley weakly, all his assertiveness gone.

"In her condition? What are you thinking of, jolting her about in that thing? Do you want to lose the bairn?"

"Oh, she's taken no harm," said Bradley. He seemed to be trying very hard to sound nonchalant, though he looked more like a naughty schoolboy.

"How do you know? Now you expect her to walk all the way up home, I suppose, by herself? Well, you can think again. Get down. I'll take the wagon back. You see her safe home."

Diana tried to assure him that she was none the worse for the day's activities (a good thing, she thought, that he didn't know them all), that the walk would do her no harm, but he ignored her; his mind was made up. So she walked home, with Bradley grumbling all the way beside her. She sensed that in some way he blamed her for this unfortunate end to the day, and consequently she felt guilty about it. Worse, she found that his mood, once set, was impossible to shift, being resistant to her many attempts to coax him out of it. She had to endure two whole days (and nights) of ill humour, before the cheerful family atmosphere of Sunday dinner drove it away. By then, their day of shared pleasure seemed like a dream. She knew there would be no more like it.

Haytime held up the renovation of Fell Cottage (and meant more work than ever for the Armstrong women), and it was not until a Sunday afternoon well into August that Bradley walked her over the fields to see how near it was to being habitable.

"Shut your eyes," he commanded, as they reached the brow of the hill. "I'll make sure you don't trip up."

So she closed her eyes, and kept them closed until he told her

40

to open them again, beside the front gate (newly painted). "Well," he asked triumphantly, "what do you think?"

She saw a tiny neat cottage, with the roof newly slated, the stonework repointed, the door and window frames painted a dark shiny green. Inside, the smell of damp and neglect had gone, and the worst of the dirt had been cleared from the floors, revealing stone flags downstairs and boards upstairs. The walls, freshly plastered though not yet painted, were a soft smooth pink. The woodwork had been painted the same green as the outside. The chimneys had been swept and the hearths cleaned out; there were new shelves in the scullery and a small second-hand range had been installed in the living room.

"Now it's up to you," said Bradley.

"Me?"

"Finish off the floors, put up the curtains and that. Mam will help you, and our Lily, they'll all help."

Mam, she found, already had curtains made, or rather cut down from some old ones of her own. They were not perhaps what Diana would have chosen, but she knew she was not in a position to be choosy, and they certainly made the rooms look immediately more homely. When she scrubbed the floors she was thankful for the first time that the rooms were so small, and when she cleaned the windows that there were only three of them, one in each room. In any case, it felt much less like drudgery to be cleaning her own house.

As for furniture, various neighbours and members of the family supplied them with cast-offs – two wooden chairs and an armchair, a table, a small double bed, the washstand from Bradley's bedroom. The most recently made clippy mat was presented to Diana, who was suddenly proud that some of her own handiwork had gone into it, though she wished it was not quite so obvious which part that was.

"There's this too," said Elsie Armstrong, on the day when the cottage was finally ready for occupation. She laid a large linen package on the table, and carefully unwrapped it, revealing crimson satin, intricately worked. "It's the quilt I made, for when Bradley was married. For your bed."

Diana was enchanted. "It's exquisite!" She examined the delicate needlework, marvelling that any ordinary human being could make anything so lovely. Later, spread on their bed, it gave the small, sparsely furnished bedroom an unexpectedly opulent look.

There was very little of Diana's own choosing in the cottage, but she had brought two pictures with her – a cousin's small watercolour of Dale House, and a seascape in oils which had come to her on the death of a spinster aunt; it showed a tranquil harbour, with boats rocking at anchor, and had always reminded her of a particularly enjoyable family holiday in Cornwall. These she hung in the downstairs room. Her few books she placed on the mantelpiece above the range, until such time as there was a more suitable place. Beside the books stood a wooden chiming clock, which had been a wedding present from one of Bradley's cousins. Outside the cottage, a cockerel and two hens strutted and scratched, and a young pig lay on new straw in the renovated sty. He came from the most recent Springbank litter and terrified Diana, who'd been told he was her responsibility. She knew nothing whatsoever about pigs.

But it was still a relief when Elsie and Lily left them alone at last. They stood watching the departing figures from their newly whitened front door step, waiting until they were out of sight before turning to one another. "Now I feel really, truly married," Diana said and, laughing, she let Bradley carry her over the threshold.

Four

"Sunday, we'll have Mam and Dad over for tea," Bradley declared after dinner, as he sat slumped in Fell Cottage's only armchair, his feet stretched towards the range.

Diana, returning to the room from the scullery where she had been washing up, felt as if her stomach had dropped below her pelvis. "Shouldn't we wait a while? Just until—" Until what? Until she'd miraculously turned into a half-decent cook? Until the shops in Wearbridge supplied cakes that might pass as homemade, at prices they could afford? Until (here was hope!) they had more than two each of plates and cups and saucers?

"No," said Bradley, before she could say anything further. "We owe them."

"What shall we do for plates?"

"Mam will lend us some." He blew a smoke ring towards the mantelpiece, a visible full-stop on the matter.

So that was it. Diana dared not argue. After all, Bradley knew the rules better than she did. In any case, it was obvious that he was right – they'd enjoyed so many meals at Springbank, even since they moved into Fell Cottage, nearly two months ago; they still went back to the farm for dinner every Sunday, and often stayed for tea as well. It was time they gave something in return.

She thought of Sunday teas at Springbank, the thick and succulent ham, the fresh bread and butter and homemade jam, the light, moist scones and the three or more delicious cakes. She knew she couldn't even begin to provide so sumptuous a feast. Yet that was what would be expected of her.

She was vexed with Bradley for forcing this unwelcome intrusion on their life at Fell Cottage. Until now everything,

43

almost, had been perfect; just the two of them sharing an idyll.
Certainly that was how it had seemed at the very first. It was
wonderful to make love in a bed that was just about large
enough, without fear of being overheard by censorious ears in
the next room. It was lovely to feel she need no longer worry
about the unspoken rules of the place, and whether she might be
breaking them. Here she could begin – given Bradley's acquies-
cence – to make her own rules. It had been like playing at houses,
only this was real, and it was all theirs. Diana had felt she was a
proper wife at last, fully grown up.

There had been shadows, of course, of which her attempts at
cooking cast the largest. She had begun with the best of inten-
tions, turning to her cookery book for assistance, imagining
herself welcoming Bradley home at night with meals such as his
mother had put before him at Springbank. No cook at Dale
House had ever managed to produce such meals, such crisp
golden pastry that melted in the mouth, such tender meat, such
satisfying puddings, though the Poultneys had always eaten
adequately. Diana would have been content to be an adequate
cook. But even with the help of her cookery book she fell far
short even of that lesser aim. Her first culinary disaster had
seemed funny, and they'd both been able to laugh about it, but
the joke had quickly worn off. A few evenings ago, faced with an
inedible stew, Bradley had simply carried his plate outside and
tipped its contents into the pig's trough. Diana had almost been
grateful to the pig for not rejecting them too.

And now she was faced with displaying her failings as a cook
before his mother, that paragon in the kitchen. The thought filled
her with terror. Elsie had always been kind to her, an ample and
generous presence, accepting her unquestioningly as a full member of the family. Yet being an Armstrong brought with it duties
as well as privileges, and for that reason Diana had quickly
learned to be a little in awe of her mother-in-law, partly because
she was such a perfect housewife, with such relentlessly high
standards, partly because of the brisk manner in which she had
occasionally put Diana right on some matter, as if amazed,
indeed only half-believing, that it should be necessary to do

so. Diana was quite sure that Bradley's mother did not yet realise the full extent of her daughter-in-law's wifely incompetence. She had no wish at all to do anything to bring that moment of uncomfortable revelation any closer.

As for Bradley's father, Diana was, quite simply, terrified of him. All she knew of him was that he was a naturally silent man of firm views who yet spoke his mind when he felt it to be necessary. She had seen how Bradley seemed to shrink before his father's suppressed anger. She hoped she was not about to find out what it would be like to be the direct recipient of it.

Still, if the tea could not be avoided, then she had to make the best of it. *Practice makes perfect*, she told herself, with renewed determination. She took down her cookery book from the mantelpiece and found paper and pencil and began to look through the book, choosing recipes and making a list of the ingredients she would need. She hoped the housekeeping money Bradley gave her from his pay would be able to cope with this sudden extra demand. She knew she couldn't hope for any more. She had discovered very quickly how alarmingly little could be bought with her weekly six shillings (which was not much more than her pocket money used to be), but by careful planning and keeping a meticulous record of everything she spent she was already learning to make it go further. It was a pity that she was not yet able to use the food she bought to good effect, but she was nevertheless rather proud of her thriftiness, as well as surprised by it. There were even a few pennies left over from last week's housekeeping.

The next morning, Friday, she walked down to the road to catch the bus to Wearbridge to do her shopping – the hill was too steep for her to attempt the journey on her bicycle, and in any case she was afraid that might damage the baby. She had been to Wearbridge as little as possible during the past weeks, though the few shops in Ravenshield barely supplied their daily needs, and it was strange to be in a place that was so familiar and yet in circumstances that were so very unfamiliar. She felt self-conscious, quite sure that everyone was watching her and remarking disapprovingly on her now obvious condition. If she saw anyone she knew approaching her along the street, she would slip into the nearest shop, for fear of the awkward conversation that might result. She was only too aware, as well, of her total inexperience of shopping – at least, of the ordinary, everyday household shopping that was the only kind she was likely to be involved in nowadays. She was always relieved when she found a shop crowded, so that she could tag on the back of the queue and, waiting her turn, observe what other people did – their manner, their actions, all the little things they took for granted but which, omitted, would only display her inexperience.

Today, she went first to the Co-operative store, whose elaborate Gothic frontage stood out against the weathered simplicity of its neighbours in Front Street. She knew there was no danger she would meet any of her parents' circle here, or their servants. They regarded the Co-op with disdain, and not just on aesthetic grounds: it was a shop for the lower orders, for those who had to watch the pennies. Since Diana Armstrong had to watch the pennies, the Co-op suited her very well.

As she waited in the long queue at the grocery counter, she heard the talk going on around her. Unsurprisingly, it was all about the possible imminence of war, as most conversations had been for what seemed like years – so long, in fact, that the probability of war seemed like a permanent state, something that was always about to happen but never really would in the end, simply remaining there as a matter for endless speculation and planning. This morning, however, there was an alarming sense of urgency about the talk, as if the speakers had actually begun to believe there would be a war, and soon. The Prime Minister, Mr Neville Chamberlain, was at this very moment in Munich negotiating with Adolf Hitler, but no one held out much hope that he would succeed in averting the inevitable. Diana, for so long bored by the subject, had not realised that preparations for war had actually reached an advanced stage, as if the government at least believed it was coming, and wished to be ready. Strange initials were being dropped into the talk – ARP, for instance, which seemed to be some means of protecting the civilian population in some way: from air attack, from that horror of the last war, gas.

"There's one thing, if war comes it'll sharp be over," said a large-bosomed woman a little way in front of Diana. "The Germans'll flood us with gas and that'll be it. All they'll need do then is march in." She spoke with gloomy relish.

"Not if we've all got gas masks," said the elderly man behind her, who had first introduced the subject – he was the only man amongst the customers.

"You think that'll make any difference?" said the woman.

"They'll never get as far as this, I reckon," said a cheerful-looking young woman in front of her.

"Won't they? I'm not so sure. Besides, I'd not want to be left, if all the towns were taken. Not to be trampled under the jackboots of a lot of Germans."

"They've got some good ideas, those Nazis, so my Alf says," murmured a meek-looking woman. "We could do worse than learn a thing or two from them."

"Good clean living," endorsed a brisk middle-class voice. That was the only woman Diana could put a name to, Miss Firbank, a retired History teacher from Meadhope grammar school; she had joined the queue after Diana. "Fresh air, simplicity and hard work. We would all benefit from those principles."

"Aye." The man sniggered. "Like the Jews. They're taking their gold off them, putting them to work. About time too. You know what they say – you'll never see a Jew-boy down a coal mine. Or a lead mine, come to that." Then, perhaps realising that if war came such sentiments might be seen as less than patriotic, he added quickly, "Mind, I'd not want this country ruled by foreigners, Germans no more than Jews. If they come up here it'll be up to us to fight them, to the last man."

"Why, yes," said the first speaker. "Fine example you'd be, Arthur Ingleton. You made sure you never saw any fighting the last time round."

"I'd have gone soon enough, if it hadn't been for my chest. You know that, Bella Hindmarsh."

After that, the conversation became rather heated and unpleasant, and Diana was glad when her time came to be served and she could leave the shop.

47

She felt depressed and even a little frightened. She was used to talk of the last war. Now, she could not help recalling what it had done to a whole generation, her parents' generation, of which so many women were growing old without the men in their lives, without a brother, a husband, a sweetheart. Elsie Armstrong had lost three brothers. Bradley's father too had lost a brother, as had her own mother. She knew her father mourned many good friends, because he'd mentioned it once and she had sensed deep emotion beneath his customary matter-of-fact exterior. Old Doctor Elliott, her father's partner, who was also the Armstrong family doctor, had lost his only son. What if she should have married Bradley only to lose him almost before she'd got to know him? Thank goodness at least that they had married, that they had been given some time together, that she was carrying his child, so that if the worst happened they should at least have had something.

Outside, deep in thought, she almost collided with a woman walking along the street – no, not a woman, a *lady*, and one known to her. Full of flustered apologies, she focused her gaze on the face of Mrs Garthorne, mother of her friend Lydia; but only for a fraction of a second. She was just about to stammer out some kind of greeting, when Mrs Garthorne stepped to one side and went on her way, her stony expression scarcely registering Diana's presence.

Diana remained where she was in the middle of the pavement, not moving. She felt as if someone had tipped a bucket of cold water over her.

So that was it. She had recognised that those who moved in her parents' circle must know why she'd made so hurried a marriage, and would disapprove of what she had done. She hadn't realised that so far as they were concerned she had ceased to exist; they had erased her from their lives. For her, it was as if the child at boarding school had suddenly found there was no way home when the holidays came, that she was for ever stranded there, away from what had once been so familiar and safe. She realised that until now she had always believed, in some part of herself, that no matter what happened, no matter how disapproving they might be, her family – especially her mother and father – would always be there if she really needed them. Now she felt that the ultimate support had gone. She was alone. She could only restore the old sense of security by becoming, wholly and for ever, an intrinsic part of her new family; or, better still, by establishing a family of her own, with Bradley – father, mother, child.

She began to walk on, slowly, because she was trembling and her legs felt as if they had no strength in them. She tried to gather her thoughts and remember what shopping there was still to do, while all the time she was looking around, fearful that she might meet someone else she knew, wondering if they would react as Mrs Garthorne had done. Robert and Angela would be back at school by now, at the end of the summer holidays, so there was no danger she would bump into them, though it was odd to think they had been so near, yet she had seen nothing of them. That was a relief, as well as a pain. She knew she wouldn't have been able to bear it if her own sister or brother had treated her as Mrs Garthorne had done. But there were other people she might meet. She quickened her pace, anxious to return to the sanctuary of Fell Cottage.

There was just Mr Emerson, the butcher, who, unfortunately, also supplied Dale House. She was half-inclined to go to the Co-op butcher, but Mrs Armstrong had declared that, on the rare occasions when they had none of their own home produce, Mr Emerson's ham was the next best thing. She dared not risk buying any other, but she peered nervously into the shop before entering it, to make sure she was not likely to risk hurt or embarrassment. She saw no one she knew, and went in.

Mr Emerson chatted as he served her, about the weather, and the possibility of war, addressing his remarks as much to his other customers as to Diana, though he was perfectly friendly. She was taken by surprise when he suddenly asked, "Did Mrs Poultney enjoy her holiday? A fine town, Scarborough. The little ones will have enjoyed the sea, I'll be bound."

So her mother had been away, taking Robert and Angela with her! Had that been deliberate, to take them where they wouldn't run any risk of meeting her, or be tempted to ask awkward questions? She stammered some kind of reply to the butcher and fled from the shop. She was sure that the moment she had gone everyone would begin to discuss her. But worse was the increased sense of rejection, from which there was no escape. It had come to this, that to have news of her family she had to listen to gossip in the shops!

She was glad to reach home, to arrange her purchases on the still bare pantry shelves, to enjoy her possession of the little house and all that was in it. Here, she had no need of anyone but Bradley, who would soon be home, wanting his supper.

Which was the trouble, of course. She tried not to think of all the previous disasters. From today things were going to be different. She was going to get it right at last. She would make a stew, using the shin of beef she'd bought, and carrots and onions and potatoes. Surely this time nothing could go wrong? As she washed and peeled and chopped (awkwardly, scraping her fingers, sending chunks of vegetables scattering onto the floor) she could already imagine the savoury smells rising from the pot on the range.

By the time Bradley came home the smell was not a bit as she had imagined, though it was, she thought, a good deal better than the last time she'd attempted a stew. Unfortunately (or was it fortunately?) that was not the first thing he noticed.

He came home perhaps half an hour before she expected him and stood in the doorway in his oily dungarees, looking around the room. The first gleam of sunshine for days was lighting it, stretching into every corner. "This place is a pigsty," he said in disgust. "What have you been doing all day?"

Diana stared at him. "Shopping. Cooking. Keeping the fire going. Feeding the pig and the hens. Collecting eggs. Fetching water. You can see – your dinner's all ready, the water's hot for you." That was perhaps the job she hated most. At first she had thought it fun to bring water in from the spring outside, heating what they needed for washing over the fire. It had all been new and exciting, a bit like being on holiday. But holidays came to an end and this did not, and the novelty had very quickly worn off, especially when the weather was cold and wet, as it had been for much of the time. She often found herself thinking longingly of the hot water that used to flow so conveniently from the taps at Dale House. "Anyway," she went on, "what's wrong with this place?" She looked about her. True, there was a clutter of kitchen utensils on the table, which she'd not yet taken into the scullery to be washed up with the supper dishes. But she could see nothing else wrong.

Bradley strode to the fire and ran a finger along the mantelpiece and brought it away darkened with dust. "Look at that! It's disgusting. Mam would never let anyone in a place that looked like this. She'd be ashamed. She'd have been ashamed to let a man come in weary from work to such a tip."

"I'm not your Mam. Besides, I can't do everything. I haven't had time to dust today."

"No time! Don't be ridiculous! I cannot believe how idle you are."

Idle, she thought – *when every drop of water has to be brought in from the spring, and every drop of hot water heated over the fire, and I have a good bus journey and a long and tiring walk for every bit of shopping, and I never stop from getting up to going to bed?* "You're always telling me to rest. But when do I ever have time to rest?"

"Mam never let things slip, even when she was having us, and it never did her any harm. I remember when our Jimmy was born. She had a bad time, but the house was spotless. She'd not have let the neighbours in if there'd been a thing out of place." Jimmy was a small brother of Bradley's who had died of diphtheria at three years old; Elsie always visited his grave after chapel on Sunday. "Any woman should be able to keep her house nice, no matter what. Didn't your Mam teach you anything?"

"We had staff for all that." Diana immediately wished the words unsaid. She heard Bradley mimic her, cruelly.

"Why now," he sneered, "poor little Miss Diana, having to shift for herself. Next thing, you'll have me weeping for you."

"Don't be so hard on me," she pleaded. 'I'm doing my best." Her heart was thudding. She felt as if every last trace of her happiness was under threat. She began to clear the table and set it ready for the meal. "Let's eat." She tried to sound calm and in control. "I'll clean up afterwards."

"You needn't think I'm stopping in this mess. I'm off to the Black Bull." That was the pub at Ravenshield where once he used to drink almost every night, risking his parents' disapproval.

When he had gone Diana began resentfully to scrub and scour. It was all right for him; he could be out enjoying himself all day. She had asked more than once if she could go with him again on the lorry – his father would not know, if they were careful. No, he'd said; you should stay here and rest.

Rest! she thought. It would have been fine if she could have sat with her feet up, reading books, varying the routine with an occasional gentle stroll. But somehow doing the housework did not count as over-exertion, as far as Bradley was concerned. Diana suspected that he didn't regard housework as work at all. Perhaps he believed women were born doing it, as they breathed, without conscious thought or effort. If so, he must now be revising his opinion.

The tea the next Sunday was every bit as dreadful as Diana had anticipated. The preparations were bad enough, and not helped by the ill-temper that had enveloped Bradley since the outburst about her lack of cleaning skills. It was hard to cook well with a heart heavy with misery. Her cakes and scones seemed to take on a sympathetic heaviness.

The Armstrong parents arrived at Fell Cottage in a cheerful frame of mind, sharing the overwhelming relief that almost everybody had felt since yesterday's good news of Mr Chamberlain's agreement with Hitler at Munich. There was no wireless at Fell Cottage, and no newspaper, but Bradley had brought the news home last night from the Black Bull, where it had lightened even his sullen mood.

"Well, at least we know there's not going to be a war," Elsie Armstrong said, as she took off her coat and handed it to Diana. She glanced at Bradley, and Diana caught a glimpse of the anxiety she had felt for her sons, grown men though they now were.

It's not her business to worry about Bradley, Diana thought, a little resentfully. *That's for me to do.* But she said nothing, simply invited her guests to be seated.

The table looked really rather attractive, spread with their one tablecloth and the borrowed plates, the slices of ham neatly arranged, the scones halved and buttered (their deficiencies were more easily concealed that way), the two cakes – one jam-filled Victoria sandwich, one seed cake – partly sliced (for the same reason). Perhaps it would be all right after all.

It was not. The ham was acceptable, of course, if not as good as Springbank's own produce. The bought bread could have been worse. The jam came from Springbank, and had been made by Elsie herself. But the scones were hard and dry, and the cakes were scorched on the outside and soggy within, and full of odd lumps and textures, flour here, butter there.

As the meal progressed, Elsie became more and more silent, more and more stony-faced. Now and then her gaze would wander about the room, to settle unerringly on something that met with her disapproval. During the past forty-eight hours Diana had swept and scrubbed and polished until she had thought there could be no possible blemish left. Now, following Elsie's gaze, she could see a film of dust on a forgotten picture frame, a stray cobweb high in a corner of the ceiling, a ball of fluff gathered under a chair.

Bradley's father said even less than did his wife, and almost all his few remarks were addressed to his son. Diana noticed too that he ate very little, for which she supposed she could hardly blame him. At the earliest opportunity, he rose from the table, accepting Bradley's offer to show him what had been done in the vegetable plot, which Bradley worked on at weekends.

Diana stood up and began to stack the plates. "It's such good news about the war," she said, conscious that she was repeating herself. She was desperate for some safe topic of conversation. "That there's not going to be one, I mean . . ."

Elsie was not so easily diverted. "Has no one ever taught you to cook?"

"Not really," admitted Diana. She felt herself reddening with guilt. "But my mother gave me a very good cookery book as a wedding present."

"Nothing worthwhile was ever learned from a book," said Elsie. Then she softened the remark by adding, with brisk kindliness, "If I'd realised how bad it was, I'd have taken you in hand before you moved up here. But it's not too late. You come down to the farm next Tuesday – come early, and I'll give you some hints on cleaning too. It looks as though they wouldn't come amiss. Then in the afternoon you can give me a hand with the baking. A week or two of that and you'll see the difference."

Diana felt humiliated. "It's all right, thank you," she said stiffly. "I know I made a few mistakes this time, but I hadn't made scones and things before, and I know where I went wrong. I shall manage."

But that night, as they got ready for bed, Bradley said to her, "Mam says she offered to teach you to cook. You should let her. There's no better cook in the whole of County Durham. She'd enjoy it."

I bet she would! thought Diana. She was angry that Elsie should have discussed her with Bradley behind her back. She was angry with Bradley too, because it was clear that he agreed with his mother's view of things. "I'm not a child, I'm your wife. You should have taken my side."

"How could I? Mam's right – you haven't the first idea about housework. I'm sick of being poisoned by your cooking. Learn how to do it properly, or I'll be down at Springbank every night, that's all I can say."

So Diana gave in, and the arrangements were made. Feeling like a disgraced schoolgirl, she went down to Springbank the following Tuesday and worked under Elsie's tuition. What made it worse was that Lily, not much older than she was, observed all she did. Her mother's image in domestic matters, she was ready with an exclamation of astonishment every time Diana revealed the depth of her ignorance (which happened very often). It was clear to Diana that each tiny error only made them despise her the more – and not only her, but her school, her family, and especially her mother, who had so miserably failed to pass on to her the most essential skills.

There was no miraculous change. But her cooking did begin to improve a little, and she learned to do some things quite well and had fewer complete disasters. Housework was another matter. Diana felt no sympathy at all with Elsie's approach to cleaning. She felt angry that she should be expected to spend every waking moment occupied with some menial task, as if such tasks were the most important things in life, instead of simply an adjustment of its background for greater comfort. What, she thought, did it matter whether the range was blackleaded weekly or not, so long as it was relatively clean and did its job properly? Why clean every window in the house, inside and out, every week, whatever the weather? The setting aside of each day to its purpose irritated her too. It seemed to imply that the daily tasks were more important than anything else and must always take priority. She felt impatient with the whole relentless system. She did not want to spend her days cleaning the house and cooking. She wanted to do something she felt to be purposeful, something that would not simply have to be done again in exactly the same way the next day, or the next week. But for Bradley's sake she developed a routine that – imperfect as it was by Armstrong standards – seemed to satisfy him.

Yet she had lost something in the whole business. Things were never again as happy between Bradley and herself as they had been in the early days of their marriage. The innocence of his love for her seemed to have been irrevocably damaged; it now had reservations and qualifications. As for his family, they were never afterwards as unreservedly warm in their manner towards her. Lily always seemed to have mockery in her expression, and Diana saw disappointment behind Elsie's warmest smiles. It did not cause them to reject her, as her own family had done, but she feared they had come to regret their initial unqualified welcome. Sometimes she wondered if she would ever again be

55

able to do anything right; if anyone would be pleased with her or praise her for what she was or what she could do.

The autumn seemed very long, though at least the weather was mild, which made the fetching of water less arduous then it might otherwise have been. Daily, she grew larger and more weary of the burden she carried. She wished the waiting was at an end and the baby born. Surely then everything would be right again?

In the evenings she sewed baby clothes – not very well, though she had done some sewing at school. Elsie made some garments too, and presented her with a cot and mattress, and a pillow with a prettily embroidered cover. Her mother's baby book warned against pillows, but Diana felt too much in the wrong already to say anything about it.

She saw little of Bradley. She felt, in a way, as if she could hardly blame him for not wanting to spend time with her. She knew she must look terrible, so ungainly and awkward, though fortunately perhaps there was no full-length mirror at Fell Cottage with which to confirm her impression. She was always tired, her hands red and roughened, her hair lank from lack of care. Bradley went out almost every night, to the Black Bull, or to Springbank, or (often) without saying where he was going. She wished he would stay with her, but she found his moods so difficult that after a few attempts she ceased trying to dissuade him from going out.

Christmas meant going daily to Springbank, to endure too many people and too much to eat in rooms that were too hot, from which they returned at night to a cottage chilled by emptiness. Diana would have liked in some way to make this her Christmas too, by inviting the family (or some of them anyway) to her little house, or by putting up decorations, or trying to cook something special, but she was too near her time to risk starting anything that she might not be able to finish.

The old year–1938–departed, with its mixture of joy and pain and bewildering change, and hope destroyed.

On New Year's Day a fierce snow storm blew up, and at its height Diana went into labour. The midwife, fetched by Bradley (along with his mother), came through the drifts to Fell Cottage just in time to assist at the birth. It was, they told her afterwards, an easy labour.

The storm had subsided before the light went from the day. The world seemed suddenly very quiet. Diana lay in bed with her son in her arms, and listened to the distant downstairs sounds of Elsie preparing the evening meal. Up here, the tranquillity of the snow-bleached room was disturbed only by the soft snuffling of the sleeping infant's breathing. Bradley sat on the edge of the bed and shyly stroked the baby's cheek, and smiled. Diana thought she had never seen him look so happy.

"This is going to be a good year," he said. "1939. This'll be the year when everything turns round." Happiness filled the room, enveloping them all.

Five

A t first it seemed as if Bradley had been right. The birth of
their son on New Year's Day marked a new beginning.
Diana luxuriated in the novel sense of being the centre of
approving attention. She had at last done something for which
she received nothing but praise: she was the mother of the first
Armstrong grandson, and he was a strong healthy child, in which
(to Armstrong eyes anyway) many resemblances to his father
could already be seen.

The baby was christened at the gaunt Methodist chapel at
Ravenshield on a Sunday in February, a cold day punctuated by
snow showers that reminded Diana of Pamela's wedding day.
That day, linked to this by the newly-born child, now seemed to
belong to another age, remote from the present in every way.

He was given the names Jackson Bradley, in acknowledgement
of both his paternal grandparents. "We shan't have to change the
name on the wagons when he grows up," Bradley declared, when
he announced his decision. Diana would have liked the baby to
have one name to indicate her part in his making (if only
Poultney tagged onto the end), but she knew Bradley would
not have agreed, so she didn't press the point. After all, the
Poultneys had not treated Bradley well. He could not be expected
to feel he owed them any favours. Besides, she knew, if no one
else did, that the child was hers, given into her care for all the
years of his growing. Sometimes, when she was feeding or
changing him, she would look on the tiny perfection of his body
and feel awed by the responsibility of it. At the christening, filled
with an unaccustomed religious feeling, she prayed that she
might be worthy of the trust placed in her.

The entire Armstrong family was present in the chapel that day, down to the most distant cousin, as well as many of their friends. By now, Diana knew some of them quite well, though she felt she would never be able to remember all their names, still less their relationships one to another. It was not until she turned to leave the church after the service that she suddenly glimpsed one profoundly familiar face in the bewildering throng, and felt dazed with shock. It was her mother – surely it was her mother? – slipping quietly out of a back pew. Evelyn Poultney gave her one fleeting, unreadable glance, and then was gone. Diana stared at the place where she had been, filled now by indistinguishable Armstrongs all jostling to get out of the church, and wondered if she'd imagined it. Surely there should have been some trace remaining of something so important to her?

"She might at least have spoken," said Bradley at her shoulder. "No present either. Stuck-up lot, your family."

Diana might have agreed with him, except that there was too much hurt in the thought. Yet she was conscious of a tiny glow of thankfulness that her mother should have taken the trouble to come. For it must have been a trouble for her, Diana knew that. She was, in a small way, making an embarrassingly public gesture, against her principles. Diana wondered if her father knew what his wife had done, and guessed that he did not. More likely, it was a small gesture of defiance on Evelyn's part, born of a love for her daughter that had never quite been extinguished. Diana, a mother herself now, bent and pressed a kiss on her baby's forehead. *I'll never turn my back on you*, she promised him inwardly. *No matter what happens.*

The christening party was held at Springbank (there would not of course have been room for everyone at Fell Cottage) with one of Elsie's lavish spreads to entertain the guests. It was a happy occasion, apart from one thing, and that was something so slight that (as with her mother's appearance in the chapel) Diana even wondered afterwards if she'd imagined it. The cake had been cut and the baby's health drunk in ginger cordial, and two of Bradley's aunts were bent over the pram in which the infant Jacky slept, exclaiming at his remarkable likeness to every male relative they could think of. Diana turned round to share her amusement with Bradley, who had been standing just behind her. But he had moved away, and she found herself looking instead at the thin figure of her brother-in-law, nine years older than Bradley and by all appearances of another generation. She did not know Jackson very well; they met on Sundays, but had talked very little. If asked, she would have said that perhaps he didn't like her very much. Now, she caught on his unwary face an expression that startled her, for it had in it something very close to hatred.

She shivered, and for a moment they stared at one another, guardedly. Then Jackson gave an odd half-grin and turned away. She watched him cross the room to rejoin his flustered wife, who was engaged in a tussle with their daughter, Irene. The toddler was probably tired of wearing her best clothes and being on her best behaviour, Diana thought. She saw Jackson speak sharply to her, at which she subsided into a mute sullenness, all the sparkle crushed out of her by her father's scowl. Soon afterwards, the three of them left, almost unobserved, without saying goodbye. Was it possible, Diana wondered, that Jackson was jealous of her and Bradley, because they had produced the first grandson, who might one day take over the family business? If so, it was very silly of him. After all, his own next child might be a boy, and baby Jacky might, in due course, develop his own ideas about a career, which might not include lorries, or quarrying stone, or farming, or selling petrol. Meanwhile, Diana had every intention of making the most of the unaccustomed family approval.

It did not last. Even by the time of the christening the warning signs were there, threatening the harmony between Diana and Bradley. It was the fault of the baby book given to Diana on her wedding day by her mother. Diana had begun to read it during her pregnancy, and finished it quickly after Jacky's birth, wanting to do the very best for him. She knew the book was written according to the most modern, scientifically tested principles of child care, of which both her parents heartily approved. She might have learned to question their views on many things, but where matters of health were concerned, she trusted them completely. Her father was a good doctor, up to date with all the latest developments, unlike old Doctor Elliott, who was close to retirement and had no time for (or interest in) modern notions. If Dr Poultney approved of *First Baby* (and she knew he must) then she was right to take it as her guide.

Fresh air, calm and quiet, a consistent routine – they were the things every baby needed, she gathered. The book was written for mothers with nurseries, into which they could put the baby's cot, and of course Fell Cottage did not even have a spare room. The cot had to be squeezed into a corner of the bedroom, which Diana had first cleaned with unusual thoroughness. As for the bedroom window, when they were first married she and Bradley had argued at some length about whether or no it should be left open at night, and more often than not, for the sake of peace, she had allowed him to close it. Now that the baby had arrived, she insisted on having it open, no matter what the weather.

"What are you trying to do?" Bradley demanded, one frosty night. "Starve him to death?"

Diana knew by now that *starve* meant freeze – it was one of the many ways in which she and Bradley spoke a different language. "He's well wrapped up," she pointed out. "Fresh air's good for him."

"If it's too cold for me, it's too cold for him," Bradley insisted, closing the window. Once he was asleep, Diana crept out of bed and opened it again. By the time he knew what she'd done, it was morning, though he complained, with manifest untruthfulness, that he'd been too cold to sleep well.

Then there was the question of the routine that must under no circumstances be broken. If it was not time for his four-hourly feed, then baby must be left in his cot or pram and not picked up or fussed over. It was unfortunate that, more often than not, Bradley would return home from work about halfway between his son's feeds, so that more than once he found the child crying in his pram under the hawthorn in the far corner of their little garden, while Diana, in the house, tried very hard to pretend she could not hear him. Bradley would run to the pram and pick him up, rocking him until he was soothed.

"What kind of a mother are you?" he would demand. "How can you treat him like this?" When she tried to explain, he wouldn't listen, so as often as not the whole thing ended in her tears and his deeper anger.

It was even worse when Bradley's parents came to call, for then Diana would find herself pounded by the disapproval of three people, none of whom had any shred of sympathy for her views. It was not just the fresh air and the neglect that they regarded as unpardonable, but also the inadequacy of the child's bedding. The first time she called, Elsie took one look in the cot and went in search of the pillow she had given and placed it under Jacky's head.

"They say," said Diana nervously, "that you shouldn't give a young baby a pillow."

"All my bairns slept on a pillow, and none of them's been any the worse for it," said Elsie, admitting no argument. "Their little necks need support." Then she added several additional blankets and a small quilt to the light but adequate covering Diana had spread over her son.

As soon as she had gone Diana removed the pillow and most of the bedding. But for all her determination, she would often find herself wavering. They were all so sure. True, the book was too, but it was only a book. It was not much of a weapon against Elsie's certainty, and her undeniably long experience. Perhaps she was right, and nothing worthwhile was ever learned from a book. And what if the book's rules were in fact untested, even by Evelyn Poultney? Diana tried to remember how she and her siblings had been raised. She'd been seven when Angela was born, and could recall some things quite clearly. But there had always been a nurse in residence in the early days, a figure of starched efficiency who discouraged visits to the nursery by grubby children. It was likely that she had favoured a strict routine, but Diana could not be absolutely sure. She wished she could ask her mother what she thought. She even considered calling at Dale House one day, but was afraid of rejection. In any case, she knew that was why Evelyn had given her the book, as a substitute for her advice.

As the weeks passed, the baby seemed to sense her uncertainty, and became restless and fretful. At times Diana found herself resenting his lack of calm, as if it reflected on her in some way – as, after all, the book suggested it did. A calm mother made a calm child, she had learned, and she was not calm. The disagreements between herself and Bradley increased daily. "I'm his mother," she would say. "It's for me to decide."

"Not if you're an unfit mother," he would retort, seeking the most hurtful weapon to hand. Yet her self-doubt was never quite strong enough to make her give way to Bradley, or not, at least, without a protest.

Some time in June, baby Jacky caught a slight cold. Bradley came home to find him snuffling fretfully and turned on Diana, half way between triumph and anxiety. "Look what you've done with your crackpot ideas!"

"What about you, coughing and sneezing all over him last week? I told you to keep your distance."

"Keep your distance! That's all I ever hear. If you had your way no one would ever touch the poor bairn." He held Jacky close to him, as if to mark the difference between them.

That evening, the weather turned wet and windy, and even with the window closed (at Bradley's insistence) the draughts found a way in. Only the chimney breast running up from the living room underneath gave any heat to the bedroom. Before they went to bed, Diana had allowed Bradley to put an additional blanket over the cot, but he was still not satisfied. "It's all right for us. We've got each other to keep us warm. Jacky must be perishing." He got out of bed. "I'll bring him in with us."

That the book expressly forbade. "No! No, you musn't. What if one of us were to lie on him?"

Bradley came to a halt. The room seemed filled with the sound of rain, lashing on the window. Jacky began to grizzle. "I know!" said Bradley. He lifted the cot, baby and all, and carried it downstairs. Diana followed, full of anxiety.

Bradley stood the cot by the range and covered Jacky with all the cot bedding he could find, which was a good deal. "You can argue till you're blue in the face," he warned Diana. "He's stopping here."

"But it's much too stuffy. It's bad for him."

"Oh, for God's sake! I've had a bellyfull of your daft ideas. I wish to God your mother had never given you that book, then maybe you'd listen to sense. I bet the woman who wrote it never had any bairns of her own. Come on, let's get back to bed."

Diana was about to suggest she sleep down here too, just in case, but reminded herself that the book had always recommended a separate room for the child. They would still be close enough to hear if he cried. For the time being he was quiet, and clearly settling to sleep. "You see," said Bradley. "He was cold, poor bairn. He's all right now. Let's get some sleep ourselves."

For a little while they lay awake, listening for the sound of crying, but Jacky remained quiet and at last they both slept, soundly, until much later than usual. Diana, waking, glanced at her watch and leapt out of bed. "He must be ravenous. He's two hours past his feed."

She felt Bradley's hand on her arm. "Wait!" She turned to look at him. "He's all right. Let him sleep. He's warm enough for the first time in his poor little life. Come here!" And he pulled her to him.

It was a long time since they had made love, and Diana hoped that it might mark a new beginning. Afterwards, she was tempted to linger in Bradley's arms – it was Saturday, so he didn't have to get up for work. But there was Jacky to attend to, so she pulled on her dressing gown and went downstairs.

The room was very quiet. There was no sound coming from the cot, not even a snuffle. She didn't know why, but she was suddenly afraid. She ran across the room and looked down at her child. He lay very still, and he was pale, paler than usual, with a strange waxiness about his skin. Her heart thudding, she put out a hand and touched his cheek. It was cold.

She heard herself scream, then Bradley came running, stumbling, down the stairs. He took the baby, rocked him, kissed him, said his name, again and again, urgently, desperately. Then he went for the doctor.

Dr Elliott, when he came, confirmed what they already knew; that Jacky was dead. "It happens sometimes," he said gently, his hand on Diana's shoulder as she sat motionless by the range. "It's not your fault, not anyone's fault. Just one of those sad things."

But as soon as he had gone, Bradley turned on her. "He's wrong. It *is* your fault. All that freezing him and leaving him and all. If you'd listened to me he'd be living yet."

She had no answer for him, because somewhere deep in herself she feared he was right. At the very least, she should have stayed with Jacky last night, as her instinct had urged her to do. But it was all too late. There was nothing they could do.

Somehow they got through the formalities of the next few days. Everyone was very kind and tried to make things easy for them, but nothing could be easy. Diana supposed she said things in reply to the many words of condolence offered by those who came to call, but could not afterwards remember anything about them. She kept hoping that her mother would come, but in the end all she received was a letter, sent by post, as if from a great distance. But it was tenderly written and apportioned no blame. '*We are so sorry to hear your sad news, dear Diana,*' Evelyn wrote, among other things. And: '*You are young, my dear, and there will be others, to bring you comfort*'. But it was Jacky she wanted, and she had lost him for ever, and there was no one to put comforting arms around her and hold her close. Their child's death seemed finally to have driven home the wedge between herself and Bradley, so that it had now made the split irreparable. They hardly spoke to one another, and when they did it was only to hurt.

Jacky was buried in the graveyard beside the chapel in Raven-shield on a suddenly perfect summer's day. Afterwards, Diana lingered on by the little grave, her eyes not on the newly-turned earth, but on the green hills rising beyond the graveyard wall. *All this*, she thought, *all that I have been through. It's all been for nothing.*

Six

J acky's crying dragged Diana from a rare interval of deep sleep. She sat up, eyes open in the darkness, poised to swing her legs over the side of the bed, to go and pick him up and feed him. Never mind if it wasn't yet time – she would do it. What did routine matter after all, if her baby was content?

Silence. The crying had stopped. There had been no crying. *Jacky is dead*, said a cold little voice.

Perhaps it had been an owl she'd heard, or a vixen calling, or some other ordinary night-time sound. Whatever it was, it had now ceased. There was nothing except a rattle of wind in the hawthorn.

She bent her head, clutched herself with her arms, trying to crush the renewed sense of anguish, the unbearable every-day, every-night pain. *Jacky is dead. He's not going to come back, ever.* One day perhaps she would know it was true, even be able to accept it in some way. But not yet, not a bare three months after she'd found him lying like a doll in his cot. Now there was only a space where the cot had been; the thing itself was put away in the attic at Springbank. But she couldn't banish her grief so easily.

She began to realise, slowly, how complete the silence was – no snoring from the adjacent pillow, not even the quieter breathing she would hear when Bradley had not been drinking, which was rarely the case these days. She was alone in the bed. She groped for the bedside candle, struck a match and lit it, so that she could see her watch. Four in the morning. He hadn't come home then.

She was neither surprised nor anxious. She was even a little relieved. He must have stayed at Springbank or (if too drunk to face his parents) at the Black Bull; at least, she supposed that was what he'd done. He had not, of course, told her anything. He had simply failed to return after whatever work had taken him out yesterday. But then she hadn't bothered to cook him a meal, having long ago tired of what was becoming a regular bedtime ritual of throwing away overcooked casseroles and stews, blackened sausages, burnt vegetables. Sometimes she felt angry that Bradley so rarely bothered to tell her what his plans were. More often she was simply relieved not to have to endure his morose presence about the house.

She lay down again, flat on her back, staring into the darkness. She knew she would not sleep any more tonight.

Bradley returned several hours later, as she was washing her breakfast cup and saucer – she hadn't felt able to eat anything. She heard the clatter of his boots on the flags leading from the gate and braced herself for his coming in. She made no move to go and meet him, but stayed in the scullery, finishing what she was doing, waiting. Perhaps for once he would come and seek her out, ask her how she was, even put an arm about her. But she doubted it, and was not in any case sure she would welcome it if he did. She could no longer recall what it felt like to be cherished by him, if indeed she ever had been.

She heard him moving about the living room, opening the door of the range, poking the fire. He swore. "Damn you, woman, there's no hot water!"

"How was I to know you were going to want some?" she asked, coming into the room. Even standing some distance from him she could smell his sweat, and the breath stinking of last night's beer.

"It's Sunday morning, isn't it?"

Diana had long since lost count of the days. "Is it?" She glanced at the clock: twenty past ten. It was too late for him to be intending to go to chapel, where morning service began at ten. Dinner would not be on the Springbank table until twelve-thirty. "You've got time to get the water heated."

"That's your job."

"Oh, it is, is it?" she threw at him. "What does that leave for you to do then? Love, honour and cherish me, as you do so very well?"

"You get your housekeeping, every week on the dot. That's more than you deserve. God knows what you spend it on, for I certainly don't get the benefit."

It was true that Bradley still paid her the weekly housekeeping money, handing it over in silence every Friday night. It was one of the few occasions when, their hands briefly touching, there was some kind of physical contact between them. For a month or so after Jacky's death Diana had continued rigorously to carry out her wifely duties, shopping, cooking, cleaning, washing, ironing. But she'd quickly realised that her efforts were wasted. On the rare occasions when they sat down to eat together Bradley did not even look at her. When he came home at night, he slept as far apart from her as the bed allowed. If by some chance – passing in a doorway, handing over money – they did touch, Diana almost felt she ought to apologise for breaching the barrier he had set up, except that she knew even then that she hadn't breached the barrier. It was as firmly in place as ever.

"Whose fault is it then, if you don't feel the benefit? You're in the Black Bull more than you're here."

He said nothing, simply stood glaring at her, as if he could think of no adequate reply. He looked older than his twenty-one years, ill and exhausted. She suspected she had much the same look, though it was a long time since she had troubled to use their one spotty mirror. She felt, suddenly, weary of it all, this living as strangers, the anger, the pain they both felt. They should be consoling each other in their loss, finding comfort together, if any was to be found, not tearing each other apart in this horrible deliberate way. Perhaps she'd not tried hard enough to reach him, perhaps he was simply waiting for her to take that large step towards him, to confide or caress. "Bradley, I miss Jacky so much. I know you do—"

He recoiled from her as if she had struck him. She thought she had never seen such naked hatred on any face before. "Shut your mouth! You're the one who killed him! Isn't that enough for you? You're not fit to speak his name."

Then he ran up the stairs, out of her sight. She heard him moving around, back and forth across the floor. Her hands shaking, her vision blurred by tears, she began to stoke up the range, putting on more coal, though quite why she did not know. He was hardly going to be moved to forgiveness simply because she deigned to heat some water for him.

He came down shortly afterwards, still unwashed and unshaven, but wearing his best Sunday suit, a clean shirt and a tie. He did not even glance at her, simply put on cap and muffler and strode towards the door.

"Where are you going?" she called after him.

"Home, of course."

She wondered sometimes if he'd ever ceased to think of Springbank as home, even during those first happy weeks at Fell Cottage, which now seemed to belong to another age. "It's not dinner time yet."

He did turn and look at her then, with the sort of impatient, scornful expression accorded to someone who has stupidly missed some essential point. But he said nothing, simply continued on his way out of the house.

She supposed she had better follow him. Attendance at Sunday dinner was something from which even the death of Jacky had not released her, though it was the worst ordeal of the week, surrounded as she then was by people who, she knew, shared Bradley's view of her, however politely they might behave towards her.

It was a morning such as she would once have enjoyed, with the last of the early mist lifting to leave the little fields of the dale stretched out in the September sunlight, taking the dreariness from those where the hay still lay mouldering after the weeks of summer rain. Today, as usual, it only made her feel more heavy-hearted, that the world should be so beautiful when Jacky was not in it any more. The warmth – unusual enough this year, and the more welcome for that – hardly seemed to touch her. She had her coat pulled about her, trying to shut out the chill that enveloped her – vainly, because it lay inside her, not out.

She came within sight of the farm, and at that point almost

turned back. Why go on behaving as if everything was normal, as if she might even find herself welcome there? Not only would she be more comfortable away from them all, but so would all Bradley's family, to whom now her presence must be a constant reminder of the disaster her marriage had proved to be.

But she was here, and it was expected of her, so she pushed open the door and stepped inside, her nostrils filled at once with the smell of roasting meat, her hearing with the usual Sunday morning bustle – but no, there was no bustle today, though the meal was clearly under preparation. No one moved, or spoke. The room was in silence, complete silence. Yet it was full of people, all the usual people, even those who would normally still have been in church at this time: Elsie and Jack Armstrong and all their sons and daughters, with their families. They were none of them busy with the customary tasks, and certainly not engaged in cheerful family gossip. Instead, they sat in frozen immobility about the room, filling every available chair and stool and the fireside settle, absorbed in listening. The radio was on, and as Diana stepped softly into the room, afraid of causing a disturbance, a lugubrious male voice was announcing: '*We are at war with Germany . . .*'

She halted, and a shiver ran down her spine. It had come, the thing they'd all been talking of for so long, expected, awaited, inevitable; yet now it was here, and real, now it had actually come, revealed to be strange and horrible, something to be feared, and faced.

It was a long time before anyone moved and longer still before they noticed she was there, even when the broadcast came to an end and the wireless was turned off. Elsie Armstrong stared at her sons, while her husband laid a hand on her shoulder; Lily had reached out and linked her arm through Bert's, as if trying to hold him safe. Amy and Jackson were gazing at one another. Suddenly everyone in the room seemed to be linked with one or more of the others, held in this solemn moment by invisible bonds that were yet tangible. Only Diana, separated by the width of the room from Bradley, who was not even looking her way, felt no one reach out to her and had no one to whom she could reach. She stood alone, isolated from them all.

Then she saw that someone *was* looking at her. She felt the gaze first, and then turned her head slightly to meet a pair of grey eyes watching her from the shadows of the further corner, near the door to the passage; grey eyes under heavy black brows, conspicuous in a sallow face, watching her with disconcerting intentness. They belonged to a boy she couldn't remember ever having seen before, a gawky, foreign-looking lad of about thirteen or fourteen, who sat hunched on a stool, so that she could see little of him apart from the eyes. As soon as he realised his gaze was returned, he looked away, bending his head so that his eyes were hidden. She wondered who he was, and why he'd been watching her so intently.

Elsie Armstrong stood up and moved towards the range, to check the progress of the joint and the steamed pudding. Her husband cleared his throat, said, "Well, there it is," and began assiduously to clean out his pipe. The menfolk gathered around him, and they talked quietly, intermittently. Annie took the Sunday tablecloth from its drawer and spread it over the table. Vera and Amy gathered handfuls of cutlery and set them in place on the cloth. May sliced carrots and cabbage, which Lily then placed in saucepans on the range. Diana hung up her coat, put on an apron and went to the scullery to wash up the implements that had been used earlier to prepare the pudding. Things were almost normal again; except that there was no chatter, no hymns sung over the range, no laughter.

The meal, when the time came, was a sombre affair, with none of the cheerful talk that usually enlivened it. The only person to eat much was the strange boy Diana had noticed earlier, who was perched awkwardly on the end of the further bench, shovelling food into his mouth as if the coming of war made the likelihood of another meal uncertain. There was a girl beside him, a thin waif with the same grey eyes – his sister, presumably. She looked both frightened and furtive. Diana was watching them, still wondering who they were, when Lily made an announcement: "We're getting married, me and Bert."

They all turned to look at her, dragged from their separate, private absorptions. Her round face was pink but determined.

72

Her hand lay over Bert's, where it rested on the table; he looked very self-conscious. "Nothing grand," Lily said, "no fuss. But we're not waiting any longer."

All the things that were unsaid hung in the air throughout the ensuing discussion of plans and projects: the quiet chapel wedding, the meal here at the farm, with all the family present, the two or three days away in the Lake District. But they all knew what was in Lily's mind as she put forward this and vetoed that, and Bert's too, as he shyly backed her up; that he, like most young men, might very soon be called away to war, that he might be killed, that Lily wanted something left of him, if the worst happened. So Diana had thought once, in what seemed another age. Now she didn't care. She had nothing anyway, nor any hope of anything. She and Bradley were man and wife only in name. Though they sat in their usual places at table, side by side, he had not once spoken to her since that chilling broadcast; but then she'd said nothing to him.

She turned to look at him, wondering if he, like her, was recalling their own wedding day, and if he felt the same regretful bitterness. She caught his eye; there was something odd in his expression, something combative, alert. He almost smiled. Then he looked away from her, laid down his spoon, cleared his throat and said, loudly, into a momentary silence, "I'm joining up now, before they send for me."

There was a wash of protest, pierced by an anguished cry from Elsie, seated on Bradley's further side. "You can't lad – your Dad needs you here!"

Bradley shrugged. "Too bad. My mind's made up."

"And how do you think we'll go on without you?" his father demanded, his lined face harsh with displeasure. "You're the best mechanic we've got."

Bradley resumed scooping spoonfuls of jam sponge and custard into his mouth. "Jackson's a fair hand with the wagons," he said, indistinctly.

Their father looked dubiously at his elder son, who said, "By the time they slap a ration on fuel, we'll not be needing mechanics. There'll be nowt left to mechanic. And they'll not be wanting stone either. They smash things in wartime, not build them."

"We'll see," said his father, grimly. His wife continued to talk in an urgent undertone to Bradley. Diana could not hear what was said, though she could guess at it easily enough. She knew, too, instinctively, that Elsie would blame her for Bradley's decision, justly enough perhaps, for was he not seizing the opportunity to break free from the bitterness of their marriage? But she had no wish to be confronted with that obvious truth. She wished the meal were at an end, so she could slip away before Elsie or anyone else could say anything. But the moment they finished eating, May began passing the plates for her to stack and she knew she would not be able to escape before the table was cleared (there were far more leftovers than usual) and the dishes washed up. She could only hope that no one would be able to corner her in the general after-dinner bustle, and that afterwards she might be able to slip quickly away. In any case, for the moment she had her own questions to ask. "Who's the boy, and the girl with him?" she asked Vera, a quiet matronly young woman who was the least censorious towards her of Bradley's sisters; they'd reached the scullery sink at the same moment.

"Oh, they're evacuees, from Sunderland. Twins. Came last week: Ronnie and Freda."

She remembered then: children – and sometimes, mothers – were to be moved from the coastal towns to safer places inland. The evacuation had begun even before war was declared. She had a dim recollection of Elsie saying that she wanted to secure a strong lad to help on the farm, and a girl who was handy in the kitchen. It looked as though she'd had her way – little Freda was as busy as any of them today, and seemed instinctively to know what to do without having to ask. Her brother had already disappeared outside, and Diana glimpsed him from the window, standing with Bradley beside one of the wagons, examining the engine under the open bonnet.

Her mind on other things, Diana carried the remains of the joint to the pantry, where she found herself unexpectedly face to face with her mother-in-law. Elsie took the dish from her, but made no move to put it on the shelf. "He didn't have to do it," she said. Diana had no need to ask who didn't have to do what. "Maybe he'd have been called up soon anyway, with no bairns. But we could have made a case for him being needed here. If he'd wanted it. If he'd had anything at home to keep him."

Children, for instance; or a loving wife to give him hope of another child. Suddenly Diana longed to have it all out in the open, instead of endlessly being skirted around. "It's not my fault Jacky died!"

Elsie gave her a long steady look. "Who's to say?" It was the nearest she'd come to putting blame into words. "Still," (more gently) "you've paid more than anyone would ask for it, both of you. It's past mending now."

So it was; so it had been for a long time. "I'd have thought," Diana ventured in a low voice, "that you would understand, a little. You lost a baby too." She was conscious of her temerity in embarking on so sensitive a topic. It had been made clear to her by Bradley, a long time ago, that one did not mention little Jimmy.

Elsie's expression only hardened. "I did everything I could for him. My conscience is clear." *As yours has no right to be*, was implied by the severity of her tone. Diana was wondering how precisely to extricate herself from this uncomfortable confrontation, when the other woman added in a low voice, "I have to say I can't help wishing Bradley had never met you."

"You can't wish it more than I do!" Diana retorted, torn with pain and anger. As she turned and walked away she realised it was true; that for the first time she had acknowledged that the whole thing had been a disaster.

She was shaking as she pulled on her coat and left the house, and did not begin to feel any calmer until she came within sight of Fell Cottage.

Bradley did not come back to the cottage that day, or during the night. For the first time, Diana found herself wondering if there was another woman in his life – not that she had any real reason to think it, for it was quite clear that he spent most of the hours away from her drinking. Would she mind if she found he had been unfaithful to her? With a dull misery, she rather doubted it. After all, what was there left for him to be faithful to?

The following morning she had been out of bed long enough to drink a cup of tea and revive the fire when Bradley returned, unshaven and smelling of cigarette smoke and sweat and stale beer. He did no more than nod at her, before going to wash and change. Then he came to the door of the pantry, where she was washing up. "Right," he said. "I'm off then."

She saw then that he was dressed not in his work clothes but in his Sunday suit, with a fresh shirt and his best tie. It was no longer immediately obvious that he'd been drinking, though his eyes were a little bloodshot and there were dark circles beneath them. "Where are you going?"

"Like I said – to sign up. I'll be back some time. Not for long though."

"Is this really what you want?" She knew she'd spoken from a lingering sense that she ought to do something to dissuade him, that she ought to try to cling to what was left of their marriage, if anything was.

"What do you think?" He reached for hat and coat. "Don't wait up for me."

As if I ever do! she thought. *I'd never get to bed if I did.*

She watched from the door as he walked away, feeling regret that there was so little left between them that he could leave without a kiss or even a wave. Then she went upstairs to tidy the bedroom. A few days more and she would have it to herself, all the time. Would she be glad when he'd gone, or would she feel suddenly, unexpectedly, bereft?

Going to throw the window wide, she saw that someone was coming over the field towards the cottage. She stayed where she was, leaning on the sill and watching. It was a woman, but not one she immediately recognised, certainly not one of the Armstrong women. Unlike them, this woman – lady – walked with the assurance that only years of careful training could bring, head high, shoulders well back. Even from this distance, it could be seen that her suit was well-cut.

She came nearer. She was not in her first youth, but not old either. Her hair under the neat little hat was fair. Diana felt her heart thud and then seem to stop altogether for a moment. It couldn't be—?

The lady had reached the gate, had her hand upon it, was looking up with grave curiosity at the cottage. Diana could see her clearly now. With a cry she turned and ran down the stairs and flung wide the door. Her heart was thudding so fiercely that she could scarcely draw breath, and her voice emerged as an undignified squeak. "Mother!"

Evelyn Poultney, as neat in her tweed suit as if making a social call upon a neighbour, stepped into the house. Her colour was high, from exertion probably – the hill was steep – though it might have been from emotion.

"My dear . . ." she began, and then stopped, pulling off her gloves with shaking hands.

They looked at one another, two women who had not met for months, who had parted on difficult terms and been kept apart by so much that was painful to recall. Diana wished her mother would put her arms about her, hug away all the anguish of the past two years. But that was never likely to happen, and she was not sure that she wouldn't have rejected such an advance, had it come; there was so much hurt inside her still, and anger. Besides, the Poultneys were not given to demonstrations of emotion, not like the Armstrongs, though Bradley's family too could be cold, as Diana knew to her cost. She knew too that her mother's 'My dear' was an effusion, in her own terms.

At last Evelyn tried to speak. "You look—" The words fell into silence, though she continued to gaze at her daughter.

What had she been going to say? Haggard? Exactly how Evelyn would expect her to look, in these circumstances her mother had never wanted for her, locked into a marriage she had tried to prevent?

With legs that scarcely felt able to support her, Diana turned away to put the kettle on the fire, set cups on the table, anything to prevent her from having to meet Evelyn's gaze, to speak, to think. She pulled out a chair, gesturing awkwardly, and her mother sat down. When the tea was poured neither of them made any move to drink it. For a long time Evelyn simply sat studying her daughter's face, as if trying to read in it all the experiences of the past months of separation.

"How is everyone?" Diana asked at last. She spoke brightly, far too brightly. This might have been a conventional social occasion requiring cheerful small talk.

Evelyn looked startled, as if she'd been forced suddenly to return from some far place and could not for a moment remember who 'everyone' was. "Oh – yes! Well, they're all well." She looked round the room, and commented on the first thing that caught her eye. "You have no blackout."

"It didn't seem necessary. We've no electricity, and we don't even light the lamps now, only candles. Ordinary curtains should be enough."

"I suppose that's true. You're certainly better off without it. It makes everything so gloomy." There was another pause, another look round. Then Evelyn's gaze settled again on her daughter. This time her voice was uncertain, husky. "How are things then? You're not . . ." Her glance moved to the region of Diana's abdomen. "I hoped there might be . . . ?"

"Another baby?" Diana shook her head, not quite trusting herself to speak. She and Bradley had last made love while Jacky lay dead; she thought she would never be able to bear to do it again so long as she lived. She said quickly, "Bradley's signing up for the army. He wants to go straight after Lily's wedding."

Evelyn leaned closer, resting her elbows on the table. "Your father's gone already."

Diana stared at her mother. "Gone? Where?" she asked, stupidly.

"To join the Army Medical Corps. Dr Elliott can hold the fort here. You know how reluctant he was to retire. In the circumstances, your father felt it right that he should go." For a moment she looked utterly miserable. Diana felt a pang, partly, simply, for her mother's sense of loss; partly for herself, because she knew nothing of that sense, in Bradley's going. "That's why I'm here; to say goodbye. We're going to Granny's."

Diana had a sudden mental picture of the beautiful old house in its ample grounds, the comforts of life with her grandmother, agreeable holidays spent there in past years. Now they would all be there without her – something else to add to the experiences from which she'd been excluded: the holidays, the Christmas festivities, the letters full of family news, the small shared everyday things.

"Of course it's only a few miles from Woodland Hall." That was the name of Angela's school, at which Diana too had once been a pupil. "Robert will be quite near too. I believe, with you—" She broke off.

Diana, watching her, suddenly knew what her mother had been about to admit – that she had made mistakes in her upbringing of Diana, and did not intend to repeat them with her two younger children. Their lives, at home or at school, would be closely supervised, their friends personally known and approved. They would be allowed no opportunity for secret meetings with undesirables like Bradley Armstrong.

Yet what Diana was recognising now in her mother's face was not bitterness or reproach, but something she herself knew only too well – guilt. Her own mother, that calm, assured source of authority and measured affection, was as troubled by guilt for what had happened to her daughter as Diana herself was for what had happened to Jacky. Diana knew that Evelyn would never admit openly to such a feeling; she was too conscious of the need to maintain the appropriate respectful distance between parent and child, the mature and responsible adult and the child whom she must see as still needing guidance and help.

And Diana longed to ask for help, longed for her mother to reach out to her with some kind of solution to everything that had gone so disastrously wrong. Yet the past stood in the way of that reaching out, the knowledge that she had once rejected her mother's advice, turned aside from what Evelyn had so clearly seen as the right choice and taken her own path; the path that had led, inexorably, to Jacky's death.

Many times since that dreadful June day Diana had found herself wondering how she would feel now if she had allowed herself to be guided by Evelyn and given up her son for adoption. Would there be some consolation to be found in knowing that he was still alive somewhere, even if she might never see him again? Would that have been worse than to know he was dead? Except that, in sending him for adoption, she would not have known that the alternative was a loss far worse. If only someone could have told her, then, when she made her choice, what the outcome would be!

But had not Evelyn come as close as anyone could to warning her what might happen? If Diana had listened, if she'd given Jacky up for adoption, not only might he still be alive, but she would now have been at home, or at least within reach of her home, of her parents' love and care, the affection of sisters and brother and friends of her own kind, the comforts of life she had so taken for granted. She would not have been sharing this primitive cottage with a man who had become a stranger, to whom she was irrevocably shackled, locked in a pattern of mutual blame.

She wanted, so much, to go back to them all. She knew what it was like to be homesick, but this was worse than homesickness because grief, guilt, unendurable pain were all bound up with it too. She wanted to cry out to her mother, "Take me with you – please, Mother, let me come!" But something held her back, some sense of propriety, along with the reserve that had always been there, a proper barrier between mother and daughter.

She heard herself say, in a voice that was hoarse yet oddly matter-of-fact: "What will happen to Dale House?"

Her mother seemed to give herself a little shake, as if she too were suppressing inappropriate emotions. "It's happened already. The first evacuees arrived two days ago – mothers and babies."

So Dale House was to be filled with the cries of children, the tender voices of mothers – the house from which Diana, as a mother, had been shut out. She wondered if any of the mothers would be unmarried . . . She'd been right not to plead for her mother's help and understanding. "When do you leave?" Again that dry, emotionless voice.

"On Wednesday." Her mother smiled faintly. "If we're ready by then. There's so much to do." A silence followed, during which Evelyn bent her head so that Diana, watching her, could not read her expression. She saw, though, that her mother's interlaced hands were pressed together so tightly that the knuckles showed white. Then she murmured, without looking up, "I wish – I wish . . ."

Silence. What had Evelyn been about to say? *I wish you would come with us?* Almost certainly, for it was clear from the next thing she said that this had been uppermost in her mind, only to be immediately rejected. "No," she said, her voice straining to repress the emotion behind it, "your place is here. I would not come between you and your duty. What I fervently hope is that in time you and Bradley – you both – will find happiness; other children; a real happiness."

But it's dead, our marriage, Diana thought. *Dead, over, for ever. If I say that now, aloud, what will Mother say? 'Then come, my dear, leave all this behind – your place is with us, your family'?* She knew she was deluding herself. Evelyn loved her daughter, truly loved her (Diana could see that now, clearly), but she was, above all, a woman of principle. She would never dream of coming between a man and his wife, even when that man was Bradley Armstrong and the wife her daughter, and the marriage one she had done all in her power to prevent. As far as her mother was concerned, Diana had made her choice, in those dreadful days in France. There could be no turning back, ever.

Evelyn glanced at her watch, rose to her feet. "I must go, my dear. I am sorry it can't be longer. I shall write to you – let us hear from you sometimes too. You know I wish you every happiness." She brushed Diana's cheek with her own. "Goodbye."

As soon as the door was closed behind her, Diana bent her head on the table and wept, for everything that had gone so terribly wrong.

On a bright day at the end of September, Lily and Bert were married and Bradley left for the army, displaying less emotion in parting from his wife than Evelyn had done. For her part, Diana shed no tears, and felt only relief.

That night when she went upstairs to bed she stood at the open bedroom window and looked out over the dale. From here, just a few weeks ago, she had seen little points of light dotting the blackness, marking farmsteads and settlements, and the occasional moving headlamps of a motor vehicle. Now there was nothing, nothing at all. The darkness was complete. *This is war*, she thought: *the blotting out of light*. She shivered at the aptness of the image, its concrete realisation.

But with apprehension, awe, fear, came something else; a sense that here was a new beginning, even an opportunity. It was no more than a vague instinct, as yet given little real shape. But it was there all the same. She was alone at last, with nothing laid before her, no expectations – how could there be, when she had never before been in precisely this position, as few people had? Perhaps at last, in some way she could not yet see, she might now make something of her life.

Seven

By the time it grew light on the third Sunday in February, Diana had made up her mind. She lay in bed, enjoying the peace and solitude, knowing that nothing at all would intrude upon it. If this could have been all her life, if she never had to leave this place except when she chose, then she thought she would have been content to remain in the dale. But of course it wasn't as simple as that.

She reached for her book, ready on the bedside chair: *Wuthering Heights*, another of the old favourites she'd brought with her on her marriage, but found no opportunity to re-read until Bradley had gone. She gave a passing thought to all those books she had never read at all, which had once filled the shelves in Dale House. *When the war's over, and I'm free*, she found herself thinking, as she opened the novel, *then I'll go home and read them all.*

Shocked, she let the book fall against the quilt. How could she have allowed such a thought to find its way into her mind? She knew precisely what 'free' meant – free of Bradley, freed by his death in action.

Yet, through the shock, she acknowledged that the thought had been with her ever since Bradley announced his intention to join up. From the moment he left she had been waiting in some part of herself for news that he had been killed – not, in fact, as far as she knew, that he'd seen any action yet. He had not written to her, but she knew, because they'd mentioned it one Sunday, that his parents had received at least one letter, from the training camp where he was stationed. She had been so little interested that she did not even know where that was.

83

Now, suddenly very sober, she put her book aside and got out of bed and dressed. This was not how she ought to behave. As her mother had so sternly pointed out, she was still Bradley's wife, a choice she had made freely, of her own accord, a choice she had fought to make. The fact that she now bitterly regretted it did not alter anything. She could be thankful that the coming of war had made it easier to be a dutiful wife, by removing her husband from her side, but that was all. It was her obligation to keep her home in order, to maintain good relations with Bradley's family, in readiness for his return.

Except that she was not going to do that, not precisely. For she had made her decision, and she held the thought of it to her as she fed the pig and hens and collected the eggs and lit the fire and ate her simple breakfast, at the table on which the Valentine's Day flowers still stood, arranged in a jam jar, since she had no vase. She smiled to herself, as her gaze fell on them. She'd found them on the doorstep on first going out last Wednesday, a small bunch of flowers, snowdrops still not open, and three celandines, tied with a pink ribbon. Bewildered by the unlikeliness of it, she had carried them indoors, and only then remembered that it was February 14th, St Valentine's day, the day for lovers. So someone had brought her a gift, a token of affection. But who? All she had known was that the flowers had not been there on Tuesday night, when she'd come in after barring in the hens. Slowly, wondering, she'd washed out an empty jam jar and filled it with water and arranged the flowers in it. Ever since, they had seemed to bring the austere living room alive, marking it with the fingerprint of spring. But four days later she was no nearer discovering who had left them. There were no men in her life now, apart from the members of the Armstrong family, and none of them was likely to have left her flowers. She had, for a moment, wondered if Bradley had somehow arranged it, and didn't know whether or not she wanted that to be so, but had almost immediately dismissed the idea. Wherever he was now, he was miles away from here, and besides it was not his style. He had never been a man for romantic gestures.

Now, gazing at the flowers, calmness came back to her, and

enjoyment of her solitude. The house that had been a place of grief and bitterness had become a haven. She loved having Fell Cottage to herself, she loved having it free of Bradley's mess and cigarette smoke and his carping, drunken presence and his unpredictable comings and goings. She loved being able to eat when, and what, she chose and go to bed (or not) when she wanted, with the window wide open, and read or write letters or simply stand in the garden and look out over the dale and breathe in the clear air. Before the worst of the winter came she had (to her surprise) enjoyed working in the little garden, digging the stony earth, creating a compost heap in one corner, planning what vegetables she would plant when spring came (she hadn't known then that she wouldn't be here when spring finally, fully, arrived). She had even enjoyed being snowed in, feeling snug and safe and happy because the drifts were too deep for anyone to expect her to try and make her way to Springbank.

But she was no longer snowed in and it was Sunday and she had no excuse to keep her at Fell Cottage. Besides, today she must tell them what she had decided. After a peaceful morning spent writing a letter to her mother, she put on coat and hat, scarf and gloves, made sure she had her identity card (like most people she no longer bothered with her gas mask, after several months during which not a trace of gas had been released, even in the most vulnerable areas), slipped on her gumboots and set out for Springbank.

It wasn't easy. In this first grim winter of the war, spring still seemed very far away. High above the dale, around the cottage, snow from last month's storms lingered on the shaded sides of walls and in every hollow. In places the remains of drifts crossed her path, and she had either to take a longer way round or struggle through, trying to keep to the tracks she had made in previous days. But the snow was very hard now, and her feet slithered on the icy surface or plunged through it, sending a harsh crunching sound into the early morning quiet.

She was not helped on her way by her inevitable sense of reluctance. Sunday dinner was as much of an ordeal as it had always been, though the food was simpler now war had come and

85

so many things were rationed. As time passed, she had found herself wondering if she dared absent herself, and if there would be any repercussions if she did. But then she would recall her mother's sense of duty, her acceptance that Diana must remain Bradley's wife. Once, she had ignored her mother's advice, and the consequences had been appalling. She would not make that mistake again. She might hope that circumstances would soon set her free; but so long as she was still married to Bradley, she owed some kind of duty to his family, unless and until war parted them for ever; or until she acted upon the decision she had made, which would make attendance at Sunday dinner impossible.

It was Annie's letter that had put the idea into her head. It had reached her parents two weeks ago, on the day Diana had first managed to struggle through the snow to Springbank, to offer her services, not simply from family duty, but because the war effort needed every pair of hands. Jackson and his father were now the only men left to do the farm work, and since they had the quarry, haulage and garage businesses to run as well, they needed all the help anyone could give – even Diana's, incompetent though she was. When she first began to work outdoors, it had seemed to Diana to be much like her first days at Springbank, as she struggled without skill or understanding to carry out routine tasks, milking cows, feeding sheep, clearing byres. She'd been greatly relieved when two land-girls had arrived at the farm; they had been there last Sunday, two hearty competent young women who made her help outdoors unnecessary. But that meant she was obliged to return to the hated domestic work, helping her mother-in-law about the house. She had no quarrel at all with doing her bit for the war effort, but she didn't want to do it as one of the Armstrong women, surrounded always by those who most disapproved of her, who constantly picked on her failings, whether outdoors or in. She wanted to make a constructive contribution.

She had thought, first, of joining the local Women's Voluntary Service. In normal circumstances (whatever they were) that would have seemed attractive. But many of its members were those who had once been her friends, or her parents' friends, people from whom she had long been estranged. She could not bear the prospect of being the object of both judgement and pity, as would certainly be the case. It had seemed that she would not, after all, be allowed to make a new beginning. She told herself that she must accept it, if she was to do her duty as Bradley's wife. At least she now had Fell Cottage, her haven and her retreat.

And then Annie's letter had come, and changed everything. Of course, her family had been very disapproving. "What on earth does she want to join the WAAFs for?" Jack had demanded, as the letter was discussed at the supper table. "A lot of spoiled rich girls, no better than they ought to be. Annie's not that kind of girl."

Diana pictured the young, lively company, the lack of parental supervision of their social lives, the purposeful work, and thought it likely that this was precisely what Annie, for so long the dutiful elder daughter, wanted for herself. It was certainly what tempted Diana. Not that she wished to be anything but a faithful wife to Bradley, so long as he lived. But to get away where no one had any preconceptions about her, to find some useful work which she was able to do well, to be accepted as she was, for herself alone – that was an immensely alluring prospect. She was not certain that the authorities would accept a married woman with a husband still living, but she pushed that question to the back of her mind, to be faced if it came. In every other respect, her decision was made.

Of one thing she was quite certain: Bradley's parents would be appalled. As she walked down the hill, she found herself feeling a little sick at the thought of the anger she might have to face, but she knew she would not weaken. She had made up her mind. They had no power to stop her.

When she reached the farmyard, she found Ronnie there, sitting in a corner amongst a heap of rusting metal, with his head bent over it as he laboured to reassemble it into whatever it had once been – an old plough, she thought, obsolete since Jack Armstrong had acquired a tractor and put his plough horse out to grass; except that with fuel rationing so tight, it might once again have its uses. It had been lying in pieces in the yard for as long as Diana could remember. Now, Ronnie had set to work on it, his strong nimble fingers busy with nuts and bolts. Even to Diana's inexperienced eye, the assortment of rusting metal was beginning to look like a useful implement again. She thought his hands must be frozen, working with metal in this bitter wind; indeed they looked red and sore. Yet he was so absorbed in what he was doing that he didn't even seem to have noticed her arrival.

"You could do with some gloves," she said.

For a moment he didn't move. She had just realised that perhaps he did know she was there after all, when he looked up and she saw that he had coloured vividly red. "I'm all right," he muttered. She had never found him easy to understand. Most Sundays he sat quite close to her at table, sometimes immediately beside her. But though she struggled to engage him in conversation she was always defeated by a combination of his extreme shyness and his impenetrable accent, so that when he did say anything she often had no idea what it was. The fact that his voice had begun to break and was liable to veer off in unpredictable directions didn't help either. Now, he said something more, which she thought might have been on the lines of how it would be hard to manipulate the machinery if his hands were muffled in gloves; but she could not be sure. She did more or less understand the last bit, however: ". . . Got some me Nan knit for me."

"Did you have a Nanny then?" She had spoken from an impulse of surprise, without thinking, and then realised she must sound very rude – though indeed he didn't look the kind of child who would have been raised by a nanny.

"Still have." His head was bent again. "We live with her, back home. Wer Mam's dead."

Diana was not much the wiser, but at that moment Elsie emerged from the kitchen to announce that dinner was ready. Ronnie answered with cheerful self-assurance and went into the house, with one odd sideways glance at Diana. A sudden startling thought occurred to her, though she shelved it temporarily and followed the others in to dinner.

Ronnie sat near her as usual, separated from her only by his sister, who had taken her place before him. Freda had proved herself a paragon, as far as Springbank was concerned. Like her twin, she hated school, but had found her niche in the life of the farmhouse as Diana had never done, learning quickly to perform domestic tasks, even though many of them were as strange to her as they'd once been to Diana. "A proper little housewife," Elsie often said, approvingly.

Diana was able to observe the boy as the meal progressed. Yes, her instinct did seem to be right. The two land-girls, Sal (large and fair) and Dot (thin and dark), who sat opposite him, subjected him to a barrage of teasing, which he deftly deflected. It had been the same every Sunday almost since he'd come to Springbank, long before Dot and Sal arrived. Taken on because of his size and strength, he had not proved the useful extra pair of hands about the farm that everyone had hoped. He could not be relied upon to carry out the tasks he was given, or not to do them well, at least. He was wholly unused to animals and never quite at ease with them. Diana, hearing how they all teased him for his failures, had felt sorry for him; she knew what that kind of failure was like. Yet he appeared cheerful enough, unabashed by his shortcomings, and everyone seemed to like him in spite of them. Even as he was, he was more a part of the farm than she had ever been. In any case, they'd soon found that, inept though he was with animals, he had a natural talent when it came to machinery.

Now Diana observed that when anyone but herself spoke to him, he was open, cheerful, quite without any trace of shyness. When *she* spoke to him it was a different matter: then he would suddenly lose all control and dissolve into blushing and stammering. Yet he continued, week by week, to seek her out, by sitting near her at table, painful though the experience seemed to be. That was not the behaviour of a boy who was naturally shy, but rather of one who had a gigantic crush on her. She thought of the Valentine's Day flowers. Was *that* where they'd come from? She felt a pang of disappointment. *I bet he stole them from someone's garden*, she thought, and then rebuked herself inwardly for her ingratitude. The gift had given her pleasure, whoever had sent it, wherever it had come from. She wondered whether to mention it at table, but decided against it. Apart from anything else, she had the matter of her decision to bring up and didn't want anything else to cloud the issue. It was going to be hard enough as it was.

She had to choose the right moment, the best moment. But the conversation hardly ever included her. She had always been aware that she was an outsider. These days, she felt more than ever like a ghost at the feast, someone whose presence was so irrelevant that it went unnoticed, ignored. Talk of what others were doing went on around her, not touching her: Jackson's wife Amy was pregnant again; fuel was rationed, causing problems to both the quarrying and the haulage businesses; the petrol station sold little petrol, but was in great demand for repairs – new vehicles were practically unknown; increasing government regulations of all kinds gave everyone headaches.

"George's back's playing up again," Bradley's father was complaining, speaking of one of his employees at the quarry. "We can ill spare him. Jackson's the only mechanic we've got left, and he cannot be everywhere." He looked down the table at Ronnie. "You've turned fourteen now, lad, haven't you?" The boy nodded. "Then it's time you left school – you're not doing any good there that I can see. How would you like to come up to the quarry, full-time? Learn on the job."

Ronnie did blush then, fiercely, with manifest delight. "Why aye, Mr Armstrong sir – please!"

Jackson glared across the table at the boy. "There's more to mechanicking than liking machines."

"As Ronnie knows full well," said the older man sternly. "I've seen what he can do. He's a quick learner too." Diana wondered if she detected a note of rebuke to his elder son in his tone; no one had ever called Jackson a quick learner. Then he returned to his more gloomy train of thought. "Mind," he was saying, "I wish that was the end of it. Jim's just got his call-up papers."

"But you put in a word for him to be exempted," said Lily. "He's the manager."

"Aye, and they took no notice of it. They could take Jackson instead, I suppose, except that he's got bairns, which Jim hasn't. So I'll be having to fill Jim's shoes, as well as do the driving. And then there's the paperwork, just as it's getting more than we can deal with. They seem to be going out of their way to make things hard for us. I'm at my wit's end, I can tell you."

"I could do your paperwork." Diana had no idea what made her say it – the impulse of a moment, which she instantly regretted. What was she doing? She was going to join the WAAFs, she'd already decided, after nearly two weeks of careful consideration. She couldn't dismiss all that in a moment. Then she saw how they all turned to stare at her, amazed, amused, bewildered, certainly disapproving, and realised that no harm had been done after all; her decision could stand.

Except that what she saw in Bradley's father's face was not disapproval, but speculation. "You've had some schooling," he said thoughtfully. "How are your sums?"

You were always supposed to hate sums, so she had never admitted to her school friends that she found a certain quiet satisfaction in the successful outcome of her calculations. "I wasn't bad," she conceded now.

"Worth a try then. Get down here at seven tomorrow morning – I'll give you a lift up to the quarry. A week's trial."

So her decision was blown out of the window, just like that. For a moment it was on the tip of her tongue to retract her offer, to refuse what Jack suggested, to say, *No, after all, I won't come. I'm going to join the WAAFs.* But she said nothing, not because Jack had already moved on to something else, dismissing her from his mind, but because some instinct told her that her impulsive words had after all led her in the right direction. Besides, if she found it all to be a dreadful mistake, it would still not be too late to opt for the WAAFs; unless of course the war ended sooner than anyone seemed to expect.

So, next morning she dressed with care, as she thought an office clerk ought to dress, in her one good tweed suit, and walked down to the farm, where her father-in-law met her in silence and helped her up into the cab of the wagon in which, in happier times, she had ridden as Bradley's mate; Ronnie was already seated inside, his head bent, not looking at her. But it was Bradley who was in her mind, for once; she tried not to think of the laughter of that stolen day, the companionship, the love-making. That was in the past, and had in any case been wiped out by many later days of misery. Today was a new beginning, entirely new.

She had passed the quarry once in Bradley's company and glimpsed distant views of it from a high point near the cottage, but never before turned up the bumpy track that led into it, away from the green world of the dale to something much larger than she had imagined, a vast arena, bordered with massive shelves of rock. When the wagon came to a halt she was scarcely aware of Jack getting out and coming to open the cab door for her to descend, so awed was she by everything around her. She knew, because Bradley had told her, that it was a small quarry, doing a modest amount of business, even in good times. But the wagon seemed tiny, the human beings who jumped down from it even smaller and more insignificant, as were the men already at work on a rocky ledge just visible from where she stood.

"Right, now. I'll show you where you'll be working." Jack led the way across the uneven, dusty quarry floor. Diana had come here with a mental picture of her new office, an orderly if austere room in a stone building, with everything in its place. But the only buildings on the site were a vast barn made of a variety of unattractive materials, with a roof of corrugated iron; and a dilapidated wooden hut, to which Jack immediately led her. He opened the door onto a cramped space cluttered with boxes, papers stacked any-old-how. There was a table, not very big, and an uncomfortable-looking chair, and there were three shelves on the further wall, as cluttered as everywhere else. Somewhere under the piles of paper lay a dusty typewriter, which looked as if it hadn't been used for years. "Here we are then," said Jack, with as much satisfaction as if it had been the most modern and palatial of offices. "Make yourself at home."

Was that a joke? Diana wondered. Her father-in-law was not generally given to jokes. She turned to look at his face, but he was already on his way out, walking away from her.

So she took her place in the hut at the quarry, amongst the jumble of papers stored without system, and the odd assortment of machine parts and tools. She began, after her first moments of despair, by putting everything in order. She worked all day, and more papers came in as she did so – forms to be filled in, invoices, delivery notes. She was still hard at work when, at the end of the day, Jack Armstrong came to lock up. He looked round the hut, making no comment, though she thought he seemed approving of the tidy shelves and the ordered desk. "Let me know if you're short of anything," he said, as they walked to the wagon. After that, he was silent until he dropped her off in the farmyard. "Early start again tomorrow," were his parting words.

She walked up the hill in a state of exhaustion, feeling truly hungry for the first time in months. She had forgotten to ask about eating arrangements, and so taken no food or drink with her to the quarry, and no one seemed to have thought of her when the break came and they all settled down to their *bait*. On reaching home, the first thing she did when she had devoured three large hunks of bread and cheese was to find Bradley's old Thermos flask and put it ready for the morning. Then she went very slowly upstairs to the bedroom to change. As she opened the door she found herself reflected in Fell Cottage's sole mirror, hanging on the opposite wall, and for a moment did not recognise the face that stared back at her. She still had in her mind the image she had seen before leaving for work, and what was there now made her laugh aloud. The tidy office worker of this morning had a face smeared with dust and oil; her hair was tangled; her neat suit as dirty as her face, and creased too. Tomorrow, she resolved, she would put on her one pair of slacks, and when she was paid she would begin saving for another pair. Pamela, and their mother too, would have felt she had sadly lowered her standards. For herself, she suddenly realised that she was as close to happiness as she had come since Jacky's death. That night, she slept soundly and dreamlessly, as she had not done for many months.

By the end of the week she felt as if she'd been working at the quarry all her life. The hut had become her realm, a place wholly under her control, where she knew where everything was, and its function too. She had found, deeply buried, a small leaflet explaining the principles of touch typing, and each day made herself spend a good half hour practising her skills, which by the end of the first week were, she felt, recognisably improving. She was still very slow and made a great many mistakes, which necessitated retyping almost every letter she wrote, but she was beginning to be able, sometimes, to type correctly without watching what she was doing, and the mistakes were diminishing, a little. She'd made herself familiar with the verbose tedium of government instructions, caught up on delayed paperwork, sent off returns that should have been in weeks ago, attaching explanatory or apologetic notes where necessary. The account books were in order, the petty cash had been made to tally (somehow) with the record. The shelves were stacked with neatly labelled files and ledgers, and the surface of the table had been rubbed clean with a duster brought from home and was now clear of everything but the typewriter, a neat array of writing implements and the particular papers she was working on at the time.

What was more, Jack Armstrong was pleased with her. He stood in the doorway of the hut on Friday night, looked about him, nodded. "You'll do," he said. He was almost smiling. She knew she had received the highest praise of which he was capable. She also received a small pay packet, which she hadn't somehow expected. She would save it, she decided. She had learned to live on the small sum allowed her as a serviceman's wife, and this money, put in the post office, would be a bulwark against an unknown future.

The work brought her new friends too, people she would never have expected to include in that category: taciturn quarrymen who teased and protected her, and guarded their tongues against anything that might offend her ears. She quickly learned their names and also, bit by bit, something about their families and their work. She learned more about Ronnie too, when he came to the hut one morning in the second week.

"Mr Armstrong said I was to bring you my card," the boy

said, handing her his identity card. She thought his accent was softening, unless it was simply that she was growing more used to it.

"I'm afraid it's another of these government forms," she said with a smile (she noted again how he blushed). "I have to have everyone's details." She was conscious of his attentive gaze as she examined the card.

It was not quite as she expected. "I thought your name was Ronald. That's not what's down here. Have they got it wrong?"

Inevitably, he went pink again, and shook his head. "Na. That's right. Roald, it is. I'm never called that."

"It sounds foreign." She looked at him with renewed interest. She'd always thought he had a foreign look about him.

"It was my Da's name, so my Nan says."

"Has he died too then?" she asked gently, though it hardly sounded like a recent tragedy.

"Don't know. He was a sailor, a foreign sailor. Told my Mam he'd come back, but he never did. She didn't know she'd fallen pregnant till after he'd gone." He saw the way she looked at him and added, "We're bastards, Freda and me."

She felt embarrassed for him, until she recalled how nearly her Jacky had come to being a bastard. She had reason to know how easily it happened. "So your mother named you after him?" And had cared for the man enough to know how he spelled his name, she thought. "Do you look like him?"

He shrugged. "Don't know."

She thought the name sounded Scandinavian, but that didn't quite fit his looks, with his curly dark hair and wide cheekbones; though his eyes, looking at her so intently, were the pale grey of the North sea on a misty autumn day. She became aware that she, like him, was staring rather rudely, and blushed in her turn and gave her attention to transferring the details of Roald Shaw to the form.

She had thought she might mention the Valentine's Day flowers to him and see how he reacted, but decided against it. That was in the past now, and besides it was better to keep things on a businesslike footing. She finished her writing and returned the card. "Thanks, Ronnie. That's it then. You can go." And, after a moment longer, he went.

By the end of a fortnight she began to find that, now and then, she had time on her hands. The work no longer filled every day. She was just beginning to feel the first hint of boredom when, one bright March morning, a harrassed Jack came to the hut and said, "You can drive, can't you? There's no one else available, and that load to get to the steel works."

She stood up. "I'll take it then." She had already assembled the papers for the journey. Normally, the load would have been taken to the station at Wearbridge and transferred to the train, but this time, for speed, it was to be delivered directly to the factory at Meadhope, a large village at the further end of the dale, a journey of about twenty miles. Her heart thudding, Diana made her way to the wagon. It was a long time since she had driven any kind of vehicle – not in fact since the day she'd taken the wheel with Bradley at her side, in this very same wagon. She put him, deliberately, carefully, out of her mind, and forced herself to concentrate simply on what she had to do today.

The wagon was laden with stone, and felt slower and heavier than it had that day. Uncomfortably conscious of men watching her from every vantage point, and of young Ronnie standing entranced at the shed entrance, she edged the vehicle forward. It juddered and jolted over the rutted, muddy floor of the quarry, out past her hut onto the track and then down to the road. Once there, she felt her nervousness gradually slipping away. She began to feel more confident. She was glad it was a calm, quiet day, with neither frost nor snow nor rain. Before very long she was even enjoying herself, relishing the good views from the cab, the sense of power. Best of all was the reaction as she passed through the dale's various settlements. Already, war had meant that women were, of necessity, doing men's work, but to see a woman at the wheel of a lorry was still unusual enough to turn heads. In peacetime she was sure there would have been censure too. Now, many people waved at her, cheerfully encouraging. After the months of disapproval, she felt exhilarated, elated.

Nervousness returned to her as she drove through Meadhope

until she came to the high wall that enclosed the small steel works. She turned into the yard and brought the vehicle to a halt.

From various sides there came the noise of construction and the whistling of busy men; but through the open doors of a large building across the yard Diana glimpsed overalled women standing over some kind of heavy machinery, a reminder that here too women were doing what had once been men's work. At that moment two more women emerged from a nearby doorway and crossed the yard, turbaned heads bent against the wind. One of them looked round, said something to her companion, and they both turned and came towards her as she jumped down from the cab.

"Can you tell me where I can find the manager, please?" she asked.

One of them ("I'm Jean, by the way") led her back into the main building and along a corridor, chatting as they went, and left her at a door with *H. A. Watson* painted on it, on which Diana knocked. Hearing an answering call from inside, she opened the door to find, with a shock, that the stocky middle-aged man behind the cluttered desk was known to her – only slightly, like most of her parents' occasional dinner guests, but she had, more than once, sat at the same table with him, trying laboriously to make conversation. He had not, she recalled, been a stimulating companion, but then perhaps he, for his part, had found her less than wholly entertaining.

"Ah, Miss Poultney – no, it's Mrs Armstrong now, isn't it?" He looked her over, as she blushed uncomfortably. She was quite sure he knew her whole sorry story, and guessed what he must think of her.

Trying to appear briskly businesslike, she handed the papers to him and he examined them. "It's heavy work for a woman," he observed then. "But I'm learning every day what women are capable of, given the chance, and it never ceases to amaze me. Now, shall I get a couple of the lads to unload for you, or do you want to do it?"

She accepted the offer gratefully, in view of the weight of the load and her own inexperience. "I'll drive the wagon to where you want it tipped, if you'll tell me where that is."

"I'll come with you. Then I can show you round while the lads see to the load."

He clearly enjoyed her company, becoming positively expansive, even indiscreet, as he showed her over the enterprise, beginning where they left the wagon, at the railway sidings beyond the furthermost buildings of the factory. "We're extending the goods yard, as you see. All these years of depression, and we're suddenly busier than we've been for years."

"It's a pity it's taken a war to do it," Diana commented, because it seemed the right thing to say. As far as she was concerned the war had so far brought her little but good.

"True. We're going over to bomb-making, you know." He had lowered his voice a little. "Hush hush, of course – though I'd guess most of the dale knows by now. Weapons of destruction, made by the gentler sex. Strange world."

Diana enjoyed her tour of the factory, and the insight it gave her into this grim part of the war effort, from which her clearest memory was the lively jokiness of the women who worked there. "We're all in this together, that's how I see it," Mr Watson said as he saw her off afterwards. "We all have our little bit to do. That's how we'll come through."

It was perhaps a trite statement, but Diana felt an answering swell of pride that she too should be fully a part of this.

Before long she had yet another task to add to those already undertaken. "I've told Jackson you'll be at the garage tomorrow," her father-in-law said to her one evening, as she descended from the wagon in the farmyard. "The books need an eye running over them."

So next morning she had to catch the early bus to Wearbridge, where she alighted at the petrol station and went in search of Jackson. He was talking to a customer in the yard where she had first met Bradley, and it was some time before he ended the conversation (it was not, Diana quickly gathered, anything to do with the car that the customer had brought in for repair). Then he turned a morose expression on her, without taking the cigarette from his mouth. "Well?"

Had Jack failed to warn his son of her impending arrival? Diana felt her heart thud uncomfortably. "Your father asked me to take a look at the books."

"Interfering old—!" He broke off, reddening a little; Diana had realised some time ago that Jackson was even more in awe of his father than Bradley was. Now he shrugged and set off towards the small office looking out over the forecourt. He gave Diana no instruction to follow him, but she did so all the same. "There!" he said, indicating a desk as untidy as the one at the quarry. He opened a drawer and took out three battered account books, which he threw on top of the other clutter. Then he flung a bunch of keys on top of them. "Lock up before you go home." He went out, slamming the door behind him.

So he clearly expected her to be there for the day! When she opened the books and began work she immediately saw why. Until the birth of their daughter Irene two years ago, Jackson's wife Amy had kept the garage accounts, after a fashion. Since then, though she still sometimes served petrol, she clearly no longer considered herself responsible for the books. Though Diana knew that Bradley had often worked in the repair yard, there was no sign that he had ever given a thought to the accounts. Nor, it seemed, had anyone else. Diana had thought the quarry paperwork muddled and disordered. This was far worse. There were whole weeks when no record of the business had been kept at all; and when a note had been scrawled down in the book, there was only rarely any kind of receipt or other proof of activity or expenses to go with it. Before the war it had perhaps not mattered very much if records were not kept. Now, when everything had to be accounted for to a higher authority, when supplies of fuel were strictly controlled, it mattered a great deal.

Determined but apprehensive, Diana cornered Jackson in the yard at a time when no one else was there and tried, as patiently and tactfully as she could, to explain just how serious it all was, and what she thought he should do about it.

He was not impressed. "My father has no idea what it's like for me," he complained. "It's all right for him. He can please himself where he works and when and how long." Diana wondered if Jackson had any idea how very hard – too hard – his father pushed himself, how few breaks he took, how often he would make a delivery long after everyone else (including, most certainly, Jackson) was snugly at home, resting behind the blackout curtains. "I've better things to do than mess on with paperwork. Stuck down here when there's any amount of work to be done up at the farm. No one to give me a hand. Bradley used to do a good half of the repair work, you know."

"That's why I'm here," Diana pointed out. "To save you work. But I shall need some help."

"I don't need a stuck-up girl telling me what to do, interfering in my business. Why don't you go back to your family? You know Bradley doesn't want you."

If he had hit her it wouldn't have made her feel any the less shaken. She thought, fleetingly, of the WAAFs, her deferred escape route. Then she drew a deep breath and said, "I'm helping your father. If you don't like it, then complain to him, not me." That, she knew, would silence Jackson; and indeed he listened while she told him what she needed from him.

She had wanted explanations and receipts, to fill in the gaps in the record, none of which were forthcoming except, grudgingly, for the past week or two, for which Jackson still sometimes remembered necessary details and had not always thrown away the evidence. By the end of that day, she had accepted that all she could do was to write off the past and begin again, with efficient records, and hope that no one in authority would check up, at least not for a very long time.

That evening, she gave a tactful version of the day's events to her father-in-law, and got him to agree that she should spend each Thursday morning at the petrol station. She also had his backing for her insistence that Jackson keep all receipts and bills and other papers in an agreed place in the office, so that she could enter up the details when she came in. She knew that Jackson, who had resented her from the moment of Jacky's birth, and perhaps before, would never forgive her for the humiliation of being at the beck and call of what he saw as a stuck-up chit of a girl, but that was simply something she had to learn to live with. It couldn't be mended.

As the weeks passed and the accounts began to display an accurate record of what was going on, it became obvious to her that things were seriously wrong with the garage business. She was not surprised to find that sales of petrol were very slow – with rationing as it was, she would not have expected anything else. But the car repair business should, she thought, have been doing much better than it was, now that new vehicles and even new parts were in short supply, and make-do-and-mend applied to vehicles as much as anything else. A good mechanic should be much in demand. A suspicion began to grow that perhaps Jackson was not a very good mechanic. Certainly, she overheard several angry exchanges between her brother-in-law and disgruntled customers, and on one or two occasions bills remained unpaid for that reason. She wondered whether to say something to Jack, but decided against it. Very likely he was only too aware of his son's shortcomings, and there was no obvious solution. There were just not enough mechanics to go round, and the haulage and quarry business must have priority, now that stone was needed for the war effort. Instead, she suggested tentatively to Jackson that perhaps Ronnie should be asked to spend some of his time at the garage, but was met with anger. "Are you saying I don't know my job?" Jackson hurled at her.

"Of course not," she said soothingly. "But maybe there's work for more than one man."

"Man, yes. If you hadn't driven Bradley away—" He made an angry gesture. "Ronnie's a bairn, and not even trained. No, my father's welcome to him."

Diana did not much enjoy her weekly half-day at the garage; Jackson's resentment of her and his general obstructiveness made sure of that. But even there she found a certain satisfaction in her own small achievement, knowing that what she did was done well and contributed to the general prosperity of the business.

As for the rest of her working life, she had not thought it was possible to feel so fulfilled, to find such pleasure in routine tasks. Her days never seemed long enough for what had to be done, and none of them were predictable. She would arrive for work at the hut, not knowing if she would be sitting all day at her desk or would suddenly be sent out to deliver a load to some local firm in urgent need of stone. She found herself setting out eagerly in the morning, even when she had to walk down the hill in rain and wind, full of excitement at the unknown prospect before her. She found that in a few short weeks her circle of acquaintances had grown. She might almost have called them friends. Everywhere, she was greeted with cheerfulness, with affectionate teasing.

She had a slight feeling of guilt at her enjoyment of her situation. After all, it was wartime, and Jacky was no less dead for the change in her circumstances. Certainly no day went by, almost no moment, that she did not think of her lost child. But the pain was growing less, fading to something that was almost endurable. War had brought such a change that, even when the anniversary of Jacky's death came round, she felt distanced from the agony of last summer, as if it were much further off than a mere twelve months. She began, now and then, to be conscious of hope.

Gradually, she became aware of something else too. Most of her working life was spent among men, and she began to realise, slowly, imperceptibly, that there were those (as well as the persistent and devoted Ronnie) who deliberately sought out her company, engaged her in conversation without good reason, casually happened to be passing – to query a bill at the petrol station, to discuss a forthcoming load at the quarry. She'd never really considered that she might be attractive, in any general sense. That Bradley had found her so, once, as she did him, she'd taken for granted; it had been a part of their mutual passion. But now she saw daily evidence that many men admired her and wanted to spend time with her. She knew that at times she was even behaving in what her mother, disapproving, would have described as a flirtatious manner. Though she felt no attraction herself for anyone she met (after all, the young and handsome had by now, for the most part, been called up for military service), it all added a certain spice to her days. Joining the WAAFs no longer tempted her, even temporarily.

It was only at the Springbank dinner table that she was reminded that not everyone was admiring of her new-found skills, or welcomed her as an essential part of the war effort of which they too were a part. Bradley's sisters – and Lily in particular – continued to treat her with scarcely veiled contempt, and there was no new warmth in Elsie's manner towards her, no softening. Diana wondered if Jack ever spoke of her to his wife, if perhaps she did not know what her despised daughter-in-law had achieved, and was daily achieving. Then one Sunday, coming into the farmhouse by the front door, Diana overheard Jack, in the kitchen, speak her name, and realised that he must have been praising her to his wife, for Elsie retorted, rather sourly, "I'm glad she's good at something then." It was, Diana realised, as close as she was likely to come to acceptance by her mother-in-law.

Then, in September, her sister-in-law Amy gave birth to her baby. It was a boy, and they called him Jackson, reclaiming the name for their own. Very soon, everyone spoke of him as Jacky. Diana felt as if her Jacky had been wiped out, not simply from life, but from every memory except her own.

Eight

D iana woke, and wondered how soon it would be before her alarm blasted its harsh sound into the near-darkness. She groped for the cold round metal of the clock, and brought it near her face. Half past midnight . . . No, it couldn't be so early: there was a faint grey light outside the window, from which she'd pulled the curtain aside before she went to bed. It must be six, or very nearly six. Her alarm was set, as always on these winter weekdays, for six; and today was Monday. Not any Monday, either, but Monday November 8th 1943, her twenty-third birthday – and any minute now the alarm would go off. She slammed down the button before it did (she hated the sound, that being the worst thing about being a working woman). Then she slipped from the warm bed into the chill of the bedroom and dressed as quickly as she could.

Downstairs, by the gradually increasing dawn light, she pulled on the old coat and gumboots she kept near the door and went out to feed the pig and hens. Tonight, if it was fine and she wasn't too exhausted, she would finish digging over the garden, all but the corner where the leeks were. Pulling them up to eat gave her enormous satisfaction.

She ate her solitary breakfast, and re-read the letter that had arrived, two days early, from her mother – the thin wartime card sat on the mantelpiece. Evelyn had never forgotten her daughter's birthday, except once, in the year of estrangement before the war. Diana doubted if anyone else even knew it was her birthday. Certainly Bradley had never marked it in any way, but then he had not once written to her during three years and more of war, nor had he returned to the dale.

She realised if she didn't hurry she would be late for work and on the receiving end of Jack Armstrong's displeasure, a rare enough occurrence for her these days, but not one she wanted to risk even so. She washed her dishes quickly, filled her flask and assembled two sandwiches (bread and marge only, since that was all she had at the moment), put on coat, hat and scarf, grabbed the bag with her extra clothing and set out at a run for Springbank.

Her father-in-law was just emerging from the farmhouse as she reached the yard; Ronnie, who still travelled with them each morning and evening, was waiting by the wagon. He looked as if he was about to say something to her, when Jack came up to them and he clearly thought better of it, though the colour lingered on his face for some time afterwards. The boy's obvious adoration of her had continued now for three years, persisting even after his voice deepened and he grew taller and stronger and became as good a mechanic as Bradley, so Jack said; even, to Diana's astonishment, in the face of obvious admiration from girls of his own age. She'd watched him once last summer at a village dance, awkwardly shuffling around the room with the prettiest girl there, and all the time stealing glances in her direction.

Jack climbed into the cab without saying anything to either of them. Diana gestured to Ronnie to climb up first, and then got in after him. She expected the wagon to move off at once, but it did not. She glanced at Jack, as she saw Ronnie was doing too. Their employer sat very still, staring ahead. His face had a distinctly greyish tint to it. "Are you all right, Mr Armstrong?"

He looked round. "Aye." He sounded as if to say as much as that took a considerable effort. But the wagon began to move.

At the quarry Diana waited until Ronnie had disappeared into the shed, then she turned to Jack. He didn't look quite so grey – perhaps she'd imagined the extent of it, or it was simply a trick of the early light – but certainly he appeared very tired. "I could do with a cup of tea before I start," she said briskly. "How about you? If you don't mind sharing a cup, that is." She saw him hesitate, torn between an inclination to give in and a lifetime's dislike of anything that seemed like shirking. "There's a letter that came yesterday which I'd like you to look at," she added, mentally sorting through her paperwork for something that would back up her story.

He glanced across the quarry, to where a group of German prisoners were standing waiting to begin work, and evidently saw something he disapproved of, for she heard him mutter under his breath. "I'll be with you when I've set that lot on."

She went to the hut, suspecting that he wouldn't come, but she was wrong. Within half an hour she heard an odd shuffling step outside, then the door opened and Jack stood there, propped against the doorpost as if it were the only thing keeping him upright, one hand clutching his chest. He looked far worse than he had earlier, with a dreadful colour, and his breath made a horrible rasping sound. Diana stood up, took his arm, guided him to the chair, discreetly closing the door as she did so. She dimly recalled some long-buried instruction to loosen the necktie of anyone fainting or otherwise in difficulties, but Jack never wore a tie for work, and his spotted cravat looked loose enough, as did the rest of his clothes. "No hurry," she said, because it made her feel she was doing something. "Just get your breath."

He gave no sign he had heard her, simply sat bent over, gasping for air. Diana poured tea from her flask, then set the cup on the table and perched beside it, waiting. She felt helpless. She ought surely to be doing more than this, but she had no idea what. She half wished someone would come and take charge, but knew that Jack would hate to be discovered as he was now, and she couldn't think of anyone who might have a better idea what to do than she had. Long ago, at home, sending for the doctor would have been the obvious course, but here they were miles from any doctor, and in any case that too would mean others knowing Jack's state. Was he ill enough for that to be justified?

She was greatly relieved when, at last, he began to show signs of breathing more easily, and even raised his head. "Could you manage some tea?" she asked.

He sipped at the drink. She saw that his face had a little more colour, driving out the ghastly greyness, and judged that he might be able to speak. "Has this happened before?"

"Aye," he said. "A couple of times." He sipped at the tea again. His breathing sounded normal now. "Don't let on. You know Elsie. She'll fuss."

"You should see Doctor Elliott."

"I've no time for doctors. They don't know a lot more than the rest of us, just have a good stock of fine words to clothe their ignorance."

Diana, who had once heard her father, in one of his more cynical moods, express precisely that view, protested forcibly, but Jack was firm. He would not see a doctor. "Now, there was a letter you wanted to show me?"

"That's all right. I'll deal with it myself," she said.

"Aye, as I thought." He stood up, slowly. He was almost smiling; she knew he'd seen through her ruse. "Thanks for the tea." He went on his way.

Diana watched him go, frowning a little. She knew Bradley's father worked hard, too hard, but until today she had not regarded that as a difficulty. This morning's little incident had suddenly reminded her that he was not immortal. She had thought, often, without effort, of the possibility of Bradley's death, but never of his father's. Now she saw, starkly, that this one member of the Armstrong family who could truly be said to have become her friend might not always be there, might not even be there very much longer. The realisation frightened her.

She tried to put the anxiety out of her mind, occupying herself with the haulage returns, filling in details of journeys made and fuel used. The most difficult part of that was getting the drivers – and even Jack Armstrong himself – to record what they did, and then to pass on the information to her; Jackson was not the only man to hate paperwork. Once or twice she'd been reduced to making up figures, for want of any others.

It was a bitterly cold day, and there was no fire of any kind in the hut. She put on an extra jumper from her bag and wore her coat and scarf and hat, and a pair of gloves that made writing difficult, but by mid-morning she was still chilled to the bone.

She was nevertheless aware when it momentarily grew colder still; someone had opened the door. She looked up. Ronnie was standing at her elbow. His face was red, as if he were near to bursting with something he couldn't quite bring himself to say. After a moment or two, during which he made some inarticulate sound, he suddenly thrust out a hand. "Happy Birthday!"

With cold fingers, she took the small object he held out and examined it: a bar of chocolate, real chocolate. It seemed years since she had seen chocolate. Astonished, wondering, she raised her eyes to Ronnie's face. "Oh, Ronnie, I can't—! Here, at least let me give you some back, for yourself, and Freda."

He shook his head fiercely. "Na – I want you to . . . All of it."

He turned to go, and then suddenly swung back again. His colour had almost returned to normal; he even looked a little anxious. "Mr Armstrong's bad," he said. "This morning – that's not the first time. There've been a few times now."

"I know," said Diana. "But he refuses to see a doctor."

"He works too hard. I try to stop him, when I can. Do things before he sees they want doing."

She was touched by the boy's obvious concern. "I think that's all we can do, for the moment," she said. There was a little silence, then she added, "Thank you for the chocolate," and he blushed again and went on his way.

She unwrapped the gift, and then, watchful in case anyone should disturb her and discover her greed, began to eat, savouring each rich, creamily melting mouthful. She didn't think she had ever tasted anything so delicious. She did, however, find herself wondering how Ronnie had known it was her birthday (she might perhaps have spoken of it to someone in his presence) and, more to the point, how he'd come by the chocolate. Better, perhaps, not to enquire. It was clear enough that the gift was an act of pure devotion, which succeeded for a moment in lifting the gloomy mood that Jack's indisposition had brought.

That afternoon Jack had a delivery to make, and she insisted he drive straight back to Springbank afterwards, rather than return to the quarry simply to give her a lift back to the farm. "I shall enjoy the walk," she assured him, though she knew it would be getting dark by then.

So she found herself walking three miles home in the dusk, by an unfamiliar lane she had once known well, having travelled it by bicycle or on horseback during many a school holiday – she chose that way today because the lane was higher than the usual road, and would catch the light later than any lower road. She pondered the day's events, wondering whether she should disobey Jack's instructions and have a quiet word with Elsie about today's incident. Could she forgive herself, if worse happened and Elsie had not been forewarned? On the other hand, surely Elsie of all people must have seen how ill Jack had looked this morning, and on a number of other occasions lately?

The lane ran up the hill, following a straight line just below the brow, and then curved steeply at a point where a rowan tree hung over the road. Beyond its shadow, heard but not seen, a burn splashed down from the bank. It brought vividly to mind the last time she'd come this way, about six years ago, riding a pony borrowed from her friend Lydia Garthorne, who had been her companion on that occasion. It had been just this time of day, the air raw and misty as it was this evening. They had talked, as always, of boys and clothes and school (they went to different boarding schools, but were the closest of friends during the holidays). By that rowan there, she recalled, Lydia had been confessing a passion for the rector's second son. Diana had pictured him, as last seen in church, comparing him unfavorably with Bradley, and then – just as they came to the place where the little burn splashed over the road after rain – she had told Lydia of her love for Bradley. Lydia had giggled, in that gasping, half-shocked way in which she responded to any scandalous gossip, and had clearly not taken the confession seriously; as Diana had not taken her friend's. She'd seen Lydia only once after that – avoiding her, at a Spitfire Fund concert in Wearbridge. She had no idea what her one-time friend was doing now.

She was ascending the slope beyond the burn when she heard the sound of wheels brushing on the road just round the corner. She stood aside as a bicycle swept past. She could see it was being ridden by a young woman in the green, grey and burgundy uniform of the Women's Voluntary Service, but it was only as the rider was passing, with hardly a glance at the roughly dressed girl at the side of the road, that Diana realised it was the same Lydia Garthorne who had just been in her thoughts. It was almost as if those thoughts had somehow made her materialise, there in the dusk. Diana, awed, even a little frightened, gave a cry, and at the same moment Lydia looked back at her, exclaimed, and screeched to a halt.

"Di!"

"Lyddie!"

Then, silence, an appraisal of the situation, second thoughts, perhaps, at the impulse that had made them acknowledge one another; Lydia had gone very red, as if recalling the overwhelmingly embarrassing circumstances which had ended their friendship. Diana wondered if she was regretting the impulse that had made her look back, and then stop; if she was wishing she had thought quickly enough to pretend she'd not seen Diana. Then Lydia said, awkwardly, "How are you?" Her voice sounded, to Diana's ears, astonishingly upperclass – 'posh', as Bradley would have said. The accent gave her words a faintly patronising sound.

"Well, thank you," said Diana, rather stiffly. Then, seeking for some way of prolonging the encounter (she could see how Lydia's feet were already feeling for the pedals, on the brink of movement), "How's the WVS these days? There can't be many evacuees left now." Most of them had long since returned home, preferring air raids to the dubious hospitality of strangers.

"Oh, we're not just responsible for evacuees. Lots of other jobs, you know. Though I'm in charge of mothers and babies – I've just come from your house. All this 'flu means we're rushed off our feet."

By 'your house' she meant Dale House, Diana supposed. She wondered what it was like now, how it had changed after such a long time in war use, but she didn't ask. She doubted if Lydia would be able to give an answer she would find adequate.

"I heard you're driving for Jack Armstrong."

"Yes. And doing his office work too."

"Well, we all have to do our bit." Lydia hesitated, then went on, "I was sorry to hear about your baby. No one would wish that on you." *In spite of everything* was implied, though not said. Before Diana could think of any appropriate reply, Lydia added, "What news of what's-his-name – your husband? Is he in the forces?" Her tone, still faintly patronising, as one might speak of a servant, told Diana that her chief fault in Lydia's eyes was not her ill-timed pregnancy, but the fact that she had married beneath her. Bradley was acceptable as the object of a schoolgirl passion, to giggle over on a country walk, but as a husband he was quite another matter. The war might have thrown together people of all classes in a common effort, so that often it seemed that their shared humanity was of more importance than their former differences, but for Lydia nothing could quite wipe out Diana's offence in making a permanent connection with someone so intrinsically unsuitable. Very likely it was what many others besides Lydia thought, though it had never occurred to Diana until now. For the first time for many years she felt a prickle of anger on Bradley's behalf, and a wish to defend him.

"Bradley's in the army. In the East." She wished for once that she had more information to give, that she could state proudly that he had seen this action or that, or could even find within her some tender concern for him which she might express. But she had told Lydia as much as she knew. Bradley wrote very infrequently, and then only to his parents, who for the most part did not trouble to tell her what he had to say – Elsie because, presumably, she thought Diana did not deserve to be told, Jack, more likely, because he guessed she wouldn't be interested.

"I'm engaged, you know," confided Lydia.

"Oh, congratulations! Is it—" She was about to mention the name of the rector's son, when Lydia spoke of a young gentleman farmer from Teesdale, temporarily an army officer, met at a dance while on leave; a young man whose family was much like that of Diana's mother, the kind of family into which she herself might well once have aspired to marry. "Of course we shan't wed until all this is over. But the war news is awfully heartening. Surely it can't be long?"

"They say the tide's turning."

"I hope they're right then."

Diana refrained from saying she didn't want the war to end, because that would have sounded callous. Yet she realised it was what she felt. For all the shortages and hardships and the occasional fear, she had never been as happy as she was now, nor led so purposeful a life.

She said goodbye to Lydia, who rode off into the dusk, her cycle lamp a faint diminishing glow. Diana walked on, considering how the war had changed her life – and indeed changed her. The wilful, unhappy girl of the weeks before the war – the girl Bradley had known – had become a mature and capable woman, who was proud of her achievements, small though they might be. She loved her work and knew she did it well. The hut at the quarry had become her realm, and she the authority on anything to do with it, to whom even Jack Armstrong deferred on occasions. Certainly he frequently asked her advice on anything to do with government regulations – on that subject, she was the only one at the quarry with anything like a full knowledge or understanding. Away from work she had the haven of Fell Cottage, the place from which all traces of Bradley's presence had now been eradicated, so that it was hers alone. She still held in some level of her mind the assumption that Bradley would not return from the war, but no longer saw herself, automatically, as returning to her parents when that happened. There had been dark times during the past years, and moments of despair, and few days when she did not think of Jacky, but she had found her place in the world and had no wish to be anywhere else.

Except that today Jack had been ill, and she suddenly saw the possible threat that this might offer not only to a man she liked and respected, but to her own way of life. Soon after parting from Lydia she reached the point in the lane where, by looking over the wall, she had a clear view down the hill to Springbank, shadowed in the dusk. The farmhouse, and the women who ruled it, remained the one blight on her life, tyrannising her Sundays.

She could see Elsie now, out in the orchard gathering in a blowing line of washing; she was alone, and it was likely to take her some time. On a sudden impluse, Diana climbed the wall and half-ran, slithering, down the hill.

By the time she reached the orchard, Elsie had finished her task and was carrying the basket of washing into the house. Diana called, just loudly enough to be heard. Elsie turned, halted, watching her with her usual impassive expression. She waited until Diana reached her, then said, "Well?"

Diana took a deep breath, then gasped out, "There's something I think you should know. Mr Armstrong didn't want me to say. But it's the second time it's happened, I think. He has these turns, when he can't breathe."

She saw Elsie's expression gradually soften, and when she replied, it was with unexpected gentleness. "I know. Ronnie said something, and one of the lads from the quarry. Besides, I've eyes in my head. I know how sickly he looks. But he won't see the doctor. You know how he is, stubborn."

Diana could not remember a time when Elsie had opened up to her as she was doing now, speaking simply as one concerned person to another, on the same level. She was even more startled when her mother-in-law added what amounted to a plea. "If you could stop him doing too much, sometimes, when you can . . . I know it's not easy."

Nor was it, though Diana promised to do what she could, having already decided that this must be her course of action, as far as possible. She found excuses for Jack to come to the hut and sit down, as often as she could. She spared him anything that might make him anxious about the business or its running. She took driving jobs even when very inconvenient, so that he wouldn't be tempted to add to an already excessive workload by doing them himself. She kept from him all her anxieties about the way Jackson was running the petrol station, and covered up Jackson's failures, so that his father shouldn't be troubled by them. That meant that she had sometimes to take things up with Jackson herself, risking his bitter anger.

Such an incident occurred the very next Saturday. She had

gone to Wearbridge on one of her rare shopping expeditions – she now grew much of what she needed – and, filling in time before the bus was due, happened to walk past the petrol station. On the forecourt a man was talking to Amy, his arms gesticulating. He was obviously angry, though from the far side of the road Diana could not hear precisely what he was saying. A moment later, he strode furiously away, and Amy waved to her sister-in-law, calling her over. A little warily, Diana crossed the road. Amy was always civil to her, but Diana suspected her of sharing her husband's view of her.

"Diana, I don't know what to do. You saw Mr Foster there – he's been waiting for his car for two weeks now. He's furious. Three times Jackson's had a go at it, and it's still not right. I've been telling Jackson he should take on another mechanic, but he says there are none to be found. He says I should be backing him up. But we cannot go on like this. It's a wonder we've any customers left at all – but then there's nowhere else for them to go. You've got to get his Dad to talk to him. He'd listen to him. I'd ask Mr Armstrong myself, but you get on with him better than I do."

Diana had in her mind a picture of Jack's weary face, pinched and grey. If there was any way of resolving the matter without involving the old man, she would find it. But she said nothing about that to Amy. "I'll do what I can," she promised.

She considered the problem all the way back to Fell Cottage, and laid her plans. By the following Thursday morning, when she reached the garage as usual, she had begun to put them into effect, and went immediately to the yard to speak to Jackson. "Your father had a word with me yesterday," she said, though it was she who had initiated the talk with Jack Armstrong on the drive home the previous evening, designed to get his agreement to a set of proposals carefully judged to cause him the least possible anxiety. "He thinks you're overdoing things here."

Jackson scowled. "Overdoing things? With business slack as it is? What's he talking about?"

"There are customers having to wait a long time for repairs, aren't there? It's not easy for you. You've said as much, many

115

times. Your father thinks Ronnie should come and give you a hand, two days a week."

"Ronnie? He's just a lad – what is he now, seventeen?"

"Eighteen, and strong with it. Besides, your Dad wants him to have some experience on cars, to widen his knowledge."

If Jackson had known the suggestion had come from her in its entirety, he would have refused. But he dared not refuse anything he thought to come from his father, though he said, with the note of grudging pessimism that never ceased to irritate her, "The next thing, the lad'll be called up and we'll be back where we started."

It was, Diana knew, the closest Jackson was likely to come to a gracious acceptance. The following Tuesday Ronnie went to the petrol station for the first time, and then again on Thursday, and after that the complaints dwindled and business markedly improved. Diana was careful not to comment on it. There was one small inconvenience to herself in the arrangement – on the Thursday mornings when she worked at the garage, Ronnie would come to the office to seek her out on the flimsiest of excuses. Even so, Diana suspected he managed to do more effective work in those hours than Jackson had ever achieved in a whole week.

On the other hand, Ronnie was missed at the quarry, and there were times when his absence put an additional strain on Jack. Diana hoped that it wouldn't be too much for him, but she couldn't see what alternative there was. Perhaps when spring came he would get better.

It was a mild winter, which was a relief, and Jack seemed to have fewer worrying attacks, on the whole. As spring turned to summer, he did indeed begin to look better, cheered perhaps by the good news of the invasion of Europe and the gradual defeat of the Germans. News from the East, where Bradley was, might be less unequivocally good, but it looked as if the tide might be starting to turn there too. In early September, Lily, returning from an evening visit to a friend in Wearbridge, reported that the street lights had been lit again.

A week later, the quarry found itself with a sudden influx of orders. Diana was despatched to make a delivery and Ronnie was brought back from the petrol station, though it was a Tuesday, to carry out an urgent repair on the second wagon. Diana took most of the day to make her delivery, but returned late to find Jack still at work, supervising the loading up of the repaired wagon. "I promised they'd have it today," he said.

"Then let me take it."

"When you've been at work all day? I won't hear of it."

"Then I'll ring Jackson and ask him to do it. I can drive the wagon down to Wearbridge and he can take it from there."

She managed to get Jack to agree to that arrangement and went to the hut to use the phone, newly installed the previous year. But Jackson refused. He'd been busy all day, he said, the more because Ronnie was absent, and he was ready for his supper; besides, Amy wasn't well and someone had to keep an eye on the children. Furious, Diana tried to argue with him, but he must have sensed it was more her idea than his father's, for he proved immoveable.

She left the hut, trying to control her rage. She had somehow to convey the message to Jack without disturbing him. She could see him standing near the loaded wagon, with two of the quarrymen and Ronnie, who was supposed to be checking her wagon, to make sure it was ready for use again in the morning. Perhaps Ronnie could take the load; he had after all learned to drive by now, and was competent enough, if a little too inclined to recklessness.

Then she realised something was happening, some kind of commotion. She could no longer see Jack, and one of the men was bending down. Ronnie called to her. She broke into a run.

By the time she reached them she could see that Jack lay on the ground, with Ronnie on his knees beside him. She knew almost at once that he was dead.

The chapel was packed to the doors for the funeral, and most of the congregation came back to the farmhouse afterwards to pay their respects and eat their way through the hams and cakes and tea that the women of the family had prepared; all, that is, except Elsie, who on this occasion was not expected to do more than receive condolences. She was tearful, but calm and dignified.

Diana felt strange, as if Jack's death had somehow reduced her once more to the status of an outsider. Her friend and ally had gone. Yet there were many people here today who had come to accept her as one of the Armstrongs, even if Elsie herself, and Jackson, were not among them. The trouble was that her fate and that of all the family businesses must now, she supposed, lie in the hands of those two individuals.

She helped carry round plates of food, and gathered up used crockery, and did a great deal of washing up, making herself useful, as if to provide some justification for her presence. As she went, scarcely noticed, from group to group, odd snatches of conversation clung to her attention, without context or conclusion. Many talked of Jack, recalling incidents from the past, some even from his childhood, acts of kindness, characteristic words or deeds. Others talked of the progress of the war, the new offensives against Japan in the East, the good news from Europe, where city after city fell to the Allies; and from whence came rumours of dark things uncovered. "Those camps in Poland – I don't believe it's true, what they're saying," she heard an Armstrong cousin say.

"Just something thought up by the Jews," suggested his companion, a neighbouring farmer. "You know what they say – Jews don't like getting their hands dirty. Stands to reason they'd hate being sent to labour camps. I'm not saying it will have been a picnic, mind, but the things in the papers – no, you cannot believe all that. Remember all those stories about murdered Belgian babies in the last war? Pure propaganda, they turned out to be. Trying to stir up anti-German feeling."

"Why yes, I'd forgotten them . . ."

Diana moved on, glad to share the relief in the man's voice. The reports she'd read one day in a newspaper left lying in the office at the petrol station had haunted her ever since. Now she recalled the disparaging comment overheard in the queue in the Co-op just before the war: 'You'll never see a Jew-boy down a mine'. Not that she knew anything about it; to her knowledge she had never met a Jew.

Then she passed the sofa where Elsie was talking to a neighbouring farmer's wife and caught a snatch of their quite different conversation. "No. Bradley couldn't get leave. We don't even know exactly where he is." They all understood that. What was happening in Europe was clear enough, and well known. But Bradley was in the East, where the war against Japan was by no means over.

"Has he been left any of the business? Or does it all go to Jackson?"

Diana was surprised by the odd look Elsie cast in her direction. There was something almost venomous about it, and yet awkward and even embarrassed as well. Then she returned to her companion. "Why no. They all get something, of course – the girls had their share when they were wed, but there's a bit extra cash for them. The farm goes to Jackson, on condition I stay here – though I'll be glad to have him living here too, and the bairns. But the rest of it, the business—" she paused, with another odd glance at Diana. "Of course, Bradley gets his share. He says he'll be back as soon as ever he can."

Diana felt a sense of shock. She realised it was the first time she had even considered the possibility that Bradley might return. She had continued, under the surface, almost unknown to herself, to believe that he would be killed in action. Of course, he still might; the war was not over yet. She wondered now, hearing the particular note in Elsie's voice, if even his immediate family had been unsure that he would come back, simply because he might not wish to return to the place where so much of his life had gone wrong. Now they all had to face, in their different ways, the possibility of his return, though for each of them it had very different implications.

It still might not happen, she thought. *He might still change his mind – or be killed. The war's not over yet.* Yet that thought, a part of her mental furniture during the past years, was now beginning to seem dangerous, a betrayal, something she must not allow, in case Bradley, if and when he returned, might be able to read her thoughts and know how disloyal she had been. She tried to push it behind her.

She quite forgot about the look Elsie had given her, at least until much later in the day, when, mourners gone, washing up done, the house quiet again, she was on the point of going home. She was in the hall reaching for her coat when Jackson came up to her. "So, you worked on him then, you bitch!"

The savagery of the attack left her momentarily bereft of speech. When she could find breath enough, she stammered, "What are you talking about?"

"My Dad, of course. Got him to alter his will and do his own children out of what's rightly theirs."

Diana sat down heavily on the hall chair, trying to understand what he was saying. "I don't know anything about your father's will."

She could see Jackson wishing he'd held his tongue. He reddened and looked angry, with himself as well as with her, she suspected. "Forget it then!" He turned to go.

She grasped his arm. "No, I want to know. I think I've probably a right to know."

That only made matters worse. "You've no rights – or you shouldn't have, if there was any justice! Besides, the will's not read yet."

"Then how—?"

"Mam knows. Think how she must feel, at this time—" He broke off. "Oh, get out! You'll know soon enough."

She knew the following Wednesday, when she answered a summons to Springbank sent to her by Mr Simmons, the Armstrong family solicitor – he was another of the Wearbridge worthies who used to dine from time to time at Dale House. She found the rest of the family crowded into the parlour; they turned to look at her as at an unwelcome intruder, which was exactly what she felt herself to be. She still could not see what Jack's will could possibly have to do with her, though she had come to the conclusion that he must have left her some small legacy. Mr Simmons, seated at the fireside facing a stony-faced Elsie, waited for Diana to take her seat on a stool in the furthest corner, and then cleared his throat and began to read.

Diana, embarrassed, wishing herself anywhere but here, sat in a daze while the formal legal terms passed over her head, largely unheard. It was only the murmuring, the exclamations, the heads turned to stare at her, that told her they had anything to do with her, though it was not until the formal reading had finished and the solicitor came to speak to her that she understood precisely how.

"The business has been left three ways," Mr Simmons explained. "Equally three ways. Between Mr Jackson Armstrong, Mr Bradley Armstrong – and yourself. And if Mr Bradley fails to return from the war, then you and Mr Jackson get half each." He studied her astounded face. "Mr Armstrong clearly thought very highly of you," he added, as if trying to prompt her to some response.

Something obstructed her throat, making breathing difficult and speech impossible. She still could not take it all in, except the one obvious fact, that her father-in-law had more than repaid her loyalty and hard work. But he was no longer here, and she was faced suddenly with a whole new set of responsibilities which she had not asked for, and most of which she did not as yet understand at all.

Mr Simmons patted her arm. "I see you had no idea."

She found her voice at last. "No idea at all. But what does it mean?"

"If you'd like to call in at the office sometime I'll explain in full. But at the very least it means you have an equal voice, on your own account, in any decision concerning the business."

No wonder Jackson had been angry! In spite of herself, she felt a twinge of sympathy for him. She would have been angry too, in his place, very angry; and hurt. She would probably have wanted to exact some kind of revenge for what had happened, from the person he held responsible – herself. One thing was only too clear, she thought: life for her was about to change, and probably not for the better.

Nine

O nce again, Diana reached the end of the day in a state of anger. The post that morning had brought another letter of complaint (the third this month) about the poor service the writer had experienced from Armstrongs' haulage, and in the afternoon another irate customer had telephoned to ask what had become of the stone he'd expected to receive by now. He had telephoned yesterday too, and Diana had been able to calm him with a promise that it would reach him the following morning at the latest, which was what Jackson, exasperated at her persistence, had eventually promised. Now, the moment she put the receiver down, she went in search of her brother-in-law – it was (unfortunately) one of his quarry days; he came here once or twice a week. But in the shed she found only Ronnie, covered in oil as usual and stretched under a wagon; he hadn't wanted to go back to Sunderland when the war ended, to his increasingly failing grandmother, whom his twin sister was now devotedly nursing. And he was too useful to the business for anyone to argue the point with him. "Do you know where I can find Mr Armstrong?" she asked of his feet.

The boy emerged, grinning, and stood up. He still blushed slightly whenever she spoke to him, but his eyes now generally met hers without embarrassment. Perhaps it was the heat of the September afternoon, but for some reason she was abruptly reminded of her first meeting with Bradley, in the yard behind the petrol station, though this young man's sturdy figure was concealed by heavy blue overalls and his eyes were not brown but that strange light grey, in striking contrast to his tanned skin and dark brows and lashes. For the first time she noticed how long and curled his lashes were. She suddenly felt very hot, and wondered if she was blushing too. "He went to seek Hans."

Hans had been a prisoner here for the past two years. His comrades had now been repatriated to Germany, but he had fallen in love with a local girl, married her and stayed on at the quarry where he had become a valued and popular workman. A broad fair man not much older than Ronnie, he nodded cheerfully to Diana as she reached him; Jackson scowled. By now they rarely met without a disagreement of some kind. "I need a word," she said.

Jackson followed her back towards the hut. "What is it now?"

"It's the delivery for the steelworks. You promised they'd have it by this morning. They've been waiting two days already."

"I'll get round to it. All in good time. Now, let me get on with my job and you get on with yours."

"Then at least let me authorise the delivery." That was a longstanding dispute now, for though there was no one to oversee the business in Jackson's absence, he wouldn't allow anyone else to take his place.

"A clerk, authorise deliveries? What do you take me for?"

She was about to retort that she was no mere clerk, but a business partner. But she knew from previous uncomfortable experience that such a reminder only served to enrage Jackson and make him more difficult than ever. Besides, as he never failed to remind her in return, he and Bradley together could outvote her at any time. The fact that Bradley was not here in person made no difference. Jackson had written to tell his brother of the terms of his father's will, and had shown her the letter Bradley had written in reply. In it he had shared his brother's outrage, but pointed out that his wife's involvement made no difference to anything. He would, of course, always back any decision Jackson made and he was sure (he added) that Diana would support him as a loyal wife should. It was the first time she had seen any of Bradley's letters, and it had seemed to come from a stranger in a far-off land. Nevertheless, it confirmed her perception that her share in the business meant very little in practical terms. After all, she had somehow to find a means of working with Jackson, without too many unnecessary clashes.

Now, she drew a deep breath and said steadily, "Then we should employ a manager, like your father did before the war." She'd heard a few weeks ago that Jim Stobbs, Armstrong's former quarry manager, had been demobilised from the army, and she'd hoped he would return to his old job. She didn't know him, but was quite sure he would be preferable to Jackson, and at the very least he would be working here full-time. But she understood he had found work elsewhere – perhaps he couldn't stomach Jackson either.

"I told you – no point wasting money. The quarry's nearly worked out, and the government's due to take the wagons off us, with their transport nationalisation."

It had been something that had worried her since she'd first heard it mentioned, during the recent election campaign. She was not much interested in politics and did not greatly care what government was in power, but she recognised that the new Labour government, coming into office a few weeks ago after a staggering landslide victory, could do precisely what it pleased. "But we don't know if they really will do it," she pointed out, at which Jackson gave a contemptuous snort. Diana persisted, "Nor do we know what the terms of the bill will be if they do. Small firms like this might not be affected. We shouldn't be giving up before anything's happened."

"Less of the 'we'. I don't care what my Dad did in his dotage – by rights this is my business and Bradley's." Then he stalked away before she could protest.

Diana returned to the hut, and angrily resumed her typing of essential letters. It was a point he made time and time again, even though a formal attempt by Jackson and his mother together to have the will overturned had failed completely. Their case that Jack Armstrong had been deranged when he made it had collapsed under the weight of evidence to the contrary. But the old man needn't have bothered, she thought. The terms of his will might stand, but in effect they had no power at all. In practice, Jackson was now in charge, and made it clear that her job was simply to do as she was told, even when, as now, it was clear to anyone of any intelligence that Jackson was wrong and she was in the right. In law she might have a right to a say in major decisions, but as far as the day-to-day running of the business was concerned she had no effective power at all, rather less; and she did not see what she could do about it. Where Jackson's father would have listened and consulted, deferring to her views in areas where she had the greater experience or was better informed, trusting her to put the firm's best interests first, Jackson had persisted in interfering and finding fault ever since he first came to the quarry after his father's death. He could not, of course, spend all his time looking over her shoulder, with the farm and the petrol station to run as well, and in his absence she simply got on with her work as efficiently as she could. But much of the pleasure had gone out of it. Many times during the past year, Diana had found herself on the point of throwing the hut key at Jackson's feet and storming away from the quarry. But she was always held back at the last minute by the knowledge, first, that this was precisely what he was hoping for, and second, of the chaos that would result. After all, if the business failed for lack of her firm hand, then were she ever to inherit Bradley's share of it, along with his voice in its running, she might find there was nothing left.

She banged at the typewriter, venting her anger on its keys, but realised she was making too many mistakes and forced herself to take a break, trying with little success to calm herself. It was hard, to find that the job she'd once loved had become a daily ordeal. And she no longer really believed that Bradley would not one day come home. The death she had somehow regarded as inevitable was becoming increasingly unlikely. He had survived so long. The war in the East was not quite at an end, but everyone could see that victory was near, so the chances of his survival were increasing every day. She tried not to think of what that might mean for her, one day. For her, the emergence from war to peace had meant an end to a sense of purpose and security and the coming of great uncertainty. The war had forced her to make her own life. In doing so, she had for the first time won approval and affection, not simply because she was a daughter, a wife, a sister, but by her own efforts, because of her own proven abilities. That had been an exhilarating experience, and she didn't want it to end.

War had also put her marriage in suspension at exactly the point it had reached on that September day in 1939, with all the strains on their relationship as they had been then, unresolved and painful. She had thought the war would offer resolution, simply and tidily, by ending the marriage, as so many had ended, with a death. Now she was beginning to realise that this might not happen, that there might not be a neat ending; that it was her time of peace and self-discovery that was about to come to an end, with a return to all the messiness of her marriage. If Bradley returned, of course. Perhaps the fact that he had never once come back to the dale in all the years of the war suggested that he had no wish to return; that the war had offered him a chance, which he'd seized, to turn his back on them all for ever. She rather hoped that would be the case, so long as he took the trouble to let them know what he'd decided, so that she would know the suspension was over.

She finished the letters a little after five o'clock, and put them in her pocket, to post on the way home. Then she put on her coat, picked up her bag with the empty flask and left the hut, locking it behind her. She went to find Jackson, who was talking to two of the men – merely gossiping, she suspected, catching a word or two. She had been surprised to find how much time he regularly wasted in idle chatter, some of it very unpleasant.

"If you hang on a minute I'll give you a lift," he said.

"I'll walk home, thank you," she said. These days she much preferred to walk. Fresh air and exercise were the best means she knew of driving away the anger that seethed in her for so much of the day. She would take the high lane that led directly to Fell Cottage and reach home with her temper calmed.

It was only as she was leaving that she remembered she'd

promised to look in at Springbank this evening and make arrangements with Elsie for feeding the men who were coming next week to kill the Fell Cottage pig. That meant she couldn't take the short way home, and would probably have to face Jackson again, for he would almost certainly reach Springbank before her – he had moved his family into the farm with his mother as soon as his father died. Still, she would be better able to face him after a brisk walk. She had only gone a few yards down the track leading to the road when she heard running feet behind her. She turned to see Ronnie following her. "I'll walk you home, Mrs Armstrong," he said.

She liked Ronnie, and would not normally have minded his company. Now his solicitude only increased her irritation. "I can find my own way thank you!" she snapped, walking faster. "Anyway, I'm going to Springbank first." Ronnie now lodged with a family in Cowcleugh, not far from the quarry.

"I know," he returned cheerfully. "But I'm going there anyway – the tractor's broke. We might as well go together."

There was no effective retort to that other than to be openly rude, so she resigned herself to his company. In fact, she found she was glad of it. He chatted of happy everyday things – the idiosyncracies of the firm's wagons, and places visited and people they both knew – and she began to feel calmer and put her anger behind her. He was, she thought, growing into a likeable young man, good humoured and easy-going, and even, she was increasingly surprised to acknowledge, intelligent, in his way. She found herself laughing at things he said, which she would have thought impossible in her present state of mind. He had a gift for telling a story, with a sharp eye for the amusing detail.

By the time they reached the farmhouse she felt much better, and was glad to see no sign of the wagon – Jackson was not yet home then. Ronnie stood back to let her go into the house ahead of him, holding the door politely. Still grinning at something he had just said, she stepped into the kitchen.

Elsie was there, of course, but standing very still near the range, with her gaze fixed hungrily on a stranger who was deep in conversation with her, a thin man in an ill-fitting suit, with a lined dark face. Feeling that she was intruding, Diana hesitated, and at that moment the man turned his head. Brown eyes, looking her over with a momentary surprise, and a sharpening of interest . . .

She felt a sense of shock. Bradley. It was Bradley, looking her up and down as any man assesses a woman entering a room. She realised, too, that, even as he realised who she was, he was finding her attractive.

It was a feeling she did not reciprocate. The young man who had so bowled her over all those years ago had gone now, to be replaced by someone much older – very much older than she was, older than his actual years – with a hardness about the eyes and mouth, and a sense of barely-contained tension that she found a little frightening.

As if he had forgotten that his mother was there he turned to face her. "Di. You look well." Such meaningless, matter-of-fact words, after all the years of separation!

Diana had no idea what to say in response. She could not truthfully say that he looked well too. But she had to say something. "Hello, Bradley."

From the corner of her eye she saw Ronnie slip across the room and out of the far door. He knew when he was not wanted. Yet she felt, oddly, as if her one truly familiar friend had gone, leaving her with an antagonist and a stranger.

"Bradley got back sooner than we expected," Elsie said. Diana could hear the emotion in her voice. So Bradley had been expected; but not by her, for no one had mentioned the possibility of his imminent return.

For nearly six years Diana had imagined herself – when she thought of Bradley at all – as the grieving widow, dignified and beautiful in black. It had been a romantic and sympathetic image, which would have enhanced her already improving standing in the dale. Now, in a moment, the image fled. She was left with the reality of her husband facing her, real, tangible, but a stranger. She felt stunned, and then frightened. In all the years she had never imagined this.

"I came about the pig," she stammered, recalling the reason why she was here.

"Not now," Elsie said. She even looked a little shocked that Diana could think of such things at such a time. "You'll stay for supper? Bradley will want a good meal, won't you, my lad? And he'll be staying here tonight." She turned to him. "You can have your old room back."

Diana was thankful that Lily was now safely installed in her own house at Ravenshield with Bert, recently demobbed, so there was no reason for anyone to object to the arrangement. It would give her time to adjust to Bradley's return. She hoped he would decide to stay permanently at Springbank. Then, with a sense of shock, she heard him say,

"No thanks, Mam. I'm going home tonight. To Fell Cottage."

There was nothing Diana could do about it. Fell Cottage was his home. He had every right to go there. And so, after a meal which Diana ate in silence, while mother and son talked, they walked together up the hill to the cottage. They had nothing to say as they went, Diana because she was chilled with apprehension, Bradley – who knew why? From anticipation? Because there was too much to say, and he had no idea where to begin? Because he was saving it all for when they were in the cottage, with the door shut behind them? That was the moment she was dreading.

As soon as they were indoors, he reached out and pulled her to him. "God, you smell good!" He began to kiss her, though she tried to break free, but his hands were already at work, undressing her. As he had every right to do, she acknowledged; he was a husband returning from the war to the wife he had not seen for so long. Still fondling her, he steered her upstairs and pushed her onto the bed, and there took her, vigorously, with enthusiasm, for a long time. She could think only that the last time they had made love in this place, Jacky had been lying dead downstairs.

Afterwards, conscious of her lack of response, he questioned her, sharply, "What's the matter? Why are you so cold?"

"I don't know you any more. We need time to get to know each other. You didn't give me time."

"You're my *wife*, for God's sake! If you don't know me by now, then who does?"

She felt that there was no adequate response to so complete a lack of understanding.

Ten

The following morning Diana's alarm rang out at the usual time, and, as usual, in one single, swift movement she reached out a hand to silence it and swung her legs out of bed. Then she felt Bradley catch her arm. It was a shock; she'd forgotten what had happened yesterday, that her haven had been invaded, that he was back. "What are you doing?" he demanded.

"Going to work."

"With your husband just home? What kind of man do you take me for? I'm not having anyone say I cannot keep a wife."

"But I'm needed there."

"You were in the war. But the war's over. I'm back, or hadn't you noticed?" He might have spoken humorously, tenderly, but there was nothing of either feeling in his tone. He began to tug at the buttons of her pyjamas.

"Not now!" she said, breaking free. She still felt sore and bruised from last night, when it had been several hours before he had exhausted his need of her. "I've got to get up. Jackson will be expecting me." *And won't he be glad if I don't turn up!* she thought. Still, Bradley didn't know that yet. She began swiftly to dress.

Bradley got out of bed. "Then I'm coming with you." There was nothing she could do about it. As with everything else, he had every right.

That was her last day in the hut at the quarry. Bradley spent some of it questioning her about her work and examining the books; the rest of the time he spent with his brother, out of her sight. When, in the evening, he came back to the hut, he found Ronnie there. The boy had come with some silly story about one of their regular customers that he thought might amuse her, which it did, and she was grateful for the relief from the grimness of her thoughts. The two of them were still laughing over it when Bradley opened the door. It was a mild day, but Diana felt as if a blast of cold air had come in with her husband. Bradley looked suspiciously from one to the other, then said to Ronnie, "If you've no work to do, then get home." Ronnie reddened, as if he had been accused of something, and left the hut. Bradley turned to his wife, "Is that how you've amused yourself while I was away, flirting with kids? Pathetic! Get your coat. I'll drive you home."

The journey to Springbank in the wagon driven by Bradley brought the past to mind, yet it was not like it at all. Bradley spoke only once, as they came within sight of the farm. "Right, from tomorrow you stay at home, where you belong. Things are back to normal."

Diana tried to argue as they walked up the hill to Fell Cottage, but it was no use; Bradley, backed by Jackson, had decided, and she quickly sensed that there was a whole store of uncontrollable rage only just held in check beneath the grim efficiency of his manner, which she would stir to life at her peril. He had said things were back to normal, but she knew they were not, nor could they be. Whatever 'normal' had once been, it was now gone for ever. Everything had changed, Bradley most of all. They were in unknown territory, and Diana knew only that it was bleakly unwelcoming.

Within a week Ronnie had left. There were returning soldiers in plenty with experience as mechanics, he was told, and he was no longer needed. Diana heard of his going from Bradley, and was sorry she had not even been able to say goodbye. She realised she would miss him. But there were other losses in her life which were much harder to bear.

A constant, if minor, irritation was the removal of control over her income. During the war, she had set herself to manage on the small allowance paid to servicemen's wives, which so many complained of. When her pay at the quarry had been added to that, she had paid most of it into an account at the Post Office, which now contained a modest but satisfying sum. With Bradley's return she suddenly found herself with no income of her own at all. Bradley (she supposed) paid himself a good wage from the business, but she saw very little of it, apart from the weekly housekeeping he gave her, which was the same as she had received before the war, even though prices had risen considerably and he expected her to meet all their bills from it. She managed on the whole, because she was good at managing, but it was a change for the worse.

Much worse was to have to share Fell Cottage again. During the war it had become her place, and now suddenly it was hers no longer. Bradley's cigarette smoke filled the air – and he'd become a fifty-a-day man since they were last together. Once she had delighted in the sense of sharing. But then she had shared with a man she thought she knew.

Then there was the drinking. Bradley had always liked to drink, and following Jacky's death had often drunk too much. Now he went drinking every night, as a matter of course, so that once he had left for work in the morning Diana rarely saw him sober. Not that she found him especially congenial when not drunk, for his moods were dark and unpredictable, and his temper always uncertain. She often felt frightened by the morose stranger he had become. At least drink seemed, on the whole, to put him in a better humour.

She didn't know how to cope with him, had no longer any idea how to behave. They had both changed, not together, but far apart, living through experiences the other could not share, more especially since neither had tried to share them. He seemed to have no interest at all, even now, in what she had been doing during his absence – apart from that rather surprising hint of jealousy of Ronnie. When, for her part, she tried to ask him about his wartime experiences, he simply brushed her questions aside with the tense impatience that was now his usual manner towards her; that, and a physical hunger for her body which took no account at all of her feelings in the matter. There was no longer any softness between them, no laughter, no tenderness. Though, looking back, she could not recall a great deal, even in the early days before everything turned sour – passion, yes, and a proprietorial concern, but not tenderness.

He had returned so suddenly, allowing her no time to prepare herself or decide how she must behave. Now she had to adjust to the fact that she was not a widow, nor even a busy wife with her man away at war. She was, in Bradley's eyes at least, a dutiful wife whose husband had returned. And who, as a consequence, quickly found herself pregnant.

For some reason that had not entered into her calculations at all. As the realisation slowly broke in on her consciousness, she first tried to repel it, as something impossible and unwanted, but at last could no longer deny it. It terrified her. All the pain of Jacky's loss came back to her, and the fear that it might happen again.

When she had first known she was expecting Jacky, Bradley had been the person she had most wanted to confide in, sure as she then was of his support and love. Now she put off telling him. That he would share her fears seemed certain, and perhaps that he would wish it hadn't happened, because of all the cruel memories that came with it. Better, she thought, to say nothing until she could not put it off any longer. She even found herself hoping she might miscarry before she need speak to him.

Towards the end of November, she made an appointment to see old Dr Elliott at the surgery in his house at Ravenshield, half-hoping he would tell her she was mistaken. Instead, he was warmly congratulatory. "Excellent," he said, as he washed his hands after examining her. "You must be delighted." He glanced at her face as she climbed down from the couch and rearranged her clothes, and must have seen some hint there of her terror. "Don't worry! No reason why everything shouldn't go according to plan this time, no reason at all."

Diana recalled how, at Jacky's death, he had said, *It happens sometimes. It's just one of those sad things.* What he said now seemed just as much a soothing platitude as those other words, bringing as little reassurance. He had done nothing to allay her terror. She moved towards the door.

"Don't you want to know when the little one will arrive?" She wondered what he would say if she were to tell him she couldn't care less. He had taken up a small notebook and was consulting it. "From the dates you've given me, it looks like the end of May next year. So your parents will be well settled in by the time their grandchild puts in an appearance." He laid down the book and beamed at her. "It'll be good to have Dale House back to its old self."

Diana felt frozen to the spot. "Are they coming back then?" She hoped she had hidden the full extent of her shock, and the hurt. Her mother had written with reasonable regularity throughout the war, and she had thought the old days of exclusion from her family were over. But there had been no mention of this momentous development.

"You didn't know?" He looked a little embarrassed. "Yes, by the end of the week. So I shall be able to retire at long last. Before we doctors are taken over by the state, like everything else. I'm too old for such nonsense. But your father always favoured something of the kind, I seem to remember." He studied her face, trying to see if he had indeed blundered in revealing something she had not known, yet surely ought to have known. Then he rose and went to open the door for her, suddenly very solicitous – too solicitous, for it only underlined the hurt. "Take care of yourself, my dear."

It would be her father's doing, she thought as she walked home; that was why her mother had not written to tell her they were on their way back to Dale House. She could imagine what had happened: Dr Poultney had returned from the war to his family (even that had been kept from her), where he had discovered, to his fury, that Evelyn had renewed contact with their errant daughter, and had immediately put a stop to it. She tried to remember when her mother had last written – yes, it had been about two months ago, in response to her news of Bradley's return, briefly and unemotionally recounted. Evelyn had expressed her pleasure that Diana should no longer be alone, and Diana had wished she felt able to retort that loneliness had less to do with solitude than with living without understanding or love. But in her reply to her mother she had said nothing of that. She had not been surprised that there had not yet been an answer. Her mother was involved in a great many local activities and was often too busy to write for long periods together. Now, suddenly, that silence looked quite different, not normal but sinister, indicative of a deliberate policy. Through all the years of separation Diana had felt herself drawn closer to her absent family, or to her mother at least – none of her siblings had ever tried to make contact or even send her a message, though she had news of them from her mother: Angela was now working in her brother-in-law's office in Surrey, near Pamela and her growing family; Robert was in London, doing something artistic about which Evelyn had always been vague, probably, Diana suspected, because she disapproved of it. She would have liked to see them again, to know that they still cared for her. But it was her mother's love that mattered most, which she knew she had never lost. Now, at the moment when she knew for certain that she was herself to be a mother again, and might hope to have her own mother once more within her reach, when she might hope actually to see and talk to her again in person, it seemed that Evelyn's love was to be snatched away from her, by her father's unrelenting decree.

She saw little of the countryside as she walked, she who normally took in every tiny sign of the changing seasons, for her eyes were brimming with tears, forced up from her anger and her pain. She was oblivious to the cold, and the mist that enveloped her as she neared Fell Cottage.

Pushing open the door, she stumbled in, treading on a letter that lay on the mat, not taking in that it was there until she had begun to remove her coat. Then she snatched it up, brushing her hand across her eyes to clear her vision. Her name and address, clearly inscribed in her mother's bold handwriting, leapt up at her.

Her hand trembled as she carried it to the table, where she sat down, staring at the envelope. So her mother was after all writing to tell her of their imminent return. But what did that mean? Would she give her daughter the news only to reject her by warning that they must not meet?

With difficulty, she tore the envelope open, struggling through her agitation to read the letter it contained. By the time she reached the end she was smiling at her own foolishness. "Idiot!" she rebuked herself. For her mother's letter was short and to the point: she and the doctor were moving back into Dale House on Thursday; Diana could imagine how much there was to do, so would forgive her for not writing more – they would very soon be able to exchange all their news in person, something both her parents were much looking forward to. '*It will be so good to see you again*,' Evelyn ended the letter.

Diana did not want her first meeting with her parents after so long to be complicated by the difficulties of her relationship with Bradley, so she hid the letter and said nothing to him about their return; just as, for the time being, she still put off telling him about the baby.

It was Tuesday when she received the news of her parents' return. On Friday morning, as soon as Bradley had left for work, Diana walked down to catch the bus to Wearbridge, as she had done so often during the past years. But it was not as it had been, for today, descending in the market place as usual, Diana then took the lane up beside the church, where she had not walked for many years, and crossed the road and made her way between the sturdy stone gateposts of Dale House.

The gravel drive was choked with weeds, the lawns badly needed cutting, the flower beds were overgrown, the shrubs unpruned. Near the front door, which stood open on this crisp November morning, a number of empty tea chests had been abandoned on the gravel. She picked her way round them and stepped into the house. She felt as if she were suffocating, so fast was her heart beating.

There was no sign of anyone, though she could hear clattering from the direction of the kitchen and vague sounds from up-stairs. She stood in the hall, uncertain, not knowing whether to call out. The hallway looked very bare, though some of the familiar pieces of furniture, rather battered now, stood in their usual places. But there was no carpet, and the paintwork of doorways and banister was badly scratched and chipped.

Then she heard someone crossing the landing, approaching the head of the stairs. She looked up. Her father stood there, outlined against the landing window, his shape suddenly overwhelming familiar. All the long years of separation seemed suddenly wiped out by it. She could not see his face. What must he think and feel, as he saw her? He was hesitating, certainly – repelled by the sight of her, perhaps?

He broke into a run, half stumbling down the stairs. She heard him call, against all his lifelong views of decorum, "Evelyn! Evelyn! Diana's here!"

Then her mother too came running from the direction of the kitchen, just as her father, astonishingly, beyond belief, folded his daughter into his arms. This man who never hugged, to whom a handshake was an expression of deep emotion, was hugging her as if afraid that she might otherwise disappear into the atmosphere and be lost to him again. She found herself sobbing, moved beyond words.

Then her mother was hugging her too, and kissing her. There were several minutes of wonderful confusion, before Evelyn, looking just a little embarrassed at this unaccountable display of family emotion, released her, and said, "Come into the drawing room. I'll ask Doris to bring us some tea. There's so much to talk about."

Everything became calm and normal, as Diana would have expected it to be. They sat on the worn chairs in the drawing room and sipped tea from the familiar green-patterned china, and her parents told her how well she was looking, and gave her news – much of which she already knew – of her sisters and brother, and asked after old friends (few of whom she knew at all these days), and tried to fill in the many gaps in the past years. Diana, conscious that there was a great deal she was not saying, in particular this week's most important news, felt rested by the sense of being at home again, the sense of normality.

Yet things were not normal; below the calm and orderly surface, Diana became aware of that as they talked, conscious of all kinds of undercurrents. Her mother looked a little older, and her fair hair was now completely white, but otherwise she was little changed. But her father, the man who, outlined against the light on the stairs, had looked exactly as she remembered him, was, she now saw, so much changed that if she had first seen him in the street, in full daylight, she might even have passed him by as a stranger. He was her father, yet not her father; he had aged far more than the seven years since they had last met. Then, he had been a man in the prime of life, strong and vigorous. Now, he was old, lined and shrunken. But it was not so much his physical appearance that troubled her as the expression of the dark eyes that had once been so bright and confident. Now they seemed to her to have a haunted look, though he smiled, and talked calmly of everyday things. She realised that in all the exchange of news he had said nothing about his own experiences during the years of separation. But that was perhaps hardly surprising; he had always been a reticent man. And soldiers did not readily talk of what they'd been through, she knew; Bradley, had told her practically nothing, and had not even confided in his mother, and she supposed it must be the same for those whose service had never actually taken them into the heat of battle.

"That's enough about us," her mother said at last, as if the minutest detail of the past years had been sifted through. "What about you? You look well. And how is Bradley? Glad to be home, I expect. I hope he's well."

"Yes," Diana said, wondering if sullen moods and frequent drunkenness could be regarded as signs of good health.

There must have been something in her tone or expression that gave away more than she realised, for after a pause her mother said, with the lowered and sympathetic note reserved for more emotional matters, "It isn't easy, getting to know one another again after so long apart. I know you'll have seen each other now and then, but it's not the same as living together all the time." Diana had not told her mother that Bradley had never spent his time on leave with her, but neither had she said anything to the contrary; her mother simply assumed that things had been normal. Now Evelyn cast a teasing glance at her husband. "I know how quickly one grows used to living alone and going one's own way. Then suddenly one has to consider someone else all over again." She laid her hand over the doctor's, as if to reassure him that in her case it had been a pleasure to make the adjustment.

But Diana realised that her mother had after all guessed that for her it had not been easy. Somehow she must have read between the lines of the uncommunicative letters and this morning's trite responses. Suddenly wanting them to see the whole picture she blurted out, "I'm pregnant – I'm going to have a baby."

Evelyn gave a little cry and came to her and kissed her. "Oh, that's wonderful! Oh, I'm so pleased!"

Diana heard the doctor say something, though what it was she could not tell. It was not until her mother sat down again that she looked across and saw that there were tears in his eyes which he was making no attempt to hide. Once again, she found herself astonished that her father could be so moved, and so uncontrolled. This could not be the man who had gone away without saying goodbye to his daughter, who had put her out of his life, on a matter of principle. "It's such good news – such good news!" he murmured at last. "When there is so much evil in the world, to come home to something so good and wholesome – it cheers the heart!" He spoke as if he were close to choking with emotion. Then he must have become aware of something in her face far removed from the expected bliss of imminent motherhood. He glanced at the hands twisting together in her lap, a kind of echo of the twisted knot of anxiety inside her. "What is it, Diana? You're not happy."

Bewildered by her father's uncharacteristic mood, the trouble and tenderness, Diana stammered, "After what happened last time . . ."

He reached out and laid a hand over hers. "Perhaps if I had been there, if I had kept an eye on you both . . ."

"Do you think it would have made any difference?"

"Who's to say? I was not there. But this time I shall be."

There was a silence, full of unspoken feeling, which Evelyn broke at last. "I know, I still have some baby clothes upstairs! I hunted high and low for them in thirty-nine, when the WVS were appealing for help, but I couldn't find them anywhere. Now they've turned up after all. Let's go and have a look before they're buried in the loft again. You can have any of them you like."

Mother and daughter went upstairs together, to kneel beside a trunk in what had once been Robert's room and sort through small, delicate garments, smelling of mothballs, which had once been worn by the Poultney infants, beautiful garments made with a pre-war disregard for economy. They exclaimed over them, laughed together, talked of memories evoked, put those selected on a growing pile. Diana began to feel happy, even optimistic. This time everything was going to be different. This time she would have the loving support of her family – or her parents, at least. "I suppose the others will come and visit sometimes – Pamela and the other two." She felt a sudden hunger to see them again, Pamela in particular, who was now a mother herself.

"They may do so, perhaps," said Evelyn. She had an odd expression, almost defensive. "Nowadays they are all so busy with their own lives. They have their own circle of friends. I expect your father and I are more likely to visit them."

Diana knew, then, that as far as her siblings were concerned, the past was not put behind her, she was not forgiven. The happiness of a moment before wavered in the face of the realisation. Then she looked again at her mother, so concerned to protect her from hurt, and felt consoled. It was all going to be all right. Evelyn lifted the little pile of clothes. "Do you want to take these with you now?"

Diana shook her head. "I can't. I haven't told Bradley yet, about the baby."

Her mother's troubled gaze rested on her face. "Why ever not?"

"I was afraid, after what happened before. And—" And what? She herself did not really understand all that lay behind her reticence.

Crouching there beside the opened trunk, Evelyn took her hands. "This little one will bring you together, I'm quite sure of it."

143

"Mother," Diana said, conscious of breaking through the barrier of filial respect – but then surely this was a day for such unconventional behaviour. "You can't have found it difficult, when Father came back?"

Evelyn smiled ruefully, "As I said downstairs, one gets used to one's own ways. It was wonderful to have him back, but there were adjustments to be made, on both sides. One has to learn to know the other all over again. But it's worth it, truly it is."

Diana recalled then, with a little shock, that her father had been home for a shorter time than had Bradley, so for Evelyn there had been less time for adjustment, though she spoke as if it had already been made. She recognised, uneasily, that she had made no attempt herself to understand Bradley's point of view or to try to help him adjust to the strangeness of his return. She had simply resented, furiously, his intrusion into her life.

"Of course," Evelyn added, her tone very grave, "in your father's case there were special factors, after his experiences—"

Diana looked at her questioningly.

"He was in Germany when the war ended."

"Was that very bad then?" Diana had never been interested in news that did not directly affect her, and had paid little attention on the whole to newspapers or radio.

"He learned," replied her mother, "the extent of the evil we were fighting."

Diana was awed by the gravity of the remark. She felt her mother watching her, trying to gauge how far she understood what was implied.

"You must have read in the papers about the camps?"

She had, of course, read about the concentration camps found by the Allied forces as they swept across Germany, and the appalling conditions that had been uncovered, but she had not paid the reports a great deal of attention, dismissing them, for the most part, as the funeral guests had done, as propaganda, grossly exaggerated. Could they all have been wrong? "Did Father see them then?"

"He was present at the liberation of Belsen." Evelyn paused before going on, as if it took a huge effort of will even to speak of it. "My dear, simply to hear him talk about it made me feel ill. It was frightful, horrible. You know that we have neither of us lived sheltered lives. We both served in the medical services during the Great War. Your father thought, as I did, that we had seen the worst that men can do to one another. And Belsen was not one of the death camps, such as they discovered elsewhere."

"Was it for prisoners of war then?"

Evelyn shook her head. "I think those camps were bad enough, by all accounts, but only as you would expect. No, the concentration camps were designed for what were to the Nazis undesirables – communists, gypsies, above all, Jews."

Diana remembered again the queue in the Co-op, and the man talking: *Quite right too, to make the Jews work. You never see a Jew-boy down a coal mine.* "I thought they were work camps? Like our internment camps?"

"I suppose that's what most of us thought. When I think how we talked so lightly of the 'Jewish Question', as if it were something real, a problem to be addressed. Well, it seems the Nazis took it seriously, and found their own appalling solution. Diana, we know now that thousands, perhaps even millions, were deliberately killed – and that is not to take account of those who died from torture and neglect and disease in places like Belsen. And I'm speaking not simply of adult males, but women and children, down to the smallest infant. I think your father feels, as I do, that we must all bear some responsibility, for having allowed such ways of thinking to take root, however carelessly." She stood up, brushing down her skirt to neatness, though Diana could see that her hands were trembling with the emotion of all she had said. "Well, let's get back to your father. I'll put these things aside, until you've told Bradley the news. But I really do think you should do so at once."

"I will," promised Diana. Somehow her own fears looked much less formidable when she thought of them in the context of what her mother had just told her.

A little later, as she took her leave of them, her father embraced her with his new unfamiliar fervour. "If you knew how much good it does me to see you looking so well, and the bearer of such happy news! And don't be afraid. I'm sure all will be well. Remember, my dear, if you have any anxieties about your health or that of your infant, don't hesitate to come and see me, at any time."

"I won't," she promised.

"You know you can come here for the birth, if that would reassure you," her mother added. Diana thought of the isolation of Fell Cottage, and was grateful. She thought she would take up the offer, when the time came.

She had ample leisure during the rattling bus journey and the walk up the hill to consider all that had happened that morning. She felt happier than she had for a long time, but her happiness, shadowed by what her mother had told her, had an undertone of solemnity about it. She resolved not to allow herself to be consumed by fear; more to the point, she would take the coming of this second child of hers and Bradley's as a sign of hope, the opportunity for a new beginning. She'd been selfish, she saw that now, thinking only of herself and her own feelings. For too long she had allowed herself to assume that Bradley had gone from her life. When he had returned, she had looked on him only as a threat to her happiness and peace of mind. Yet he was her husband, whom she had once loved deeply, and promised to love as long as she lived. She had made her choice long ago, for good or ill. She could not simply discard it because she had tired of it or did not like what it had become. As she toiled up the hill the resolution grew and hardened in her. From this moment she would throw herself heart and soul into her marriage, to turn it into something good, if it lay in her power to do so. From this moment she was going to put her resentment aside and look to a future as Bradley's wife, sharing the task of raising their child in love and security. Since he had come back, then she must make the best of it and learn to know him again. Surely it was not impossible that they might rediscover the love that had brought them together so fatally before the war? Or if that was irrecoverable, then perhaps they could somehow find a new kind of love, more practical perhaps, without the passionate impulsiveness, but the more enduring and profound for all that.

The new child must, surely, bring them together, if they allowed it to.

For once, Bradley came back to Fell Cottage after work, not to see her nor even for supper, but to change into a clean shirt before going to the Black Bull; there was no denying that he needed one.

Diana, glancing quickly at his face as he came in, knew with relief that he was not yet drunk. She went to him and took his hands, though he immediately pulled them free. She hardened herself against the hurt. "I've something to tell you."

She felt her heart thud as he halted, looking down at her, though with no softness in his eyes. "Well? I'm in a hurry."

"I'm pregnant."

She could not read his expression. There was certainly nothing like the mixture of emotions she had seen on that first occasion, on her return from France. But at the end she saw something unexpected, yet unmistakable – pure delight. And for the first time in years he embraced her with what seemed like real affection.

Bradley did not, after all, go out again that evening. Instead, he stayed at home with her and ate the supper she set upon the table (with some hurried rethinking, since he so rarely shared this meal with her), and afterwards sat facing her by the fire as she worked her way through a pile of socks in need of darning, and talked of the coming child and what they would all do together. It did not once seem to enter his head that anything might go wrong. She even found herself wondering, with a tinge of resentment, if he had forgotten all about Jacky.

For her part, she made herself listen to his voice – the voice that had once had the power to turn her insides to water – and watch his face, trying to see in it the man she'd once loved, and for whom she had given up so much without a second thought. That man, she told herself, was still there, and still loveable. And indeed, happy as he was, and proud of her, he seemed to have more of that man in him today than she had been able to find for a long time, and already she was sure she could feel the difference. If she could achieve so much in so short a time, then it must grow easier, as the days passed.

147

Then he stubbed out his fifth cigarette of the evening and said, "Of course, we can't stay here." She had no idea what he was talking about. "The flat's standing empty all this time – you know, at the garage. It makes sense for us to move down there, so I can keep an eye on things. That's where our main business is going to be, once nationalisation comes in. I thought to shift all the repair work down there anyway. And it'll be much better for you and the baby – handy for the shops and the doctor and all. Besides," he grinned, "we want him to grow up where he can learn about wagons, right from the start."

She was so appalled that all her good resolutions were overturned in an instant. "You can move there if you like. I shan't."

"Why ever not? It's a good big flat, two bedrooms, a nice kitchen, a bathroom too. You'll love it."

"There's no garden and everything stinks of petrol and – and it's not here . . ." she ended weakly. How could she begin to explain what Fell Cottage, even shared with Bradley again, had come to mean to her?

They argued for a while, but in the end, to her surprise, Bradley dropped the subject without having resolved it. She sensed that he was so delighted that she had achieved pregnancy that he was unwilling, for the time being at least, to cause her distress.

Bradley had been sure, right from the start, that the baby would be a boy, so sure that he'd refused to discuss any but boys' names. He was wrong. This time there was no heir to the haulage business, to rival Jackson's son: the baby, delivered without trouble at Dale House early the following June, with both Diana's parents in attendance, was a girl.

Diana, waiting in bed for Bradley to come to her, braced herself for his disappointment, even perhaps for a return to the drunkenness he had almost entirely put aside since he first heard she was pregnant. As so often since that day, he surprised her. He gave her a kiss and then bent over the Poultney family crib and caressed the cheek of the tiny sleeping creature. Diana could not remember having seen such a look of tenderness on his face

148

before. There was not one word of regret for the son for whom he had so volubly planned.

"I thought perhaps we might call her Pauline," Diana suggested. Unlike Bradley, she had thought of several girls' names, and this was her favourite.

"Carol," he said, without looking up from the crib. "She's Carol."

Diana dared not ask him why, did not even want to, when she thought about it. Perhaps there had once been some woman in his life of that name, a woman who had meant a great deal to him. But the past was behind them, over and done with. Now there was only the future, for herself and Bradley and this new, beloved daughter.

Eleven

It had begun to snow again about an hour ago, and the wind had risen with it. Great white gobbets now clung to the window panes, so that indoors there was none of the usual snow-lightness, but a growing twilight. Diana tried to peer out, but could see only a white blur. Would Bradley have reached Spring-bank before the snow started? She thought it unlikely.

She went to the front door and wrenched it open. Fierce grains of snow lunged in on the wind, rattling on the flags around her, stinging her face. She could see nothing from here either, except the blizzard. She struggled to close the door, against the force of the wind and the bank of snow that was toppling over into the opening. First thing this morning, Bradley had laboriously cleared a way out, but now, three hours later, the drift was already half way up the door again.

Once the door was shut, Diana paused to gather her breath before going yet again to check on Carol. There had been no argument with Bradley lately about their treatment of their daughter – even with its window tight shut, their bedroom was freezing, so cold that they found it hard to sleep there themselves. The cot remained downstairs, where the range did little more than keep the room at a bearable temperature – the fire was kept permanently damped down, as a means of ekeing out for as long as possible the little fuel they had left. Carol who, unlike her parents, seemed oblivious of winter, slept soundly when required, laughed and played, and fed well.

But Diana was still afraid. Fear had, to a greater or lesser extent, been an intrinsic part of her life since she'd first known she was pregnant. She had imagined in the early days that, once

Carol was safely past the dangerous six months point at which Jacky had died, the fear would go, if not immediately, then gradually, steadily. Perhaps it would have done, if it had not been for the snow that had arrived late in January and now, two weeks later, showed no sign of lessening.

There had been severe winters during the war, but they had, at the worst, been no more than inconvenient, meaning a difficult walk to work, or (sometimes) not getting there at all. More often, Diana had revelled in the sense of being cut off by the weather, isolated, with only herself to please.

But this winter of 1947 was different. She was not alone. She didn't want to be cut off from everyone in Bradley's company. Least of all did she want her child to be cut off. Yesterday, Carol had sneezed, twice, in quick succession; coincidence, perhaps – but what if it should be the start of a cold? She'd seemed well enough this morning, had laughed at Bradley's teasing, and played happily in her cot after her feed, before settling to sleep. Now, checked again, she was found to be still sleeping soundly, soft brown hair – quite long now – curled about her plump face, her cheek, when her mother laid a hand against it, warm to the touch. But Diana was not reassured. She wished Bradley had not gone out.

He'd done it for the best, of course. By now food was getting low. The bacon was finished and the tea had almost gone. They had some flour and oatmeal left, though not a great deal, but the three hens were not yet laying and still had to be fed, as did the pig, with no leavings from their own meals to be used – they ate all there was. Bradley threatened to kill one of the hens, but they were scrawny and would make a tough meal, and only as a last resort would they deprive themselves of the prospect of future eggs. There were leeks in their little plot, but they were buried deep under the hard-frozen snow. By now, Diana should have been well into the process of weaning Carol, but that would only have added an extra strain to their anxieties about food, so she continued to breast feed, though her daughter no longer seemed quite satisfied by it. She wondered what she would do if, for lack of her own nourishment, her milk were to dry up.

This morning, while Bradley cleared snow and saw to the hens and pig and emptied the bucket that served them, in this icy weather, as a temporary substitute for the netty, Diana had fed Carol and then set about mixing melted snow (the spring was frozen) with flour, which she then slapped, a thick tasteless dough, onto the hotplate of the range. It was warm and it was food, which was as much as you could say about it. It would not have been enough to keep Bradley going through a day's work, but then he had not been able to get to work for two weeks now.

Now she wished he'd had something more substantial inside him. For, after breakfast and the usual playing with Carol with which the day always started, he had put on coat and hat and muffler and announced that he was going to try and get to Springbank. "We've got to have food, before we run out. Besides, I want to know what's going on." There had, after all, been two Sundays when they had not made it to Springbank for dinner. The first Sunday the blizzard had been so intense that there had been no question of trying. The following week, the snow having ceased in the night, they had set out, but got no further than the end of the garden. It had taken so long to get so far, and the drifts were so deep, that they had given up. A little later it had begun to snow again.

This morning too they had found that the snow had ceased in the night. Perhaps they had even believed that, this time, the storm might be over. "Coming this late in the winter, you know it won't stay long," they had said, when it first started. Each lull in the storm had seemed like the end of it, and this morning had been no exception. Diana had watched Bradley set out from the cleared doorway of the cottage and had then occupied herself with the usual tasks. She did her best to wash the soiled nappies in more of the melted snow – tepid this time. Her mother would have said Carol should be more-or-less potty-trained by now. Perhaps she had a point, when washing was so difficult. Afterwards, with cold hands, she draped the damp squares of towelling over the clothes horse at the other end of the fire from the cot. It was then she had realised, from the increasing force of the wind and the rattling on the window, that it had begun to snow again. And then she had been afraid in deadly earnest.

What if Bradley should be cut off at Springbank, she had thought, unable to get back to them? How could she possible manage, alone, with a young baby? What if Carol should be ill, with no one able to go for the doctor, no hope of help from any quarter?

Around noon, Carol woke, wanting another feed and then to play. It was far too cold for her to be allowed on the floor to crawl, so Diana put her, well-wrapped, back in the cot, which served these days as a sort of play pen. She jumped up and down, clinging to the rail and grizzling. Diana told herself it was just that she wanted more freedom than the cot allowed – temper, Evelyn Poultney would have called it – but the niggling, anxious voice wondered if the child might be sickening for something. By now the storm seemed only to be growing wilder and Diana found a new fear – what if Bradley had foundered on his way down the hill, and had never reached Springbank? How long would it be before anyone knew what had happened?

She who for all the years of the war had imagined Bradley's death as something almost to be hoped for, now feared it above everything. The past months of parenthood had, as she'd hoped, brought them together. It was not perhaps as it had once been, at its best, but he drank rarely these days, and adored Carol, and often seemed to enjoy his wife's company too. In bed, he had become rather more considerate, so that Diana was sometimes able to find pleasure again in his lovemaking. Above all, she realised now, he took care of his wife and daughter, as far as he was able. She didn't know if what they had rediscovered together amounted to love, but without him it would be as if, in the most literal sense, she and Carol were to be exposed, unprotected, to the full blast of the winter storm.

She sat down close to the cot with her knitting – a cardigan for Carol that was slowly taking a curiously malformed shape, with bulges and indentations where they should not have been. She'd always hated knitting and had never even been competent at it, but felt duty bound to make the effort. The child grizzled more persistently than ever, her voice drowning the sounds of the storm. In the end, her nerves in shreds, Diana put the knitting aside and took Carol from her cot. *You're making a rod for your own back*, her mother would have said, but she didn't care. She needed the comforting closeness of her now happy baby to distract her from her fears.

It was growing dark in earnest by the time she heard the stamp of boots outside, the noise of someone kicking a way through the snow, the sound of the door scraping open. She returned Carol – fed again, and sleepy – to the cot and went to meet Bradley, as he came in on a blast of snow and forced the door shut behind him. He carried a bag, which he flung down on the table, before allowing Diana to help him out of his wet clothes.

"You're soaked through! Oh, Bradley, I was so worried! Did you get to Springbank? What's it like? How are they all?"

He sank down in the armchair and thankfully took the hot drink she brought him – some of their precious tea, which he gulped down. "They're doing all right – better than us. But it's bad. Nothing's getting through. The roads are all stuck fast – snow high as the wall tops." He put down his now empty cup and reached for the bag, taking out one thing after another. There was bread of his mother's baking, a meat pie, bacon and a few of last year's wrinkled apples. "We'll have to make it last. They've not got that much for themselves."

"Never mind," said Diana, examining the bounty. "This is a feast!"

He got up then, exhausted as he was, and went over to the cot, where Carol had been shouting for him since he walked in the door. "How's my bairn then?" He swung her into his arms and kissed her. "Who's my best girl?" Then he sat down again with the child on his knee and looked up at his wife, his face suddenly grave. "One thing's for sure," he said. "As soon as the thaw comes, we're moving, down to Wearbridge. I'll not spend an hour more up here than I have to."

A few weeks ago Diana would now, as usual, have marshalled her arguments, to counter his: it might be that, once the government had nationalised road haulage, there would be nothing left to them but the garage, but she was sure there would be ways round the legislation for a small firm like Armstrong's, ways to survive – they should wait and see if the present haulage strike had any effect (though how anyone would even notice that there was a strike in this weather, she could not imagine). More to the point, the flat over the garage would never be free of the stink of petrol, the dust from the street; here there was fresh air, the little garden, the open fell, space and beauty, to stretch the limbs and the imagination of a growing child. But today none of these often exercised arguments would come to her lips. There was that other vision in her head, of a sick child for whom no doctor could come, or could only come too late. How could she, Carol's mother, deny her safety?

Sick at heart, yet resigned, she agreed that Bradley was right.

Fell Cottage had never looked lovelier than on the May morning when they moved down to the flat over the garage. The pig and hens had already been taken down to Springbank, so that the outbuildings were empty. But they left behind curlews calling in the clear blue air, and larks singing, and the sweet scent of wind-blown grasses and peaty earth, and the bleating of the few strong lambs that had survived the snow.

Slowly, laboriously, they loaded their belongings onto a hand cart and jolted them down to Springbank, where Jackson had a wagon ready; and then made their way to the petrol station. Behind the pumps the grey facade rose, pierced by an arch that led through into the repair yard where Diana had first met Bradley – *I must think of it as a good omen*, Diana thought, though she could not repel a shudder at the bleakness of everything. They mounted the narrow, dark stairs that led to the flat above the ground floor office. As Bradley had said, the rooms here were larger than at Fell Cottage, and there was even a small spare bedroom, so that Carol need no longer sleep in their room. But from the windows there was a view only of the road and, across it, a wall and two houses. The whole building stood in the very bottom of the valley, so that even so early in the day it was already in shadow. Outside, there were no trees, not even stunted and bent by the wind, no flowers, no earth, no grass, only the smell of oil and the noise of traffic. The grim memories of the winter were already beginning to fade a little, and Diana's heart ached with longing for what she had left behind and for what her child would never now know.

I'm going to make the best of it! she reminded herself grimly, as she unpacked boxes and decided, without really caring, where the furniture should go or where to hang her pictures. She gritted her teeth against the irritating incessant sound of Bradley's cheerful whistle. He at least was thoroughly happy. So, it seemed, was Carol, gurgling and laughing from the confinement of her cot while the work went on around her; though perhaps she simply enjoyed the unusual entertainment provided for her.

Later, Diana left Bradley to finish the unpacking and went, fighting low spirits, to cook dinner for them in her new kitchen – and had to admit that the electric cooker was a great improvement on the temperamental range at Fell Cottage. Very likely, as Elsie always claimed, it was inferior in performance to any range, but then Diana had never been able to cook really well on anything and probably never would. At least the cooker was consistent, predictable and easy to clean. She notched it up in her mind, as a single point in favour of the flat. She was going to need all the evidence she could muster to raise her spirits.

Later still, when preparing for bed, she had to admit that the bathroom, with its adjacent lavatory, was another advantage of the move. There was an immersion heater, allowing hot water to run blissfully from the taps into basin or bath, and no need any more, at any call of nature, for that chilly walk down the garden, or the undignified bucket in the corner of the bedroom. A little later, as Bradley undressed for bed (he was developing a considerable paunch, she noticed), he suddenly said, 'It's a good place, this. We'll be all right here. Only pity is, Mam won't be able to see it. She'd never manage the stairs, the way she is now." That, Diana thought, was a very considerable point in the flat's favour. She slept soundly that night.

The following morning, glancing out of the window as she fried bacon and eggs for breakfast, Diana saw two boiler-suited men crossing the forecourt, presumably on their way to work in the yard; and a girl, who disappeared out of sight somewhere immediately below. Diana put her head out of the open window and looked down, and saw that the girl was in the process of unlocking the office door. She appeared to be about sixteen, slight and fair. "Who's that down there?" she asked Bradley, who was seated at the small kitchen table, smoking while he waited for his breakfast. He came to look.

"Rita Emerson. She's just started in the office, last week."

Diana turned to him. "You didn't say anything to me!"

"Why should I? It's business."

"But I could do it. I did it all through the war; I know the work inside out. It's a waste of money to get someone in."

"Oh, so you'd do it for free would you?"

"What I earn would go to us both, you know that; and to Carol too, of course. And I'd only want what the business can afford."

"No one's going to say I cannot afford to keep a wife. Besides, you've got Carol to look after. You're a mother now. That's your job."

"I could do both, easily. This flat won't take much looking after. We'll get a play-pen for the office."

"Don't talk rubbish." He stubbed out his cigarette. "Am I getting any breakfast this morning? I'm late already."

She knew there was no point in continuing the argument for now, but resolved to return to it later; whatever Bradley might think, the matter was by no means closed. Even so, anger and resentment seethed inside her, boiling away long after Bradley had gone, invigorating the dusting and sweeping and polishing she turned to as a demonstration of how little time it took to reduce the flat to spotlessness, when there were no ashes to clear (it was too warm today to need a fire in their one hearth), no water to fetch from the spring, and the few rugs could be cleaned with a vacuum cleaner, powered by electricity. Carol slept peacefully through all the bustle. She was a very biddable child, sleeping at all the right times, as if determined to offer no excuse for her parents to quarrel about her routine.

Bradley came back to the flat for his dinner, without apparently noticing how clean everything was, and still refused to consider Diana as any kind of part of the business. All the renewed discussion succeeded in doing was to reduce him to extreme ill-humour – which, Diana thought as he returned to work, made two of them.

It was a sunny afternoon, so Diana carried Carol downstairs to the pushchair that was stored by the door (like the vacuum cleaner, it was a new acquisition) and pushed her across the road and along the river path and then up to Dale House. Her mother waved to her from the far corner of the garden, where she was kneeling beside a flower bed, handfork busy among the new weeds, and then came to meet her. "What a lovely surprise! I thought you'd be much too busy to spare us any time. Come on in. Your father's showing the new partner round – they're at the surgery." Once, the surgery had been here in the house, a large room on the ground floor, but during the war, Dr Elliott, who lived at Ravenshield, had opened a new surgery not far from Wearbridge church, and the old one had now become simply her father's study. Evelyn led the way indoors. "A nice young man, Dr Stephen Hewitt, with a pretty little wife – you must meet them sometime. Your father has high hopes of him. He will be sorry to miss you – your father, I mean. Perhaps if we have a nice lazy cup of tea, that will give him time to join us. How did the move go?"

Following her mother into the house, Diana thought that perhaps it would after all be bearable to live in Wearbridge, even in the bleak little flat; perhaps the advantages would very soon be seen to outweigh the losses. It might even be bearable to have spare time, in which she could call like this, on a whim, on her parents.

The best thing of all about the move, of course, was that the fear which had been with her since Carol's birth at last began to recede from her life, for in spite of everything the child thrived. She showed no sign at all that she missed Fell Cottage. Unlike her mother, she slept through the sounds of traffic from outside. With more space indoors to move around, she quickly learned to pull herself to her feet.

Bradley came home after work one day to find Diana on her knees at the far side of the room, watching their daughter, who stood clinging to the seat of the armchair. She in her turn was looking at her mother, who cast a delighted glance at Bradley. "Watch this – she's walking!" She held out her arms to the child. "Come to Mummy, sweetheart!"

"Mummy!" Bradley mocked (not for the first time). "You'll make her a laughing stock." He ruffled the child's hair. "Walk over to your Mam now, there's a good girl!"

Diana hated 'Mam', but before she could say anything Carol had picked up the word and was repeating it as a kind of humming tune: "Mammammammam . . ." Then she laughed and tottered the two steps towards her father, where she fell against him, chuckling and clutching his legs. Bradley gave a shout of triumph and swept her up into his arms. "Who's Daddy's little girl then?" he crowed delightedly.

Diana wondered why 'Daddy' should be acceptable while 'Mummy' wasn't, but, not wanting to spoil the occasion, said nothing and went instead to set the table. Bradley, carrying Carol, followed her into the kitchen. "It's her birthday next week," he said. "One year old. We'll all go up to tea at Springbank."

Her temporary softening towards Bradley gave way to a prickle of irritation. "Why can't we just stay here? And what about my parents? Don't they have a right to share in the celebration?"

"They can look in here, if they want, while I'm at work. But you know Mam can't get out much. We owe it to her to go up there. Anyway, Carol will like to play with her cousins."

That, Diana conceded, was true enough, at least as far as Jackson's two daughters went – Irene, a prim ten-year-old, had a motherly streak, and cheerful Susan adored Carol, two years her junior. But young Jacky, a noisy, restless child to whom no one in all his seven years had ever said 'no', was inclined to torment his small cousin. He made the visits to Springbank more unappealing than ever, as far as Diana was concerned; that he should carry the name of her dead child only made matters worse. On the other hand, Elsie's increasingly arthritic limbs were an unarguable fact. "All right then. As long as you watch your nephew. You know what he's like." As he did; she'd noticed that, like her, Bradley could never quite bring himself to refer to the boy as 'Jacky'.

So to Springbank they went, on Carol's birthday, and the child, for once the unrivalled centre of attention, enjoyed every moment.

Beyond the enclosing hills of the dale, the Transport Nationalisation bill passed into law. It had little visible effect on Bradley and Jackson. They had already run down the haulage side of their business, and the two ageing wagons did no more than carry stone to the nearest railway station. When one of them needed major and expensive repairs – it was the very same one in which Diana had ridden on the long-ago happy day with Bradley – it was left to rust in the yard at Springbank, providing a place of refuge and exploration for cats, chickens and children. It seemed unlikely in the extreme that anyone would find it worth their while to take the remaining wagon into public ownership.

Now, the quarry and the garage provided the chief business, apart from the farm. The quarry would be worked out within five years, Bradley asserted, so the garage was supremely important, being their main source of income for the foreseeable future. Jackson's heart was, and always had been, in the farm. It looked, Diana thought resignedly, as if they were likely to be tied to this place for the rest of their married life. Her only hope was that, one day, there would be something better for their daughter.

Yet there was joy in her life again, of a kind she had once thought gone for ever. For much of the time, Bradley too was a happy man, sharing with her their love for their growing child. Though they now lived within easy reach of several convivial pubs, he did not return to his old drinking ways, as Diana had feared he might. She herself was able to spend more time than ever with her parents. After enduring a couple of Dale House afternoon teas, Bradley would never visit them with her, except on special, near-compulsory occasions, like her mother's birthday, but Diana didn't mind. She much preferred to see them without him.

Carol learned to walk properly, and to talk. She was constantly on the move. One moment of inattention, and Diana would find she had disappeared into some other corner of the flat, and was already deeply engaged in some forbidden pastime. Perhaps, she thought ruefully, more than once, it was just as well she wasn't trying to work in the office after all.

One autumn morning, while Carol was fast asleep in her cot, Diana seized the opportunity to take Bradley the packed lunch he would need today – after completing a minor repair in the yard, he was due to go to the quarry, but she had not had time to prepare the sandwiches before he went to work. Bradley had made a gate for the top of the stairs, but it was awkward to close, so she left it open, knowing she would only be gone for a moment. He was not in the yard, and she eventually tracked him down in the office, sorting out some confusion over a bill with Rita Emerson. As soon as he had the sandwiches, Diana ran back upstairs, closing the stair gate as soon as she was through it. Then she went to peep in at her daughter. The cot was empty, the side let down.

Diana felt as if her heart had stopped. She ran from room to room, looking under tables and chairs, behind curtains, anywhere that might possibly conceal a mischievous child. There was no sign of Carol anywhere. It became clear at last that she was not in the flat.

Dear God, let her be safe! Diana implored, as she unfasted the gate again – the useless gate! – and stumbled down the stairs. There was no sign of Carol on the forecourt, in the office, on the road. Time was passing, and she could already have toddled off into real danger.

Diana went through the archway into the yard, followed by a now deeply anxious Bradley.

And there, raised on an upturned box before the open bonnet of a car, stood their daughter, a chubby barefoot figure in liberty bodice and knickers, listening intently while Norman Peart, one of the mechanics, gravely explained the function of every visible part of the car, just as if she were his newest apprentice.

Diana ran and snatched up the child, and was immediately

engulfed in a storm of rage. Carol yelled and shouted and hammered her mother with her bony heels and struggled so hard that Diana was afraid she would drop her. She was, momentarily, relieved when Bradley took the child from her.

"Now, my little lass, let's have a proper look round, shall we?" he said, and began to carry her about the yard, from vehicle to vehicle, into the sheds, pointing everything out to her. Carol gurgled and chirruped and laughed, and tried to repeat the strange words her father said. "She's a true Armstrong," he declared with pride, when at last the tour was complete and he brought her back to her mother. "You can see that."

Diana looked at the curly brown hair, the fair skin smudged with oil, and had to acknowledge that he had a point. Even the green eyes Carol had inherited from her mother were bright with excitement at what she had seen.

"You shouldn't reward her for being naughty," Diana reproved Bradley, but was thankful that this time Carol merely grizzled as she was carried back upstairs. Safely in the flat, with the gate closed, Diana found *The Tale of the Flopsy Bunnies*, which her parents had given their grandchild, and sat down with Carol on her knee to read the story. The novelties of the repair yard were quickly banished by the adventures of Beatrix Potter's rabbits, and Diana was relieved to see it. Of one thing she was completely sure: her daughter was going to have a better future than this place offered, a future full of limitless possibilities and wide horizons.

Twelve

Diana watched Carol come out of school, a small figure wearing the green jumper her Grandma Armstrong had knitted for her, with a green, red and yellow kilt and grey socks; the socks, in spite of the garters, were, as usual, wrinkled about her ankles. This morning her golden-brown hair had been neatly plaited. Now one of the green ribbons had disappeared and the other trailed down from its last precarious knot. Diana smiled ruefully. Other little girls – like Carol's cousin Susan, Jackson's youngest daughter – emerged from the school day looking scarcely less tidy than they had at its start. But not Carol. Diana had no idea what she did in school, since she frequently indicated with seven-year-old relish that Miss Burton was very strict, but she always looked as if she had spent the whole day in riotous play.

As her daughter reached the gate, Diana stretched out a hand and Carol took it, with the gap-toothed grin that would have melted the sternest heart.

Diana gazed down at her and shook her head. "Just look at you! And we're going to Granny Poultney's for tea."

Diana tried not to be hurt by the wry twist that came to Carol's mouth, though the child stood meekly while her mother replaited her hair – tying both plaits behind with the one remaining ribbon – and pulled up her socks and tried to remove the worst traces of schoolyard dust from her face and her clothes. Then they set out up the hill past the church towards Dale House. "Will Dad be there?"

"Not today." Nor any day, if he could help it. "He's got an urgent job at the garage." And a bad hangover from last night, which had slowed him down all day, Diana thought bitterly. There had been no sudden change in Bradley from the relative abstemiousness of the months following Carol's birth, only a gradual rise in the number of times a week that he went drinking, and an increasing tendency for him to come home seriously drunk. It was still a fairly rare occurrence for him to be as incapacitated as he had been last night, after an evening with a friend who was emigrating to Australia, but it had filled Diana with dread. She felt that things were slipping from her, as if her resolution somehow, in spite of everything, to build a good marriage, was unravelling, falling away. She clutched Carol's hand tightly, to reassure herself that, all else failing her, she still had her daughter.

Carol tugged her hand free. "Ouch, you're hurting!" Then she began to run on ahead. Diana noticed ruefully that her plaits were already beginning to come loose again.

At Dale House, the Poultneys' greeting was warm, for them. but as Diana watched her mother take Carol's hand and lead her into the drawing room, where the tea trolley stood ready, she could not repel a mental image of Nana Armstrong's hugs and kisses, and the little girls sitting on her knee; of the cousins with whom she could play in farmyard and fields, of Bradley's tenderness. Here, for all the new and more equal relationship that Diana now had with her parents, there remained a belief that children must be kept kindly but firmly in their place, if they were not to become selfish, disruptive and generally disagreeable. There was always a certain correct distance that must not be crossed; a concern with manners that made Carol sit very upright in the large armchair, with none of her usual uninhibited chatter. In many ways Diana considered that her parents were right, and she knew that their coolness did not mean that they loved their granddaughter any the less, but she could not blame Carol for believing otherwise, for preferring the generous effusiveness of her father's family.

Evelyn took her seat beside the trolley and poured tea for the adults, and milk for Carol, who would have liked to be offered tea like a grown up, but knew better than to ask. The milk was served in a mug too, instead of a pretty china cup with matching saucer, and not even an interesting mug at that, since it was a plain cream colour; at home, for the past week, Carol had been using her brand new Coronation mug, of which she was very proud, particularly as the coronation of the new Queen Elizabeth had taken place on her birthday, an event they'd watched on the television that Dad had bought for the occasion. She wanted very much to talk about these things, but decided against it. Granny and Grandad did not like it when she spoke without first being spoken to, unless there were no other adults present. Besides, they probably knew all about it anyway, even though they hadn't mentioned it. Her other piece of news would be unlikely to interest them at all, since it concerned car engines.

Granny handed round the sandwiches, and Carol took one as the plate reached her at the end of its tour; meat paste, she saw with disfavour, but she was too hungry to spurn it. There was seed cake too, which she really disliked. She resigned herself to a trying visit.

"Is the denationalisation bill going to make any difference to Bradley's business?" the doctor asked Diana. He knew, from his daily reading of *The Times*, that the Conservative government, coming into power the previous year, had quickly kept its promise to denationalise road haulage.

"Not immediately," Diana said. There was, to be honest, very little in the way of a haulage business left, for the quarry had all but finished production and the only other use for the one remaining wagon was to do a favour when a friend had some kind of load in need of cheap transport. "But it does mean he'll be able to develop the haulage side again if he wants to," she added. In her opinion it was the ideal opportunity to do so, with former government-owned vehicles being sold off relatively cheaply. If she had been in charge of the business she would have snapped up as many of them as she could afford (taking out a loan if necessary), so as to be ahead of any possible rivals. But, of course, she was not in charge. Jack Armstrong's legacy was worthless, so long as Jackson and Bradley worked together, as they always would so long as the alternative was to work with her.

"Is there enough business going to make it a practical proposition?"

"There are plenty more quarries in the area, in need of transport, and not all of them within reach of a railway line. Then there are the lead mines – there's a huge demand for fluospar nowadays."

"Yes, I heard they were reopening Cowcleugh. I suppose in the past the fluospar was simply cast aside as so much rubbish?"

"That's it – and now they're even going through the spoil heaps to get out what they can. Cowcleugh isn't the only mine to be miles from a station. And we've no rivals in the upper dale – it's a real opportunity." *Or it would be,* she thought, *if only Bradley would see it.* But for all his interest in mechanical things, he seemed to her to lack his father's enterprising spirit, and Jackson, of course, had never really cared about anything apart from the farm. She itched with frustration to have a say in what was done, but Bradley stubbornly excluded her, refusing even to discuss business matters with her. She was left to learn what she could about his plans (or lack of them) from Rita Emerson (a gossipy girl), or from what she overheard by chance on her frequent trips to retrieve Carol from the repair yard – the child had never lost her first fascination with the place and spent every spare moment there. She had soon become a kind of mascot for the mechanics, who adored her.

Feeling excluded from the conversation, Carol began vigorously to swing her legs, and Diana reached out a hand to still them. Her father, though he believed very firmly that children should endure boredom with politeness and in silence, softened towards his grandchild. "And how was school today, little Miss Carol?"

Carol shrugged, exactly as Diana was always warning her not to do. "All right," she said. Though not overtly unhappy, she had never really taken to school. "I changed the distributor cap on the Ford yesterday," she added, with all the shining-eyed solemnity of someone announcing a significant achievement.

The doctor, quickly suppressing his astonishment, smiled at her. "Did you now! I can see you're going to be a very useful granddaughter to have around."

After that, the talk lumbered on at a trivial level, but Diana became increasingly conscious of something unusual in the atmosphere, some sense of suppressed excitement. She caught her parents exchanging frequent glances, as if signalling to one another, agreeing on the right moment for some announcement. It came at last, after Carol had been allowed to leave the table to go and play in the garden, being warned first to wash her hands, sticky with cake crumbs. When she had gone – walking to the door, then skipping her way across the hall – Evelyn Poultney looked again at her husband and then said, "We're going to Surrey, for the christening of Angela's baby."

"I know," Diana said, surprised that this should be the result of all the furtive signals. Had she misread them? "You told me." They had shown her Angela's letter too, which as usual had contained no message for her. Though her parents never explicitly said so, it was clear that as far as her sisters and brother were concerned, she had ceased to exist. "It's next month, on July 12th. You'll enjoy seeing them all again."

"We hope to see a great deal more of them," Evelyn went on, speaking with what seemed to Diana an odd carefulness. "You see, we shan't be coming back."

Quickly, the doctor added, "We wanted you to be the first to know, outside the practice." Another glance at his wife, then back to Diana. "I'm retiring, you see."

"We're moving back to Surrey," Evelyn enlarged, "to live with Granny. She's finding it very difficult to manage that great house. It all seemed to fall into place."

"That's wonderful for you!" Diana congratulated them warmly on a decision that clearly made them very happy, and entered into their discussion of their various plans and hopes, but underneath she was swept by a dismaying sense that life was repeating itself, that she was once again being abandoned by her parents. Except that this was different. The last time they had left Wearbridge it had been wartime, and Bradley had gone too. Rather than loneliness and abandonment, she had then found a new sense of liberation and fulfilment; the departure of her parents, like the departure of Bradley, had given her an opportunity. This time, she would not be left alone. She would still have Bradley, tied to her in a marriage that she feared might be about to disintegrate beneath her, but her mother, whose sense of right conduct had fired her own resolution to keep that marriage going, would no longer be here to remind her, as often as there was need, of what she had resolved. Nor would her parents be at hand to support and cheer and encourage her when things went wrong. More to the point, she would have to raise Carol without what she saw, however uneasily, as their civilising influence.

"You'll have to come and stay with us," said her mother cheerfully, though Diana was sure that she sensed her daughter's unhappiness.

"That would be nice." But her grandmother's house seemed to belong to a distant past, which no longer had any real existence as far as she was concerned. She rather doubted, thinking about it, that Bradley would let her go so far away, especially if it meant taking Carol with her; and she would not, under any circumstances, be prepared to leave Carol behind, in Bradley's unreliable care. He loved his daughter and would never knowingly allow any harm to come to her, but he rarely tried to check her in anything she did, and when he had been drinking he was only too ready to forget that she existed at all.

Diana left Dale House an hour later feeling as if a leaden weight had lodged itself inside her. Carol chattered away at her side, as she always did when released from the constraints of her grandparents' house, but Diana took in little of what she said, merely making some automatic response from time to time, hoping that she was missing nothing of importance.

When they came within sight of the garage she was dimly aware, from the corner of her eye, of a car drawing up in the side road beyond the forecourt, and a man getting out of it. Diana would not have given him a second glance, except for the way he walked to the front of the garage and then stood looking around him, in the manner of someone trying to estimate the value of a property. He was young, smartly dressed, good-looking enough to attract attention. It must have dawned on him that he was being watched, for he turned to glance at her; and then his gaze sharpened. Diana continued to walk towards the flat door, conscious of the interest in his eyes – light grey eyes under black brows. Did she know him? None of Bradley's friends had quite that prosperous look. He approached her, and she realised that he at least knew who she was. "You don't remember me, do you?" he said. He had a deep voice, with a marked accent that was local but not of the dale.

There *was* something familiar about him, something about the eyes in particular that tugged at her memory, but she could not place him; he was somehow out of context, away from the things – the clothes perhaps – that would have brought recognition. He prompted her gently: "Ronnie Shaw?"

Ronnie! So *this* was Ronnie – the shy, awkward evacuee who had so adored her; the boy so much her junior, who had touched her with his furtive gifts and amused her with his stories. And here he was facing her in the garage forecourt, a well-dressed young man who seemed much of an age with herself and whose attraction she had to acknowledge. "Good gracious!" she stammered. "I'm sorry, you're not – well!" She felt herself blushing, as once he had blushed, though he was not blushing now. On the contrary, he seemed very sure of himself.

He crouched down suddenly, bringing himself on a level with Carol, who gazed, solemn, unblinking, back at him. "So, you're Mrs Armstrong's lass then. What do they call you?"

"Carol." Still no smile.

"That's a pretty name. A bonny little lass too, almost as bonny as your Mam. You've got her eyes."

Carol shot a glance at her mother, as if surprised to think of her as 'bonny', and seeking evidence to bear out the description. She did produce a smile then, her enchanting gap-toothed grin; her eyes sparkled. Ronnie reached into his pocket and took out a rather battered-looking toffee, wrapped in shiny blue paper. "Not rationed any more, hinny, so here's one for you." He glanced up at Diana as he spoke, and she was sure he must be remembering the bar of chocolate that had been his birthday present to her long ago. Carol took the sweet eagerly, and actually remembered to say thank you.

Ronnie stood up again.

171

"What are you doing here?" Diana asked.

"Oh, just business," he said.

Diana was intrigued. Somehow that didn't sound like Ronnie. "What sort of business?"

"I'm branching out into haulage. A good line to be in at the minute."

"You've got your own firm then?" She tried to keep the surprise from her voice, but did not quite succeed.

"Why yes." He'd noticed the surprise then, and was amused by it. "I bought a repair business when I went back home – my Nan left some money when she died. Not much, but she'd managed to put a bit by. Anyroad, we put it into this little business and I've built it up and it's doing well. Seemed a good time to think of branching out, now we've got some money behind us. So we're putting it into wagons."

"We?" She suddenly sensed a woman in his life, and was astonished at the slight but very real pang of jealousy that shot through her. She realised she thought of Ronnie as her admirer and did not want to find she had been displaced.

"Our Freda and me. She put her money into it too."

"Oh!" She could barely bring to mind Ronnie's dark, busy twin. "Does she run the business with you then?"

He grinned. "That's not her line. She keeps house for us. But she takes an interest."

Then there could be no other woman in his life, Diana thought, not if he shared a house with his sister. "That doesn't explain why you're here," she went on.

"I'm seeking a base up this way, and any wagons that are going. You know Tommy Nattrass at Meadhope? I've bought him out – not much left of the haulage business, but good workshops. We signed on the deal this morning. He was glad to see the back of it."

"He's been in poor health for a long time, I know," Diana acknowledged. She knew many of his neighbours were astonished he had not gone under years ago. "Then have you come to look us up for old time's sake?" Or for her sake, she wondered to herself, holding her breath for his reply.

"I had in mind Armstrong's might favour a sale. I know the quarry's finished, but it would give me a base in the upper dale. There's the odd wagon left, I gather, but it's no problem getting hold of wagons these days. Then there's this place—"

"Oh no, Bradley would never sell!" Not the garage anyway – but the rest? She was not so sure. Jackson had no real interest in it, and Bradley apparently very little. How would she feel, to see the loss of the business in which she might have played an active part, if things had gone differently? Would she feel any better to know it was in Ronnie's hands? She was sure that if she'd been running the business it would have been quite a different proposition by now, so successful as to offer a rival to Ronnie rather than a tempting buy.

"He might, if the terms were right," Ronnie suggested. "And your husband's not the only one, is he? I've just come form Springbank. His brother's only too happy to sell the lot."

Your husband's not the only one. Nor, she recalled suddenly, was Jackson. She too had a voice in the business, even if it had been effectively silenced for years. So long as the brothers agreed, she could do nothing. But now, if they were to find themselves on opposite sides – at long last she would be able to play a part! What if that part should be simply to vote for selling off the enterprise that for more than a hundred years had served the dale, adapting to whatever needs arose, moving with the times? Would that not be the ultimate betrayal of old Jack Armstrong? She guessed that Ronnie had no idea that she had a share in the business. The family had kept the matter very quiet, and no one outside their immediate circle had been told. Suppressing the rising sense of excitement in her – after all, if Bradley should be in agreement with Jackson, she would be as powerless as ever to intervene – she tried to change the subject a little.

"Anyway, how are you going to a run a business in the Dale – or will you move up here? Sunderland's a long way off."

"I'm putting a manager in – I've got someone in mind. But let's not cross bridges." He gave her an odd look, half-smiling. She sensed that there was in his mind at that moment something quite different from the buying of a haulage business. She realised suddenly that if he were to succeed, then he must, inevitably, make frequent visits to the dale. But before she could consider what she felt about that, he said briskly, "Is Mr Armstrong about?"

Diana glanced at her watch. Half past five. Bradley might still be in the yard, though she could hear no sound from there. The gate was still open, however, "Carol, be a good girl and run and see if Daddy's in the yard. Tell him there's a gentleman to see him. Then come straight back. I don't want you getting oil on your good clothes."

Carol skipped happily away, but returned very soon, looking disappointed. "Dad's not there."

"Then he'll be upstairs." She turned back to Ronnie. "Do come up."

She was conscious, through all the polite exchange, of an undercurrent within herself. Had Ronnie always been as attractive as this? She felt his strength and warmth, and a vitality that was far removed from Bradley's taut edginess. She was aware of him behind her all the way up the stairs, of his nearness, so close he was almost touching her, but not quite. She scarcely saw Carol, running ahead, though the child must have been eager to get her message to her father, for Bradley was waiting for them when they reached the top of the stairs. He was unsmiling, but thoroughly sober. "Do you remember Ronnie Shaw?" she said. "There's something he wants to discuss with you. A business matter."

"Then you'd better come down to the office." Bradley reached into his pocket for his keys. "Bring us some tea, Di," he commanded casually as he led the way back down the stairs.

Diana felt angry at her exclusion, though it should hardly have surprised her. For the time being she said nothing. "Can I go down?" Carol pleaded.

"No. Go and get your school things off."

Diana made the tea and carried the cups down on a tray. Did Ronnie still take two sugars, she wondered?

She was not to find out. When she reached the office Bradley was outside it, locking the door. There was no sign of Ronnie, and his car had gone.

"You can take that back up." She could see at once that Bradley was in a towering rage. "Did you know what he wanted?"

"He dropped a hint or two," she admitted cautiously.

"The cheek of it, offering to buy us out!" As if Ronnie Shaw would be good for anything if it hadn't been for what my family did for him."

She followed him up the stairs again, conscious that she had not yet begun to prepare his evening meal and that he was in no mood to tolerate any dereliction of duty on her part. "I thought you might be glad to part with the quarry and the wagon."

He swung round to glower at her. "Is that what you told him?"

"No. Though he'd already seen Jackson, I understand – I expect he told you that. I said I didn't think you'd want to sell at all. But I think you're forgetting something. By law I have a third share in this business. And you haven't asked me what I want."

There was a silence, and she realised she was right: he had forgotten that uncomfortable fact, ignored for so long. "You'd not oppose me." It was not quite a question. Then, as if he were afraid she might answer in the affirmative, "We'd be fools to sell up just when anyone in their right mind's thinking of expanding. Ronnie Shaw's not the only one to see an opportunity."

She caught her breath. "I thought you didn't want any more wagons."

"Who said? But I'll do it my own way, in my own time. And one thing's for certain: I'll not see Ronnie Shaw bigger in the dale than Armstrong's." He clasped her shoulders. "You're with me in this, aren't you?"

She saw her chance, and seized it. "If you'll let me have a real say, be a real partner."

He frowned, and she thought he was about to push her angrily from him. Then he nodded. "Anything you want. Just don't oppose me."

"I won't." She reflected that Ronnie had achieved what her reasoned persuasion had quite failed to do. Had he also given her the opportunity she had longed for?

The very next day Bradley started negotiations to buy two ex-government wagons. It looked as if the expansion of Armstrong's had begun.

But Diana played no more part in that than she had in its decline. The moment she tried to assert herself, the brothers closed ranks and opposed her. She realised with helpless anger that they would never again risk allowing a gap to open between them by which she might gain a toehold in the company.

Thirteen

Bradley was not at the station to meet them, though Diana had written to tell him the time of their arrival. Carol stood gazing morosely along the emptying platform, as if still hoping that her father might suddenly appear round the corner of the station buildings. Diana, who knew he would not, heaved resignedly on the handle of the large suitcase. "You carry the other, my dear."

"But it's heavy – and it's miles!" Carol lifted the smaller case, however, and began to walk on at her mother's side. "I never wanted to go away anyway."

"So you never tire of telling me," said Diana wearily. She had so looked forward to the holiday with her parents in a small Torquay hotel, and seen it as an opportunity for them to get to know their granddaughter, who was fifteen now, with four years of convent schooling behind her. Carol too had seemed eager enough when the invitation came, and it was her pleading rather than Diana's which had finally persuaded Bradley to allow them to go. But from the moment her parents met them on the platform at Torquay, Diana had known it was not going to work. She had seen how her mother's eye settled disapprovingly on the low neckline of Carol's favourite summer dress, and how she flinched at the accent which marred the girl's cheerful greeting and which her schooling had merely softened a little. She had quickly abandoned her hope that her parents' influence might help to curb Carol's increasing rebelliousness, which had even begun to disturb Bradley. During the subsequent fortnight, they had only succeeded in making their granddaughter more rebellious than ever.

177

Now mother and daughter plodded in weary silence through the teatime quietness of Wearbridge. Just as well it wasn't raining, Diana thought. She was not altogether surprised that Bradley had failed to meet them, but wondered precisely what had prevented him. The most acceptable reason would have been pressure of business; it was also, she knew, the most unlikely. Much more probable was a desire to show them to the end that he didn't approve of their jaunt, in spite of having agreed to it; or even more likely, he was drunk. She hoped, rather despondently, that it was not that, because of what might meet them when they reached the flat.

A lorry came rattling along the road behind them, and then unexpectedly drew up a little ahead. Diana had just noticed the *Shaw's Haulage* painted in blue on the tailgate, when Carol began to run. Someone in the cab was speaking to her, and she called to her mother. "Mr Shaw says do we want a lift!"

She did not wait for a reply, but was already handing up her case, and following it into the cab. Diana had no opportunity to refuse – if that was what she would have done; it was certainly what Bradley would have wanted her to do, rather than accept a lift from the man he regarded as a brash and ungrateful intruder. But then Bradley was not here to help carry the luggage. Within seconds she too was seated in the cab, her case at her feet, with only Carol between her and a grinning Ronnie. "Thought you looked a bit overloaded," he said. "Where to now?" He made a sweeping gesture with his hand. "Whitley Bay? Paris?"

"The garage, if you don't mind," said Diana rather stiffly. "It's very kind of you."

"Not at all. I'm going that way anyway." His tone perfectly matched her own. It was a long while since they had met, though from time to time over the years she had glimpsed him in passing, driving his smart Riley or (less often) as now, behind the wheel of one of his wagons. If he saw her, he would wave to her, as to an old acquaintance. She had heard, now and then, that his business was said to be doing well, something that never failed to enrage Bradley, but she had no idea how he was in himself, whether he still lived in his grandmother's old house in Sunderland, whether his sister still lived with him, or had married; whether he had married.

The wagon began to move forward. "On your way back from holiday then?" he asked, without taking his eyes off the road.

Carol snorted. "Some holiday! Two weeks stuck in a stuffy hotel with two old fogies who won't let you do anything you want."

This time Ronnie glanced at Diana, his eyes twinkling. "Sounds bad. Is your Mam an old fogey then?"

"She might as well be. She let them boss me about just as if they were *my* parents, not hers – only miles stricter than Mam and Dad ever are. Grandparents are supposed to spoil you, not stop you having any fun."

"Why, I don't know about that. I can think of a few times my Nan laid into me, when I didn't do what she wanted. I never thought any the worse of her for it."

"Bet she didn't make you go to bed at half past seven – it's not even *beginning* to get dark by then. That's when I'm just going out at home—"

"That's not strictly true," Diana intervened gently.

"And nothing I do or say is ever right," Carol went on, as if her mother hadn't spoken. "They don't like my accent – it's not ladylike – and they're always nagging you to say 'please' and 'thank you' and 'please may I get down' and 'I beg your pardon' and never never talk at table."

"It's interrupting they don't like, not talking," said Diana.

"They think children should be seen and not heard. And I'm not a child, not any more."

"I can see that," said Ronnie diplomatically. "How old are you? Seventeen?"

Carol, who didn't look anything like seventeen, beamed with pleasure. For a moment Diana thought she was going to yield to the temptation to claim that great age. But she was, on the whole, a truthful girl. She said, rather grudgingly, "Fifteen." Then she began to ask him about the wagon, and was soon in a detailed and very technical discussion of the merits, or otherwise, of wagons in general and this one in particular, from which Diana, for all the knowledge she had gleaned during the war, was necessarily excluded. "Soon as I'm seventeen I'll be driving for my Dad," Carol said. "I can drive already, round the yard. Up at the quarry too. I wish they'd let you take your test at fifteen."

All that convent education, thought Diana ruefully. She had dreamed of (at the very least) secretarial college, perhaps even one of the growing number of new universities, but Carol remained passionate only about the yard and all that happened in it. Diana could only hope that her daughter might be brought to raise her sights during her last year of compulsory education.

"So – you'll be working in your Dad's garage when you leave school?"

Carol glanced at her mother, conscious of being on controversial ground. "Maybe," she said.

"She needs some qualifications before she can think of leaving school," Diana put in. It was one of the few things she and Bradley agreed about, though they talked of it very little. She had in fact been surprised that Bradley had agreed to pay for their daughter to go the convent school, when she'd tentatively brought the matter up four years ago, after Carol failed her eleven plus exam, so losing hope of a place at Meadhope Grammar School. Bradley's family, staunchly Methodist, looked with the deepest mistrust on all things Popish, but his expansion of the business had paid off and both the petrol station and the haulage concern had been doing well, and Bradley's pride in his own success combined with his pride in his daughter had led him to agree. He wanted the world to see that only the best was good enough for an Armstrong. Carol seemed happy at St Margaret's, but only, Diana suspected, because there were so many rules to break, so many restrictions to fight against. She was a natural rebel, and had many times been in serious trouble at school. Letters from Mother Conceptua, the headmistress, were a common enough occurrence in the Armstrong household. And the school made little difference to the company Carol kept out of school. True, she had many friends at the convent, and was universally popular. But that simply meant she widened her circle of friends, not that she dropped the old ones to whom she continued to be unfailingly, and regrettably, loyal. Nor did it mean she spent less time in the yard. She was still at her happiest in oil-covered overalls with her head stuck under the bonnet of a car or a wagon – or, sometimes, when one of the men could be talked round, driving a vehicle about the yard.

Diana realised suddenly (and with surprise) that Ronnie had taken her side. "Quite right," he was saying to Carol. "That's the thing I regret most, that I didn't pay more attention to my schooling. You need to be able to turn your hand to everything to run a successful business. I've never got the hang of the books. I leave all that to my sister. If she ever gets wed I'll be up the creek."

Diana watched him, under cover of Carol's eager response, reminding herself of his face, seeing what was new. He looked well, a good-looking man in the prime of life. The strong angular bones of his face had been there since he was a boy, only gaining in force and definition as he grew older, and now softened by an increasing layer of flesh, which she thought suited him. The wide mouth and grey eyes had developed laughter lines at their corners, and his brows had thickened to form an emphatic bar marking off his broad forehead. His dark curls were cut short, but his face still had a boyish look that reminded her of the youth she had known. He must be nearing forty now, she supposed, but if anything he was more attractive in maturity than he had been in youth, exuding strength and vigour, from the assertive set of his head on his strong neck, to the relaxed control of his broad hands on the steering wheel.

He must have become aware of the intentness of her gaze, for he suddenly broke off in the middle of something he was saying and turned to look at her. One fleeting moment in which his eyes seemed to express all kinds of intense but enigmatic emotions, and he had looked away again and was bringing the wagon to a halt outside the garage. "Here we are. Safely to your door. Hang on and I'll get your cases down for you."

Feeling inexplicably shaken, Diana sat in a daze while Ronnie lifted down the cases and then realised he was reaching up to help her too. His touch seemed to scorch her.

She wondered afterwards what might have happened if Carol hadn't been there, and then told herself she was being foolish and fanciful. She was a respectably married woman accepting a neighbourly lift in broad daylight in her home town, and to read anything else into it was silly. Except that there *had* been something else, as far as her own feelings went.

As it was, she did not recall thanking Ronnie, or saying goodbye, though she supposed she had, for he drove away, on up the dale to deliver his load, leaving them standing alone on the forecourt. The garage was, of course, closed by now and the yard gates were firmly bolted. But the flat door was locked too, and there was no sign of Bradley – fortunately Diana had a key. Saying nothing, she put on the kettle and looked in the cupboards and the fridge (a recent acquisition) for something to eat. Clearly Bradley had done no shopping in their absence. There was a bottle of milk, unopened but sour, a hardened piece of cheese and two eggs. The bread bin was empty. While Carol unpacked, Diana set to work with the remnants of the ham sandwiches that had accompanied them on their journey, dipping them in beaten egg and frying them. Carol, happy to be home, pronounced them to be 'fabulous,' which seemed to be the latest teenage term of approval.

The happy mood lasted only until Carol went to her room after the meal and emerged wearing the same summer dress that had met with Evelyn Poultney's disapproval. Neither Diana nor Bradley liked it much either, regarding it as too tight across the chest for someone so young, too short and far too low-cut. A rather larger friend of Carol's, outgrowing it, had passed it on to her, and no amount of parental displeasure would stop her wearing it. "I'm going out," she announced casually, moving towards the door.

"Carol – come back here!" The girl turned, but stayed where she was. "You're not going out. You've only just got home." What had happened to this generation of children, Diana wondered, to make them behave so impossibly? Her own generation had been meek and mild in the extreme, compared to this. For them, there had been childhood (during which one was more or

less dutiful and obedient to one's parents), which then gave way
to adulthood, with all its responsibilities. In those days there
were no clearly marked teenage years to strike terror into
parental hearts. Could it all be put down to the war? Struggling
against an inclination to lose her temper completely, trying hard
to be reasonable, she said, "It's youth club tomorrow night. You
can go out then." She didn't much like the youth club either, it
being full of undesirable young people whom Carol had known
since junior school days and from whom Diana had hoped that
St Margaret's would separate her; but at least it was run by the
chapel and provided organised activities with proper adult supervision.

Carol, already standing with her hand on the door knob,
turned to glare at her. "I've not seen anyone for a whole two
weeks. Besides, Granny and Grandpa aren't here to stop me
now."

"But I am, and I'm your mother!" Diana pointed out with
exasperation. Tired, her nerves frayed, she sought for some
unanswerable argument. "You've had a long day. Besides, when
your Dad comes in he'll want to see you."

"You know he's in the pub. He won't be back for hours."

The bluntness shocked Diana; she'd never before heard Carol
admit to knowing of her father's weakness. "That's not the point.
He wouldn't want you to go, and neither do I. You will stay
here."

"Give me one good reason why I should?"

"Because I say so." Then: "Because decent girls don't hang
about the streets by themselves."

"I shan't be by myself. I'm calling for Sandra. There'll be lots
of other people."

"Like Kenny Byers, I suppose?" Kenny was two years older
than Carol, a feckless youth of no obvious appeal that Diana
could see, unless you took into account his powerful motorbike.

"So what if he is there?"

"You're too young to go around with him. Besides, he's—"
She broke off, recalling her own mother's disapproval of Bradley, and how it had only served to make her defend him more

fiercely. She had no wish to drive her daughter to the same extremes of disobedience and ultimate misery.

But it was too late. Carol knew quite well what she'd been about to say. "He's not good enough for me – that's what you mean isn't it? You're a snob, Mam. You want me to be like your snotty family. But I'm not – I'm an Armstrong!"

She stood there, defiant, angry. Diana gazed at her, hair backcombed away from her pretty freckled face, angry lips brightly pink; this beloved, exasperating daughter of hers, whose green eyes were gleaming, now, with something close to loathing. The next moment Carol had turned and left the flat, slamming the door behind her. "Be back by nine!" Diana called after her.

Feeling limp with exhaustion, she went to the window and watched the girl emerge onto the forecourt and run happily toward the centre of the town, her anger already discarded. Diana sighed. She had long ago begun to realise that loving a man (even one like Bradley) was a simple uncomplicated thing, against the love of a mother for her daughter, this most profound and enduring of loves, unwavering, constant, yet open always to the sharpest of hurts, the deepest of angers. The odd thing was that she knew, from her experience with her own mother, that for her daughter it was not complicated at all: beneath the surface, Carol was utterly confident that, whatever she might throw at her mother, Diana's love would still be there for her, always. It was as simple as that.

But understanding all this did not take the hurt from what Carol had said. As she tried to occupy herself with unpacking and then with tidying a flat disordered by Bradley's sole occupation, Diana found herself haunted by the girl's declaration that she was all Armstrong, in which her mother's family had no part. Yet Diana herself was merely an Armstrong by name, who only for a few brief months during the war had felt she belonged in any real way. On the other hand, she could no longer truly claim to belong to the Poultneys either. These days, she had very little part in her parents' life, and no existence at all as far as her siblings were concerned. She thought: *What am I? Nothing; wanted and accepted by neither*. Then she told herself not to be self-indulgent. Besides, it was not wholly true; it was all rather more complicated than that.

Bradley came home rather earlier than Diana had expected, but fortunately after Carol had returned (only a little after nine) and gone to bed. He was pretty drunk, and quite unrepentant that he hadn't been at the station to meet them. "You got back didn't you?" he retorted, when she (mildly, for fear of his temper) expressed her disappointment in him. He was in no state to ask how her holiday had been, and did not even kiss her or express any pleasure in her return. He managed a slurred goodnight before stumbling into bed and falling asleep. The room was soon filled with his snores and the stink of stale beer. When she was ready for bed herself, Diana undressed and then stood looking down at him, considering the narrow triangle of space he had left for her. After a time, she shrugged, pulled the shabby crimson quilt from under him and, wrapping it about her, curled up on the armchair in the corner of the room; it was something she had done all too often before. Several times during the long aching night she found herself wondering why she stayed with Bradley, why she had not simply remained with her parents when their holiday ended. But she knew the answer perfectly well, of course. The reason lay asleep in the small bedroom, her brown hair tumbled on the pillow about her flushed face, unaware – perhaps – of what her parent's marriage had become, and certainly unwilling to make a new life with her maternal grandparents.

The next day Carol seemed to be restored to the sunniest of moods, presumably because she was happy to be home. Within a week the school term had begun, opening as usual with a mass for parents and pupils together in the convent chapel. Bradley shuddered at the very thought of attending – besides he had work to do – but Diana put on her neatest and most discreet suit (she fully understood the sensitivity of the young to their parents' public appearance), tied a headscarf over her hair and accompanied Carol on the morning bus down the dale to Meadhope.

She enjoyed the service, the ritual, the murmured prayers, the unfamiliar but emotional hymns, the opportunity for quiet reflection; above all the sense that she was sharing a part of her daughter's life, though she knew quite well that to Carol school mass was simply another of the boring routines to be endured.

Afterwards, when the pupils had filed out to their classrooms and the few parents present had left by the main door of the chapel, Diana found herself with an hour to spare before the next return bus was due. She drank a slow cup of tea in the village café, and then wandered along one of the back lanes. It led through neat suburban villas towards what looked like open countryside, but before she could reach the distantly glimpsed fields and woods she passed a high wall, evidently enclosing some kind of business. The throaty roar of an engine being revved hard reached her from behind it. She came to a pair of green gates, open wide. To one was attached a neat notice, in familiar colours: *Shaw's Haulage*.

She stopped, peering with interest into the yard beyond. So this was where Ronnie had his business! The yard looked busy and prosperous, with one wagon under repair, and a second clearly about to leave. Someone went towards it with papers in his hand, which he passed to the driver. At that moment she saw who it was, and realised too that he'd seen her. She stepped hastily back out of sight, waiting until the wagon had driven away before turning to retrace her steps. Ronnie emerged at that moment from the gates. "Mrs Armstrong!"

She halted. She thought it safer to match his formality of tone. Safer? How ridiculous! What possible danger was there in this chance encounter in broad daylight? "Mr Shaw."

They stood looking at one another. "What brings you—?" he began.

"I was just—" she said at the same moment.

They laughed, awkwardly.

"You first!"

"No you!"

"I was just going for a walk." She explained, rather confusedly, how she had come to be here, feeling ridiculously breathless as she did so.

"Would you like a look round the yard?"

There could be no harm in it, so she followed him, a smartly dressed visitor in that half-familiar territory. She felt odd, shivering with excitement, alert to everything about her companion, and little else. Yet it was a commonplace enough matter, for him to be showing an old friend round his business, proud of what he had achieved. She was quite sure that for him that was all it was, nothing more. Especially as the old friend had a considerable knowledge of the haulage trade and could ask informed and intelligent questions – as she did not, for her mind was too bewildered with conflicting and confused memories, with dizzying impressions, for her to be able to formulate any. So much here reminded her of walking with Bradley – the young Bradley – about the Wearbridge yard before the war, the smells of dust and oil and metal hot in the sun, and of sweat-drenched men; the dazzle of light on headlamp glass and polished brass; the clamour of tools on metal engines, the noise of wagons being loaded or unloaded, men whistling, or singing a snatch of the latest hit song. *Wooden Heart* it was at the moment – that was different anyway. What was it everyone sang, in those early days? *The Way You Look Tonight*, that was it. Lying in bed at night, she used to imagine Bradley singing it for her alone, but he never had, quite, though he'd often hummed or whistled the tune, casually, when they were together. She felt a sudden pang of regret and loss, and with it a conviction that she should not be here, at Ronnie's side, on this sunny autumn morning. She was Bradley's wife. But Bradley was not the ardent youth of her memory. Bradley was an angry drunken man who did not even seem to like her any more; as she no longer cared for him, in any way, as far as she could see. Once, Bradley's yard had looked something like this, a place of ordered busyness, but now there were signs everywhere of neglect and muddle, the only too clear evidence of a once-prospering business on the decline: Bradley's first energetic response to Ronnie's offer to buy him out had propelled him into a brief prosperity, which was now rapidly dwindling as his drunkenness increased.

Ronnie talked as they went, not simply about his business, but telling little stories about the men who worked there, though never unkindly. She remembered how he used to cheer her with his tales during the war. He was still able to make her laugh, even today.

"Well, that's it!" he said at last. He turned to face her. "Cup of tea?"

She did not want yet another cup of tea, and it was nearly time for the bus. She knew she ought to leave. Duty, common sense, everything warned her against accepting Ronnie's simple, friendly offer. "That would be nice," she heard herself saying.

"We'll go up to my office then." He led the way, and she followed. It means nothing to him, she told herself; just a polite gesture, such as would be offered to any visitor. Bradley would never have been so courteous, but then Bradley had none of Ronnie's instinctive friendliness.

She followed him across the yard, through a doorway and up a flight of concrete stairs, austere and dark but spotlessly clean. At the top they came to a room containing a stone sink, a desk, two chairs and a telephone, with a small window allowing an over-view of the yard. "Have a seat." Ronnie filled an electric kettle at the sink, and then made tea in a battered pot, poured into two enamelled mugs, producing a tin of digestive biscuits to go with it.

Diana put her handbag down on the desk and sat on the chair furthest from the window, her legs neatly crossed. From here she could neither see out nor be seen; though of course there was no reason at all for furtiveness. "Do you work from here all the time?" she asked after a moment, taking a biscuit. Her hand was shaking a little, she noticed. She was not in the least hungry.

"Why no, I'm back home most of the time, in Sunderland. That's my main business. But I'm over here once a week, Thursdays mostly." Today was Monday. "Depends if they're short-handed here, or there's a driver off sick. This time it's the manager's holiday."

"You're obviously doing well." Had she said that before, down in the yard? She really couldn't remember.

He perched on the edge of the desk, very near to her, un-comfortably so. Her skin seemed to prickle with his nearness, her nerves tingle. She couldn't get her breath or think clearly. She wished he would move to the other chair, at the further side of the desk. Yet part of her didn't want him to. "Pretty well," he agreed. "The future's in haulage, as I see it. I guess the railways are on the way out, the small lines anyway. They're making massive losses. When they go, that'll be our opportunity."

"You can't really think they'd do away with the railways? It would kill the countryside." What was she saying? His grey eyes were on her face, watching her; did he think she was talking nonsense? He was smiling faintly, a warm little smile; his mouth was not thin like Bradley's, but wide and flexible. She felt the hot colour flooding her face, and could no longer look at him. She fixed her gaze on his hands instead, broad brown hands, cradling the mug. Gentle hands, surely, hands made to caress . . .

She stood up suddenly, knocking over the chair in her haste. "I'm sorry, it's later than I thought. I'll miss the bus." She had not even looked at her watch, had no idea what time it was. She reached past him to put the mug on the table, her hand brushing his arm. She felt the shock of it through her whole body. Her body ached, shivered.

He was standing too, and had put down his mug also. Though they were not touching, she could feel him, smell him. This was the moment to turn away and walk to the door.

She stayed where she was, very close, facing him, saying nothing at all, for she had no words. She was looking at him now, held by his eyes. He raised those broad hands and took her by the shoulders, pulling her closer. The next moment, without words, without conscious choice, without hesitation, they were kissing.

His hands *were* gentle, but firm too, assured. They found their way under her neat box jacket, to her waist, tugging at her blouse, moving up to the fastening of her bra, to her breasts.

She had never wanted anything so much as she wanted this, not just what he was doing to her, what his hands were doing, and his mouth, but more, much more. Some tiny residual voice warned her someone might come, warned her to stop. She tried to push it away. She had never been so strongly tempted. For years she had struggled to keep to her old resolution, to be a good wife to Bradley. Those years had been easy, set against this moment.

But, yes, someone might come; or she might get pregnant, and Bradley never slept with her these days, being incapable most of the time. She could not face what that might do to her or to Carol. She wasn't thinking as clearly as all that, but the understanding was there, and the consequent decision. Somehow she found the will to struggle free from Ronnie's embrace, to push him from her. "No!" she gasped, but with anguish.

He was leaning back against the desk, smoothing his hair, his face red. "Don't go," he said, breathlessly.

"I must." With shaking hands she fastened her bra, tucked in her blouse, groped for her handbag, and a comb to tidy her hair. "You know I must."

"What sort of life do you have with Bradley?" His voice was rough and urgent. "You don't owe him anything, from what I hear."

What had he heard? He could not possibly know what her life with Bradley was like. That was a private thing, never talked of, from loyalty, because of a resolution she'd made at the end of the war. "I'm a married woman," she said.

"Then you shouldn't have come up here."

"You offered me a cup of tea. Not anything else that I recall." She put her comb away and snapped her bag shut. "I'll find my own way down," she said, not looking at him.

"I'll come with you."

He did, following her down the stairs. There was just long enough for her to get herself under some sort of control, so that perhaps no one in the yard, looking at her, would know what she'd almost done; or she hoped not.

Out in the fresh air everything looked exactly the same, but under a brighter sun, a sharper light. She heard Ronnie say, "I might try for Armstrong's again, before long."

That helped her mind to clear. "Bradley wouldn't sell, under any circumstances. And Jackson won't agree unless he does."

"From what I hear they're not going to be in a position to refuse much longer."

What was he trying to do, make her hate him, after all that had happened, or not happened? Perhaps he was getting his own back for her sudden frustrating access of morality. She felt ashamed of Bradley, but angry with Ronnie. "You should know better than to listen to rumours," she said, though she realised afterwards that by doing so she had simply confirmed what he had said.

They parted without warmth, and she didn't look back as she walked briskly down the lane. She felt dishevelled and uncomfortable, full of guilt, above all angry with herself for giving in to that impulse to accept Ronnie's invitation. There had always been more to it than a mere tour of his business.

When she reached the market place she found she had another half hour to wait before the next bus, having missed the one she meant to catch. Bradley, coming up to the flat for his dinner, had found her absent and been forced to make himself a sandwich. He was in a foul mood for the rest of the day, refused the evening meal she prepared and went earlier than usual to the pub. She heard later that Janet Watson, Rita Emerson's successor in the office, had handed in her notice that morning, though no one seemed quite sure why. Diana guessed that she was simply tired of dealing with a constantly incapable boss.

Diana was not in the sunniest of moods herself. She was unable to shake off her sense of shame, but recognised that under it was something else, which was more than simply unsatisfied desire, though that was a part of it. What had happened this morning seemed somehow to have crystallised within her all her discontent with her marriage, all the things – many, small and large, over the years – that she disliked in Bradley, or blamed him for. She could not bear the thought of the long years that stretched before her as Bradley's wife, tied to him irrevocably, by vows taken long ago, when she was a foolish child, dazzled by passion. The worst thought of all, one that came to her though she tried to push it away, was that one day Carol would almost certainly leave home – to work perhaps, to marry – and Diana and Bradley would be left alone, with only one another for company. It was an unbearable prospect.

That evening, Carol stayed in, ostensibly because she had homework to do, though Diana knew it was because there was a favourite programme on the television. They ate their evening meal together, and Carol chatted about school and friends (though certainly, Diana thought, a very expurgated version of both), and, when the time came, went dutifully to bed, only a little after what Diana regarded as an appropriate time.

Then she was alone, with the curtains pulled against the night – the nights were drawing in so! – and only her thoughts for company, though she left the television on in the hope of distraction. She found herself wondering, as she had not done for a very long time, what it would have been like for her if Bradley had indeed been killed in the war. Would she then have been able to influence the way the business had developed, so that it might by now have been a large and prosperous enterprise? And when Ronnie reappeared in the dale – what then, if she'd been a widow?

She shivered. If Bradley had not returned, then there would have been no Carol, and that was an unbearable thought. She was horrified that she could have given room to any kind of daydream, however transient, that meant wiping her beloved daughter from her life.

It was a relief when someone knocked on the flat door – though a surprise too; they never had visitors at this time of night. She was less pleased when she opened it to find Ronnie standing there, his face illuminated by the flickering greyness of the television. But in spite of her annoyance she felt her insides turn a somersault. "What are you doing here?" She kept her voice low, in case Carol was still awake, though it was a good hour since she'd gone to bed.

Ronnie was unsmiling. "I know where Bradley is – where he always is at this time of day. No one saw me come up." He too spoke in little more than a whisper.

"But I'm not alone. Carol's here." She held the door as if to shut it in his face, but he reached up to keep it open.

"I had to see you. About this morning: I'm sorry. It shouldn't have happened."

She felt her anger fade as her colour rose. She released her hold on the door. "It was as much my fault as yours. I'm sorry too." All the breathlessness of this morning was back, all the disturbance; as it was for him, she saw. "It mustn't happen again, ever." She knew she ought to say, 'Please go!' but somehow the words would not come.

He was leaning against the doorpost. They were as close as they had been this afternoon, just before it happened. "Is that really what you want?"

She forced herself to find the words she knew she ought to say. "It's what I must want."

"Marriages end sometimes. They don't always work. There's such a thing as divorce."

Her heart was thudding. "Because of what happened today, one little incident?"

"Was that all it was? Not for me. You know I've loved you since the first, since the war."

"You were just a boy then." But a man now, a good-looking man, sober, well-dressed, his eyes on her face, as if he wanted to devour her.

"Some things you know from the start."

She took a step back, putting a safer distance between them. "You may; I don't. Today was a mistake. I don't know how it happened, but it's over. I'm not that kind of woman. Besides, I hardly know you." It was true in its way, for she had seen little of him in recent years. Yet did she really know him any less than she knew Bradley? "Thank you for coming," she whispered. "But please go now."

She thought he would refuse, and didn't know how she would respond if he did. Part of her certainly wanted him to refuse. But after a momentary hesitation he leaned forward suddenly, dropped a light kiss on her cheek, and then whispered, "Goodnight," and turned away. She watched him disappear into the dark stairwell, and then closed the door.

193

Fourteen

A large black car drew onto the garage forecourt and came to a halt in front of the pumps. Diana felt her heart give an emphatic thud. Of course it wasn't Ronnie, she told herself: he never called here for petrol, and after last week had even less reason to do so. She stood up, taking a deep breath to steady shaking limbs, and went out to serve the customer – old Mr Featherstone, who was one of the dale's few truly wealthy farmers, and a relatively regular customer.

She took the money he handed her, went to get change, and then returned to the office. It was some time before she could concentrate properly again on checking the June accounts; she liked to get the books to balance at the end of each month, and it did not usually take long – they had been efficiently kept since she took over last autumn. The petrol business was doing reasonably well. The repair side of things was another matter – good mechanics and drivers rarely stayed long with a business that was so clearly failing, and as a consequence all but the most loyal customers left too. As for the haulage business, Diana was allowed to know little about it, except that for a long time Bradley had been accusing Ronnie of snatching valuable contracts from under his nose. It was run from the old quarry as an entirely separate part of the company, and the accounts were kept up there. Diana had no idea who looked after them, or indeed if anyone did. Bradley had resisted a suggestion that she might take a hand with them too. His pride found it hard enough to bear that she was working in the petrol station, sensible though that decision had been. Diana knew he still regularly drove lorries, though she doubted if he was ever really sober enough to be wholly safe behind the wheel. But on the two or three occasions when she tried to point that out he had been enraged by what he called her interference.

He had also resisted Ronnie's most recent offer, just last week, to buy him out. Last Tuesday, Diana had been sitting at her desk when Ronnie's Riley – gleaming black, like Mr Featherstone's – had swept onto the forecourt. Her heart had thudded then just as it had this morning, but with more reason, as she had known when Ronnie stepped out and strode purposefully towards the office. Flustered, blushing like a schoolgirl (or like Ronnie himself, years ago) she had smoothed her hair and brushed imaginary dandruff from her shoulders, and tried (quite unsuccessfully, she knew) to look calm as he briefly tapped on the door and then came in. He had clearly been surprised to see her, and the shock for a moment overturned his usual assurance. "Oh! I – er . . . Good morning!" He cleared his throat, straightened his already neat tie. "I didn't know you were—"

"I've been working here for a long time now."

"And very efficiently, I'm sure." She thought they were probably the first words that had come into his head. After that he fell silent, looking at her. They had not met properly since the night, nine months ago, when he had called at the flat to apologise. They must both be remembering that occasion only too clearly. Now, recollecting himself, he said, "I've come to see Bradley, if he's about. They said up at the quarry I'd find him here."

She knew then why Ronnie had come, and went in search of Bradley, who came truculently, and insisted on discussing the matter out on the forecourt. Diana watched from the office, trying to gauge what was said from the way the two men moved and stood. Bradley was the taller and could look down on Ronnie, but his slouching posture took from him all appearance of superiority. Flabby, pale, unshaven, his face grey and blotchy, his eyes red-rimmed, the stub of a cigarette stuck in the corner of his mouth, he confronted Ronnie, who stood with legs planted firmly, head back, shoulders broad and steady, eyes clear, a man who knew what he wanted and where he was going. He had begun to speak, easily, with calm gestures, but Bradley had scarcely waited for him to begin before he interrupted, gesticulating angrily, and then turned abruptly and walked away, looking round once with what Diana knew from his expression was a final jeering taunt. She thought that Ronnie, faintly smiling, returned the insult calmly, before he made his way back to his car. He did glance towards the office, though, to wave to Diana, as carelessly as if everything had gone as he'd hoped. Perhaps, she'd thought as he drove away, he simply assumed, having seen how Bradley looked, that with patience he would be sure of getting what he wanted; if it was still worth having by then.

At the time, she had felt mortified by Bradley's behaviour, seeing how much a wreck he had become of the man she had known and even loved, how poor a thing face to face with the person he saw as his greatest rival. Afterwards, she'd felt ashamed, that she should be so censorious of her own husband, who ought to have been sure of her loyalty and support, in everything. Life had not been always been easy for him, after all, and if he was not as strong and resolute as she was in the face of misfortune and difficulty, then perhaps that was not his fault; it might even have been hers, in part, though she couldn't quite see how. Instead of judging him, she should rather have been angry on his behalf, suppressing all the feelings that Ronnie evoked in her. But in the week that followed she had found herself thinking of Ronnie more than ever, and had twice dreamed of him; erotic, deeply disturbing dreams.

This morning, she was relieved when her thoughts were interrupted by the arrival of another customer. She served petrol, took the money she was paid, and was making her way back to the office when she happened to glance round at the sound of the car driving away, and found her eye caught by someone slipping furtively towards the door that led up to the flat: Carol, who should have been at school.

She caught up with the girl at the foot of the stairs. "What are you doing here?"

There was an odd expression on Carol's face. Diana could see defiance and guilt (a very little) and other things she couldn't decipher.

"I've left school," said her daughter, with a lift of the head.

"You can't leave school just like that!"

"Why not? I'm old enough."

Diana was uncomfortably aware that Stan Hall, the mechanic, had emerged from the yard and was watching them with overt interest. She could only be thankful that Bradley had gone to the quarry today. "But it's the middle of the term," she objected, dropping her voice a little. "We've not given our permission."

"I don't care. I'm not going back."

"And what has Mother Conceptua to say about it?"

Carol blushed, but tilted her head at a more defiant angle, as if to deny what the blush might suggest. "She agreed."

"Then I think I'd better go and see her."

"No! No – don't do that!"

Diana glanced round, to see that Stan was still avidly watching. "Then you'd better come in and tell me the truth, all of it."

They went up the stairs and Diana sat down on one of the chairs in the kitchen, though Carol remained standing, as if she were better able in that way to assert her superiority. She was not quite sure why, but Diana was suddenly reminded of the painful interview with her own mother on that day in France when her pregnancy had become known. She shivered, and hoped there was no disclosure so terrible waiting for her today. "Now," she said. "What's all this about? You've always seemed happy enough at school."

Carol shrugged, then stood scowling for a few moments, and then thrust a hand into her blazer pocket and drew out a crumpled envelope, which she slapped down on the table in front of her mother. It was addressed to Mr and Mrs Armstrong. Her eyes still on her daughter, Diana took it and opened it and pulled out the letter, and then gave it her full attention. Mother Conceptua's outrage leapt up at her from the page, released from the neat and orderly writing. '*Let down . . . undesirable influence . . . immoral literature*', and the unequivocal, unambuiguous conclusion: *'no alternative but to ask you to remove her from the school'*.

"You've been expelled! Oh, Carol!" She looked in distress at her daughter's sullen, resentful face. "But what have you done? What is this immoral literature she's talking about?"

"Oh, we clubbed together and got a copy of *Lady Chatterley's Lover*. That was last term. We've been passing it round." She gave a sudden rueful grin. "It fell out of my bag right in front of Sister Lucy."

"Oh Carol!" said Diana again, exasperated, yet momentarily almost amused, in spite of herself, though she hoped Carol hadn't noticed; this was serious, after all. Then she seized on something her daughter's words seemed to imply. "But it wasn't just you then? You said you clubbed together?"

"Why, I suppose it was my idea. I bought it, in Durham. You know, when we went to get my new blazer."

Diana had been annoyed that Carol had outgrown her blazer so near the end of last term, necessitating a trip to the expensive draper's shop that supplied St Margaret's uniform. There had been other errands to complete while in the city, too, including books needed for school, and she'd been relieved when Carol had offered with cheerful helpfulness to finish the shopping while her mother rested her feet over a cup of coffee in Doggarts' café. "I'll do all the House of Fraser things," she'd said brightly. "After all, they're my books." She'd been quite quick about it, and at the time Diana had been grateful. Now, knowing what else had been purchased in the respectable academic bookshop, she felt much less pleased. She had heard news reports of the *Lady Chatterley* trial, which had ended two years ago with the novel's publication, but it had never occurred to her that Carol might be interested in a book claimed as literature, one of the many subjects she disliked.

"It's a boring book anyway," said Carol, unrepentant. "Except for the – well!" She sat down then, looking, Diana thought, absurdly young – as, indeed, she was; too young to embark on adult life.

They heard the sound of someone coming up the stairs. Carol clapped a hand over her mouth. "Dad!"

Bradley should not have been back for hours yet; but here he was, breaking in on the tense atmosphere. Diana scanned his face: not yet drunk, she decided, though he'd already had a few, as usual. "Called in with a message for Stan – he says Carol's come home." He looked from one face to the other. "What's going on?"

Diana handed him the letter, which he read quickly, and then Carol again told her story, with less embarrassment this time, a greater certainty of being heard with sympathy. She had always been sure of her ability to win her father over, no matter what the circumstances.

Bradley heard her out, then dismissed the subject with, "Stupid woman! Then that's nuns for you." He looked down at his daughter, shaking his head, his face full of the tolerant affection that was Carol's alone. "What are we going to do with you?"

"Give me a job in the yard," said Carol promptly. She looked happy, eager.

Bradley laughed, acknowledging the joke. "Why yes, I can just see that!"

"But I mean it!" She was clearly a little hurt. "You're always saying you're short of good drivers and mechanics."

"I'm not so desperate I'd take on my own daughter."

"Why not? If I was a lad you would."

"But you're not a lad. Office work's fine for a woman, if she's not wed, but mechanicking – no, never. That's man's work, dirty hard work."

"But I've been doing things in the garage all my life!"

"That was a bit of fun. You were just a bairn. You'll soon be a grown woman. What man would wed a lass who's always covered in oil?"

Carol looked at her father in bewilderment, as if she could still not quite grasp how the man who had always been so noisily proud of her enthusiasm for the garage could suddenly become so conventional a father. "Maybe I don't want to get married," she suggested.

"Of course you do. It's what every lass wants – husband,

bairns. You'll make someone a fine wife one day. Look, I tell you what—" He was suddenly being reasonable, coaxing. "I'll see what I can do. I'm sure we can find you something in the office, here or at the quarry."

Exasperated at his obtuseness, Carol cried, "I don't want to work in an office!"

Bradley lost his temper in his turn. "And I said I'll not have a daughter of mine doing owt else, except get wed when the time comes!"

"Right then," Carol exploded, "if that's what you want – I'll get wed!" She swept out of the room, slamming the door behind her. They heard her feet clattering down the stairs.

Diana looked at Bradley, full of reproach. "Why did you have to say that? Why shouldn't she work in the garage? It's all she's ever wanted to do."

"I thought you wanted her to go to university?" It was an old taunt, that Diana had ideas above herself; after all, no Armstrong had ever gone to university, or thought of it as a possibility.

"I did. But if she doesn't, well, that's her choice. But to get married, at her age! She's much too young."

"And how old were you when we got wed?"

That's just it, she thought, *I know what I'm talking about.* But she could not quite bring herself to say it aloud. "I can't see what's wrong with her working in the garage."

"She's a lass. It's no place for a lass. Think of the language."

"I worked at the quarry during the war, remember? No one said a thing about language then."

"War's different. Things are back to normal now."

Aren't they just, thought Diana bitterly. But she was not yet ready to give up. "If she's got marriage in mind, it'll be Kenny Byers she's thinking of. You surely don't want him as a son-in-law?" Bradley had often enough complained of the Byers family as work-shy layabouts. How Kenny could afford a motorbike, Diana didn't know, since he had no regular employment, simply helping out on his parents' land (more a smallholding than a farm) and otherwise doing any odd short-term work that was going: potato picking, beating for one of the local shoots, digging ditches.

"She'll not wed him. It's just temper. She'll soon see sense. She'll be back here in no time, begging for a suitable job, you'll see. You can train her up in the office."

Diana shuddered, recalling a couple of disastrous occasions recently when she'd taken Carol with her to the office. She tried a different approach. "She's like you – she hates being stuck indoors. What she really loves is wagons. Think how you'd have felt if your father had made you do office work." As she spoke, she found herself wondering if working in the yard was what she really wanted for her daughter; she who had dreamed of much higher things, even if during the past years she'd been forced steadily to lower her sights in acknowledgement of Carol's true abilities. But then anything was better than a precipitate marriage to the wrong man. Working as a mechanic was not something irrevocable, a lifelong commitment from which there was no easy escape.

"That's different," Bradley said, persisting. "I was a lad."

The argument went on for some time, but Diana could make no impression on Bradley. In the end she decided to leave it for the moment. Like his daughter (and she fervently hoped he was right about that), he might in time see sense.

Carol did not reappear until much later, when Diana was in the middle of preparing the supper while Bradley sat slumped in his favourite chair. "We've seen the minister," she announced to her recumbent father.

Diana emerged from the kitchen. "What are you talking about? Who's we?"

"Me and Kenny. About our wedding. We can have the first Saturday in August."

A bride should look happy, Diana thought; *Carol simply looks defiant, ready for opposition. Even I must have looked happier than that.* "You can't marry Kenny!"

"Why not? What have you got against him?"

Where to begin! Diana restrained herself. "Nothing," she lied. "Except that I don't believe he's right for you. You're more interested in his motorbike than him."

"What do you know about it? Anyway, it's my business who I marry."

"Not if you're under twenty-one. You need our permission."

"Are you going to refuse then?" she challenged. "We'll go to Gretna!" Then she glanced at her father, watching in a bemused silence from the armchair. "Dad?"

Bradley, who gave the impression of having just woken into the middle of the conversation, growled, "You don't want to wed Kenny Byers!"

"I've just said I do. You want me to get married. You said so."

"Aye, but—" He shrugged. "Please yourself. It's your funeral." Carol giggled, and he gave a reluctant grin and corrected himself: "Wedding." He stood up and ruffled her hair, a rare gesture these days. "If you want him, you can have him. And God help him!"

"You'll give your permission then?"

"If that's what you want."

"It is."

"That's all right by me then." He stretched and reached for his coat. "Tell me in the morning what I have to do. I'm off out."

"Wait a minute!" Diana broke in. "I haven't given *my* permission."

His eyes, turned on her, held none of the tenderness they had for his daughter. "She doesn't need yours. Don't put your neb in where it's not wanted." He moved towards the door.

"You haven't had your supper!" Anything to keep him here, to delay this horrible, inexorable process.

"I'll get it later."

Diana knew he wouldn't, because he would by then be too drunk to eat, but there was nothing she could do about it. Besides, it was their daughter who was uppermost in her mind. When the door had closed behind Bradley, she took the girl by the shoulders. "Carol, I know you're angry with us, but you don't have to go this far."

"I don't know what you mean," Carol said coldly.

"Marriage isn't something one should do out of pique."

"It's what you want, isn't it?"

"Of course n—" Diana broke off. Was she to say, *It's what your father wants, not what I want?* That would be the ultimate disloyalty, an admission that they no longer had any interest in common. "We want what's best for you. We want you to be happy."

"I *am* happy," Carol said fiercely, though Diana could see only desperation in her eyes.

"We can find some other way. I'll think of something. Just be patient."

"Oh, you don't understand!" Carol exploded. Then: "I'm going round to Kenny's."

In the following days there seemed to be nothing Diana could say or do to make her daughter turn aside from the disastrous path on which she had embarked. Carol went on with her plans as briskly as if she were indeed eager to marry, and her father soon entered into the spirit of it; he seemed to have forgotten completely his certainty that Carol would see sense. He behaved as if Kenny Byers were the son-in-law of his choice. He even drank less for the four weeks leading up to the wedding, and readily dipped into their scanty funds to provide Carol with a white wedding dress and flowers and a modest reception in the church hall (the chapel schoolroom would have been more convenient, but wouldn't have allowed them to toast the couple in anything but soft drinks). "My girl's having the best I can do in the time," he announced to Diana, when she tried to reason with him – not because she resented the expenditure, but because she so disliked the whole purpose for which it was to be used. She was convinced that, for all her disclaimers, Carol was not happy and would have been relieved to find herself facing immoveable parental opposition; she'd taken this step on an angry impulse and was now too proud to back out, but would have been secretly relieved for someone else to prevent it taking place. But when Diana tried to persuade Bradley of this, he wouldn't listen. The momentum of it all had swept him up too. "What are you on about, woman?" he retorted, when she tackled him a week after the visit to the minister. "All right, maybe Kenny Byers isn't the lad I'd have

204

picked for her, but he's what she wants and that's good enough
for me. Your Mam and Dad didn't exactly approve of me, did
they?"

No, and how right they were! thought Diana. Besides: "This is
different. I don't believe she does want him. If you told her she
could work in the yard tomorrow, he'd be out of her life without
a second thought."

"Well, I'm not going to."

"So she's to ruin her whole life for a piece of small-minded pig-
headedness?"

"No, she damned well isn't! She'll have a husband to keep her
and a home, and bairns, soon enough. She could do a lot worse."

"I don't want *she could do a lot worse* for Carol!" Diana
objected. "I want the very best. And so should you." Then: "You
know they're talking of living with his family?"

"Aye. There's a room over the hay byre, it seems. I said they
could have Fell Cottage, but Carol said she wasn't going to be
stuck up there miles from anywhere. More sense than her
mother," he added pointedly.

Odd, Diana thought, how tiny resentments, long past, had
been dragged up by the two of them during the past days.

On the morning of the wedding, Diana helped her daughter to
dress, while the two small bridesmaids (the whole thing had
somehow grown to draw in Kenny's small sister and Jackson's
first granddaughter) danced around the room and got in the way
and prevented any intimate talk between mother and daughter.
Carol looked pale, Diana thought, and was unusually silent. She
had eaten very little breakfast.

Then the car arrived for the bridesmaids and Diana, who was
supposed to travel with them, hung back long enough to say to
Carol in a low, urgent voice, "It's not too late, you know, my
dear. You can still back out. I'll support you to the hilt, if that's
what you want."

For a moment she thought she saw an answering glimmer of
hope in her daughter's eyes. Then Carol stood up and went to the
mirror. "Why should I want to back out? Don't be silly, Mam."
She put her veil straight, while her mother watched. Bradley

shouted angrily up the stairs. "You'd better go," said Carol, dismissing her.

Everything went without any apparent hitch. At the reception, Carol was in a mood of hectic excitement, laughing wildly, chattering, as if she were intoxicated before even the first sip of Asti Spumante had touched her lips. Afterwards, she went to change into her neat going away suit (another of Bradley's extravagances) and the young couple left for a week's honeymoon in Blackpool, also paid for by the bride's father.

A few weeks later they heard that Carol had passed three O-level exams taken just before her expulsion from school, in Geography, Cookery and French. The achievement meant absolutely nothing to her. She had returned from Blackpool still in that slightly hectic state, with photographs to show her parents – 'Me and Kenny on the beach', 'Me and Kenny up the Tower', and so on. Diana thought they showed her looking less than happy, her smile correct and fixed, but when she mentioned it to Bradley he said she was imagining things. Perhaps she was; certainly Carol never attempted to confide any unhappiness to her mother, who saw very little of her.

Time dragged by. Everything seemed empty to Diana, the flat, the garage, the interminable days. It seemed as if she and Bradley no longer had any reason to talk to one another at all, except, very occasionally, about business matters. The winter that followed was the coldest since 1947, with snow and frost and bitter winds, which seemed to go on for week after week. Petrol sales were slow; people drove only if they absolutely had to. The haulage business came to a complete halt for days at a time. Now and then Carol, coming into Wearbridge to shop, would call to see her parents, but she never stayed very long, and Diana was too wise to beg her to come again soon. Yet she felt as if all the purpose had gone from her life. After all, what else had there been but Carol, since Bradley came home from the war?

Spring came at last. Around Easter time, the Beeching proposals for the future of the railways were published, and seemed to involve closing almost every line in the country except the few truly main lines. It looked as though the dale would be among the areas left without a rail service. Diana, hearing the news on the radio, remembered a hot day in Meadhope, and Ronnie talking, randomly, while underneath they both knew that quite other things were in their minds. He had guessed, even then, what the future might hold – and seen the opportunities it would offer. But when she spoke about it to Bradley he seemed completely uninterested. He was much more excited by the endless news-paper stories about the misbehaving government minister, John Profumo, and the network of spies and call-girls gradually being exposed.

One Thursday night just after Easter, Bradley came home so drunk that he had to be carried up the stairs by two friends. The next morning he had a load to deliver, since the firm's only remaining driver was unavailable. He dragged himself out of bed at the shrill of the alarm, refused breakfast with a shudder, pulled on his overalls and stumbled down the stairs, unshaven and unwashed. Just as well he'd eaten nothing, Diana thought, for they were nearly out of bread.

Mid-morning, when things were relatively quiet, Diana asked Stan to keep watch for customers wanting petrol and hurried along the street to the baker's. On the way she passed the Victorian house where Dr Hewitt, young and untried no longer, would just be finishing morning surgery. The last patients were leaving, among them a slight young woman, well-wrapped against the wind: Carol.

Diana halted on the pavement, waiting, gnawed by anxiety, for her daughter to reach her. "Is anything wrong?"

Carol, she realised then, looked close to bursting with excite-ment. "I'm pregnant." She gave a small skip, like a child; but then she was little more than a child.

Diana wanted to hug her, but they were in the street, full in the public gaze (the Poultney correctness would never quite leave her), so she simply took Carol's hands in hers and stood smiling at her. "That's wonderful! So I'm going to be a grandmother!" The word shocked her, even as she said it. *I'm only forty-two*, she thought, *and I'm going to be a grandmother*. Yet for all that she was delighted, though also apprehensive. "You must take care," she said aloud. "You must look after yourself."

Carol laughed. "Of course I will, Mam. Don't be silly."

"Have you time for a cup of tea?" Diana tried to keep the note of pleading from her voice.

"I've to get back. There's Kenny to tell."

Diana went to wave her off at the bus stop, and then walked home with a curious mixture of feelings inside her. She felt as if she had aged years in a few seconds, yet she was also full of hope. A new phase in her life was about to open; a new phase in both their lives perhaps, hers and Bradley's. Surely the coming of a grandchild must encourage him to reduce his drinking, just as Carol's arrival had done, for a time? Could they begin again, and make things work this time, or was it already too late?

As she reached the garage she remembered that she'd completely forgotten to buy the bread. Grinning at her excusable absent-mindedness, she was about to turn round and go back for it, when she saw that Stan was standing outside the office, talking to Sergeant Burton, one of Wearbridge's two policemen. Seeing her, Stan quickly walked away, back into the yard, almost as if he felt guilty. The policeman came to meet her, removing his helmet as he did so. He looked very grave. A cold hand seemed to close suddenly about her heart. She stood still.

"Please come inside and sit down, Mrs Armstrong. I've some bad news."

She followed him into the office and sat down, and then heard him tell her, awkwardly, painfully, how a wagon had been found, overturned in a ditch, just over the Cumberland border. Bradley had been trapped underneath. He must, they said, have been killed instantly.

He would never know, now, that he had been about to become a grandfather.

Fifteen

The death Diana had so confidently expected throughout the war had come at last, when it was not expected at all. Once, she used often to imagine this scene, or something like it: herself the grieving widow in black, following the coffin of her husband from the chapel to the graveyard for the burial.

But somehow now it had come, on this April day in 1963, it was nothing like she had imagined it would be. Many of the participants in that long-ago reverie were themselves long dead, of course: Jack Armstrong, most of the aunts and uncles; and Elsie was too infirm to attend. Instead, Carol was at her mother's side, sobbing beyond consolation, so that Diana feared for her health and that of her baby. Kenny walked a pace or two behind, once or twice reaching over awkwardly to pat his wife on the shoulder, but otherwise clearly wishing himself anywhere but here. Both Diana's parents were present too, and as she followed the coffin out of the church she caught a glimpse of Ronnie, alone in a back pew, though she registered his presence with no more than a mild interest: Bradley's death had changed everything, including her feelings – or perhaps it had merely revealed her true feelings. She had not felt real grief in that old daydream. Now to her surprise she did, though perhaps grief was not the right word; regret was nearer the mark, and sadness, for what might have been and never now would be, in spite of all she'd done or tried to do.

They were glad to get out of the wind after the funeral for the tea laid out in the kitchen at Springbank, where Elsie could preside, as she always had done, in spirit if not in fact. She looked unremittingly sombre, which Diana might have taken for the old disapproval, except that she knew how inconsolable the old woman was at her son's death, and could only feel for her in her grief. Whatever their disagreements in the past, she would not have wished such a thing on any mother, so near the end of her own life. She was grateful to Carol, who sat beside Elsie and held her hands and talked to her about Bradley, while tears ran down both their faces. It would help Carol, too, she thought, as she could not, because her own feelings were too complicated and painful for her to know what to say to comfort her daughter.

Her parents made the conventional, proper remarks that were expected at funerals. She could not of course blame them for not grieving for Bradley, whom they had never liked; to the end, they had regarded her marriage as a disastrous mistake. But she felt the inadequacy of their response, while being grateful that they had made the effort, considerable at their age, to come to the funeral and give her their support. They were concerned for her, too, as no one else seemed to be. They brought her tea and a plate of ham that she didn't want, and sat beside her in the otherwise deserted parlour – the right place for Poultneys, Diana reflected, remembering the first time she'd come to Springbank. So many memories bound up with this place, and not all of them bad . . . She was just recalling the moment when Bradley had come home to find her sitting here, on her return from France, when her mother broke in:

"I don't suppose you've had much time think about anything. But have you any idea what you'll do now?"

"I don't know," Diana admitted. She felt disorientated, as if her whole world had been overturned, destroying all the familiar landmarks.

"How have things been left?" her mother asked next, still in that over-solicitous tone. "Did Bradley make a will?"

"Yes." She had been astonished to find that he had ever done anything so methodical, though it had been drawn up a long time ago, in the euphoric moment when he had first learned she was pregnant with Carol. He had left his share of the business to be held in trust until any son of their marriage came of age. Almost as an afterthought, he had added that, failing the birth of a son, everything went in full to his wife, but it was clear that he'd been sure that their child would be a son. Diana thought too that he had probably forgotten he'd ever made the will, though it had never been superseded. "I get all he had, for what it's worth," she said. "So I'm the proud part-owner of a petrol station and a failing haulage business." She thought now, as she had when she first heard about the will, that if only Carol had waited for one year, then she would not have felt the need to marry Kenny. Everything would then have been different – or would it?

"So what will you do?" her mother's voice broke in.

"As you say, I haven't had time to think about it." Nor did she want to, yet, though she knew she couldn't put it off much longer. Both the businesses had been closed since the day of Bradley's death, but the petrol station at least would have to be opened again soon.

"You could," said her mother slowly, "come back with us. You know there's always a home for you there."

She considered that word 'home' – was that where her home was now? With her parents, in the house that had been her grandmother's, a place she'd known well long before she met Bradley; long before she'd seen Springbank or Fell Cottage or the flat above the petrol station. Once, it would have been all she asked. But that was a long time ago, and she was another person now, changed yet again by the events of the past days, and she no longer knew what she wanted. "I don't know," she said. She gave a faint, apologetic smile. "I think it might be difficult living with you as a daughter again."

"Then sell up here and buy somewhere near us," suggested her father. "Properties aren't cheap round our way, but we can help. Since your grandmother's death we've had more than enough for our needs. No point in having money sitting around doing nothing. We'd be delighted to use it to help you – wouldn't we, dear?

"Of course we would."

"I'll think about it," Diana promised.

The mourners began to leave. Bert, Lily's husband, offered to run the Poultneys back to the Queen's Head at Wearbridge, where they were staying. "Kenny's father will run me home," Diana reassured her parents. "I'll come and see you first thing tomorrow."

She saw her parents on their way and went to find Carol, who was still with her grandmother. "I'll stop here a bit longer," the girl said softly. "You'll be all right won't you?" She had stayed at the flat with her mother during the days since Bradley's death, but it had been a difficult time, for their reactions to their loss were so very different. Diana had been glad of her company, but had been conscious too that Carol needed something she was unable to offer. Even the memories they shared meant something different to each of them. Now, she wondered whether she ought to discuss her future plans with her daughter. How would Carol react if she were to suggest that she might move away to Surrey? Would she mind? Diana decided it was much too soon to burden her daughter with the question; after all, she didn't want to consider it herself at the moment. "I'll see you tomorrow," she said, and went to find her coat. Halfway across the room she was met by Jackson.

"Glad I caught you," he said. "I need a word." He steered her to the parlour, empty now of mourners. "I've had an offer for the business."

Diana caught her breath. "Already! That's a bit soon!" She felt as if everything was conspiring to give her parents what they wanted.

"Aye, well, maybe. But to be honest I'll be glad to be shot of it all, as I guess you will too. It's a good offer too."

"Who's it from?" But she knew, of course, even before Jackson replied. She felt a surge of anger that Ronnie should be so insensitive as to step in before Bradley was even properly buried. She was surprised too; she'd thought better of him than that. "He doesn't waste much time," she said with distaste. "What did you tell him?"

"I said I'd ask you, but I didn't think you'd have any objection. I used to think it was your doing Bradley wouldn't sell, until he put me right on that." Diana wondered what lay behind that admission, what angry scenes between Bradley and his brother had taken place without her knowledge. But it didn't matter now, of course. It was all over. "I have to say I want to take it," Jackson went on. "You know how things are."

"I know about the garage; not the haulage business."

"Then you can guess, I'm sure. And of course, there's one wagon the less now. If anyone's willing to pay good money for what's left, they're welcome to it. I could do with the cash for the farm. I don't know what your plans are, but I don't doubt you'd welcome a bit of ready cash too."

"What about the petrol station? Does Ronnie Shaw want that as well?"

"He said so, but he might agree to you hanging on to it if he could at least get his hands on the yard. I don't know. To be honest, I didn't think you'd want to be bothered with it any more."

"I'll have to think about it. It's all a bit sudden."

"Fair enough," Jackson conceded. "Only don't leave it too long. I said I'd give him my answer after the weekend. The longer it's left hanging, the less it'll all be worth. We don't want to be losing good money."

It was, Diana reflected as she travelled back to Wearbridge, the most calmly business-like conversation she had ever had with Jackson, yet it left her feeling limp with exhaustion. So many pressures on her, so many people urging her to make decisions that must affect her entire future, before she'd even begun to come to terms with Bradley's death! It was all much too soon, and much too difficult.

She slept very little that night, but by early morning, for all the thoughts that had tumbled about her head during the past hours, she was no nearer to being able to think clearly about her future. All she knew was that she needed time, and solitude. Yet she had promised to call on her parents . . .

She went down to the office and telephoned the Queen's Head, leaving a message to say she had matters to attend to and would call on her parents at lunchtime. Then she found the keys to the quarry office, which had been returned to her with Bradley's other effects after the accident, and borrowed the van he'd kept for his personal use and drove to the place that had once been so much a part of her life, and unlocked the door of the hut.

It was in chaos, as disordered as when she had first begun work there, and it took her some time to find the account books. She sat down on the familiar but now very battered chair and studied the books as best she could. They had been kept only spasmodically, and in an informal manner which would never have been tolerated in her day. All she could really deduce from them was that Jackson was right: anyone who wanted to buy the haulage business was welcome to it.

Afterwards, locking everything away, she drove, not back to Wearbridge, but onto the high narrow road along which she had walked so often in the past. She parked the van just before the road ended, and walked on up the slope and across the fields towards Fell Cottage.

It looked much as it had when she first saw it, before it had been restored for their use: an abandoned place, with only the twisted thorn tree as she remembered it. She stood in the little garden – impossible to tell now that it had ever been cultivated – and gazed out over the dale, with the cold wind whipping colour into her cheeks.

What was she to do? Long years ago, in the months after Jacky's death, she had wished she might wipe out that one disastrous mistake and return to the home of her childhood, to the way of life she had deliberately left behind when she married Bradley. Now she was at last being offered that possibility, if she chose.

Did she choose, or was it now many years too late? She tried to examine the alternatives before her with an open mind. The benefits of accepting Ronnie's offer, selling up and moving near her parents were obvious enough. She would have all the comforts she had once taken for granted, the way of life she had once regarded as normal, a pleasant house in pretty countryside. Around her she would have her family and the circle into which they naturally fell, a circle of professional, moneyed people, comfortably off, assured, confident, in control of their world. People of her own kind.

Or were they? Where then did that leave the people among whom she had lived and worked during the years since her marriage; where did that leave Carol, her daughter, and the coming grandchild? If she moved to Surrey they would no longer be part of her life, in any real sense. And though she loved her parents, it was her daughter who mattered most to her. She doubted if Carol cared very much one way or the other – at the moment at least. She was wrapped up in her new life, helping with the Byers' family smallholding; she had turned her back on Diana and the business in which she'd been refused a part. But once she was a mother herself, she would come to feel closer to her own mother again, so Diana guessed, taught by her experience. More to the point, if things went wrong with her marriage, as still seemed only too likely, then it was to Diana she would turn for support. And whether Carol needed her or no, she herself did not want to be cut off from Carol, far removed from her and the coming child.

There was another thing too. She knew what kind of life she would live in Surrey, because she saw its pattern in her mother's life. Busy, purposeful in many ways, it revolved around a succession of voluntary activities – membership of the Women's Institute, arranging church flowers, serving on this committee and that. Such activities held no appeal at all for Diana. What attraction could there be in flower arranging for a woman with an extensive knowledge (if a little out of date) of running a haulage business?

From this high point she could see a lorry making its way westward along the dale, though she was too far away to make out its colour or the words painted on its side. Once she could have been reasonably sure it was an Armstrong wagon. Recently, it was much more likely to be one of Ronnie's. If she accepted his offer, then he would have the upper dale in his grasp, all this area that was not served by the railway. And very soon the lower dale would have no railway either; Ronnie had long ago seen the possibilities of that development, and it was certainly why he wanted what was left of Armstrong's. It was, after all, the best time to be thinking of developing and expanding a haulage business. Ronnie clearly had the ability to look ahead and see what others had not even begun to guess at, and it was this that made him the success he was. Could she, Diana, develop that same ability? Had she any of those same qualities? She had no idea, for she'd never really been put to the test.

She could, however, see that the mass closure of small railway lines would have momentous consequences. After all, goods still had to be carried, even without the railway. And who was to carry them, if not local haulage companies, familiar with local roads and local ways?

Yet to try and make Armstrong's into a successful enterprise again would be a gamble. What had once been a moderately prosperous business had fallen away almost to nothing. The takings from the petrol station were not sufficient to balance those losses. What was really needed was a massive injection of capital. 'We can help', her father had said, speaking of the move they were urging on her. 'No point in having money sitting around doing nothing'. But what if she were to ask for help with some quite different project? Would her parents be as generous then?

You're an idiot! she rebuked herself suddenly. *Armstrong's is a lost cause. Jackson's right: selling is the only sensible thing to do. If it's ever going to be successful again, it needs not just money but good management, by someone with years of knowledge and experience, someone like Ronnie. And Ronnie won't agree to the sale without the petrol station and the workshops behind it. They're the only bit that's worth anything. And, after all, I don't have to move to Surrey, even if I agree to the sale. I can buy a nice little place in Wearbridge if I want to.*

The sensible choice, the only sensible choice . . . She realised she was beginning to get cold, and turned to go. Then she glanced once more at Fell Cottage. *I could move back here*, she thought. *I'd have enough money to restore it properly.* Then: *No, that won't do. I have to consider what's best for the business.*

She laughed out loud. That unbidden thought had given her the answer. Without knowing how or when, she had made her decision. She was going to do the foolish, reckless thing. She was going to keep her share of the business, and buy Jackson out, so that it was all hers, to manage as she chose. Of course, there were many things still to be arranged, not least the loan she would need from her father, who might well not agree. There were many obstacles to be overcome before she could think of it as settled. And even then that would only be the beginning.

She could still just make out the wagon on the dale road. She imagined it now with new words clearly painted on the side: *Diana Armstrong, haulier*. She laughed again, from a mixture of exhilaration and fear. Not long ago, following Carol's wedding, she had felt as if the useful part of her life was over. During the past hours, she'd seriously considered a life of comfortable semi-retirement. Now, instead, she had decided to turn her back on safety and predictability and set out instead on a path that was full of risk and the possibility of failure.

Smiling to herself, she walked briskly back to the van. She felt alive again.

01 COW